THE BIG BOOK OF ORGASMS

VOLUME 2: 69 SEXY STORIES

EDITED BY
RACHEL KRAMER BUSSEL

CLEiS
PRESS

Published in the United States by Cleis Press, an imprint of Start Midnight, LLC, 221 River Street, Ninth Floor, Hoboken, New Jersey 07030.

Printed in the United States
Cover design: Jennifer Do
Cover image: Shutterstock
Text design: Frank Wiedemann

First Edition.
10 9 8 7 6 5 4 3 2 1

Trade paper ISBN: 978-1-62778-314-9
E-book ISBN: 978-1-62778-527-3

Contents

INTRODUCTION: BIG Os ALL AROUND

The sixty-nine orgasm erotica stories you're about to read will take you to many places, from sex clubs to stables to space to locations much closer to home. Everywhere, though, these characters of varying genders offer themselves up to different ways of experiencing pleasure. Sometimes, it's with sex toys, sometimes it's with a new lover, sometimes it's by pursuing a sexual fantasy to its ultimate conclusion.

They meet their lovers in a variety of ways: at work, outdoors, at yoga. Sometimes they reconnect with a partner and discover a whole new way of being intimate with them. In others, they get to know their own bodies in ways they never have before.

In Kristan X's "A Birthday Gift," a woman discovers that orgasms are hers for the taking, as often as she wants. "In between, the pleasure suffuses into her skin and tingles there like electricity, waiting to be discharged." While that's not the case for every character here, the energy X explores, that pleasure that overwhelms the senses in the best way possible, whether it's ardently pursued or easily available, is what animates these stories.

In addition to tales of wild abandon, there are also many moments of deep tenderness here, such as in "Lights Up" by Veronique Veritas, when Samuel reveals his biggest sexual fantasy to Genni, hoping she'll say yes to making it come true (spoiler alert: she does). In Ruby Barrett's powerful "Our Fragile Mouths," the sensual power of oral sex helps a couple reconnect in a time of need. She writes, "His mouth. His beautiful mouth, his soft tongue, and warm breath. He swears against her lips while he fucks her with his mouth."

Whether they're having anonymous sex, public sex, exploring BDSM, engaging in a hot masturbation session, or any of the many other types of sexual delights you'll find in this anthology, these characters are open to the possibilities of what can happen when they let go of their inhibitions and embrace their deepest desires.

There's a power to not only naming those desires, but acting on them, no matter how wanton. In "First Day" by Katrina Jackson, a new job also means a chance to get hot and heavy with two extremely hot new bosses. "This is all so inappropriate. I know that, but I don't care. *This* is what I've been dreaming about every night while in bed with my favorite vibrator: shivering between Monica and Lane, overheated skin, hard nipples, and a wet, aching pussy," she writes. Many other characters here go after their dreams, as others discover opportunities for sex their minds never could have conjured without the help of a talented and daring partner.

While each of the stories here is short, the authors have managed to pack so much desire, lust, and passion into each and every one, offering a gamut of human emotion, sexual scenarios, fetishes, and ways of getting it on in the pursuit of orgasms and so much more.

My hope is that these varied orgasmic tales offer you a way to rekindle your own desires, whether picking up ideas you want to try or simply transporting you for a few pages into a sex story that sizzles with the rush of looking, showing off, tasting, touching, and discovering the thrill of exploding from the inside out, of letting the body take over.

Rachel Kramer Bussel

LOOKING THROUGH THE WINDOW

Louise Kane

Kay loved Riley's apartment at night. Riley's entire living room wall was glass, and with only candles lighting the space, it afforded a clear view of the tree-lined park across the street and the surrounding high-rise apartments dotted with well-lit tableaus of strangers' lives.

Warm arms circled Kay's waist and she leaned her head back as Riley asked, "What do you see, sweet girl?"

Kay grinned as Riley's mouth found her neck. "I see lots of people not ready for sleep. And a few who would probably enjoy watching something other than reruns."

"Is that so?" Riley bit down, earning an undignified yelp from Kay that quickly turned into a groan as Riley licked the small hurt. They'd been teasing all day, and it didn't help when their hands slid under Kay's shirt to play with her tits.

"Take this off," said Riley, lifting the hem of Kay's tank top. Kay obediently raised her arms and was rewarded with the caress of a breeze through the window.

"These too," said Riley, tugging at Kay's black briefs. Kay wriggled out of her underwear, sticking out her ass more than necessary to press against Riley hard enough to verify she'd guessed right: they were packing.

"You made such a point of mentioning how bored our poor neighbors look," murmured Riley, hand tracing errant loops over Kay's stomach. "How do you feel about putting on a show?"

Kay jolted at the spark Riley's words sent to her cunt. "What do you mean?"

"I mean," said Riley, trailing fingers through the dark curls at the top of Kay's thighs and drawing a low moan from her lips, "I think they'd enjoy watching you fuck yourself. Don't you want to be a good neighbor, sweet thing?"

Kay whimpered. The thought of playing out a shared fantasy turned her on as much as Riley's fingers finding her clit and rubbing until she couldn't think.

Until they stopped.

Kay cried out, but Riley only laughed. "What do you think? Do you want to give them a show? If you do a good job, maybe you'll get to feel my cock inside you. Would you like that?"

Kay bit the inside of her cheek, hot desire building in her chest to please Riley—and to be watched.

"Yes."

"That's what I thought." Riley stepped back, and Kay gasped at the loss of contact. "An eager girl like you . . . I bet there isn't anything you wouldn't do, is there?"

Kay whimpered. "No."

"Exactly." Riley moved to a spot along the far wall, leaving Kay alone in front of the window. "You may begin."

A soft *click* and the overhead light flickered to life above Kay, throwing the apartment and her naked form into sharp relief. Kay struggled not to cover herself as her reflection stared back at her. Swallowing hard, her hands began their exploration.

Kay's tits ached from a day of tension, and she moaned low in her throat as she plucked at her sensitive nipples. She twisted the right one hard enough to elicit a yelp and sighed as she floated through the aftermath of the pain.

As Kay's hands passed her navel, she opened her eyes. Riley hadn't told Kay she couldn't shut them, but it felt like she was cheapening the experience by pretending no one was out there. Kay breathed out, pushing through the embarrassment as her hands drifted lower until they were nestled in curls.

Kay played with her clit while her other hand found her cunt slick with want. She moaned as her fingers glided across her opening, anyone outside the apartment

—outside herself—forgotten. Distantly, Kay heard her moans filling the room. Turned on by her own want, she finally thrust one, two, three fingers into her cunt.

"Fuck," breathed Kay, one hand shoved against the glass to keep her upright as she slowly fucked herself. She thought about every single one of those pinpricks of light staring as her rhythm sped and tension built in her stomach. Built and built and—

"Fingers out," said Riley, voice low and quiet.

Kay whined but dropped her hand as Riley moved to stand behind her. Head hung and arms limp, Kay's moans became labored breathing, caught between an almost-captured orgasm and arousal so painful that her cunt pulsed in time with her heart.

"You like that they can all see you, don't you?" asked Riley, making Kay gasp as their cock grazed her entrance. She hadn't noticed them unzip their pants. Whimpering, Kay pushed her ass back into Riley. They only chuckled.

"Always so eager," said Riley. "You're nothing if not consistent, sweet girl. The moment a cock appears, you lose your head. You forget I told you to stop fucking that pretty pink cunt, but I never told you to stop playing with yourself."

Kay shook her head even if she didn't dare turn around to plead her case. Every feather-soft pass of her fingers over hips, stomach, tits sent sparks straight to her cunt. She was distantly aware that her hips hadn't stopped moving.

Riley traced the roundness of Kay's ass, squeezing it sharply as they planted a quick kiss on the side of Kay's neck. "Do you want me to fuck you, sweet girl?"

"Yes, please," whispered Kay. "Please. Please."

"Well, when you beg so pretty," said Riley and thrust into her, filling Kay's cunt until she let out a strangled scream. Riley's labored breathing answered Kay's as they pushed her forward until she was pinned between Riley and the outside world.

Kay became a hurricane of *yes* and *please* and *harder* and *more*, spinning tighter and tighter around the eye of it until screams were all she had left. She was inside and outside of herself, focused on Riley's cock and the watching neighbors, and getting closer to coming.

"Don't you think your audience deserves a grand finale, sweet girl?" murmured Riley, stilling inside Kay as their hands slid low on Kay's hips. Kay cried out from the loss of friction, but Riley didn't move. "It doesn't seem fair to not give them what they've been waiting for."

Kay was past words, so wild with want that frantic nodding was all she could offer. She was so desperate for release that she would've agreed to anything.

"Use your hands," said Riley. "Rub your clit."

With a sigh, Kay slid one of her hands down the glass toward her clit. She moaned as she pressed down hard, sending a jolt of electricity through weak arms and thighs. Riley resumed their movement, sliding in and out of Kay at a pace just quick enough to ease her frustration.

But soon, even the edge of that was lost as Kay rubbed quick circles over her clit. Her breath fogged the glass until it was as slick as her cunt. Then Riley shifted, finding that perfect spot, and it became too much. Kay screamed, unleashing the orgasm that had been building all day as her final act.

Fully spent, Kay collapsed against the glass with a giggle, fully aware that everyone could still see her— and past the point of caring.

There would definitely be an encore performance.

FOR RESEARCH PURPOSES

Bridget Midway

" *You can't stop the feeling when it hits,*" Tristan
said.

Yesenia shook her head. "Nope. Cut out 'said' and
let the characters feel it." She deleted the last word of the
sentence she had written and grimaced. "Stop fucking
editing yourself as you write and just get the damn story
down."

Even as she told herself that, typing on her laptop
while sitting cross-legged on her king-size bed, she
still made changes. She found that writing late at night
worked best for her creative juices, especially writing
sex scenes, which as an erotic romance author, encom-
passed much of her content. When she wrote intimate
scenes, her heart raced, her clitoris throbbed, and sometimes she would have to take a cool shower to calm

herself. It helped that she had an incredible husband, who also made her heart thrum. Right now she had to focus on the writing.

"You can't stop the feeling when it hits." Tristan *punctuated his statement by palming Aya's breast*—no, wrong word—*tit through her thin shirt.*

Yes, he would think "tit" and not "breast."

Aya moaned as Tristan ran his thumb over her distended nipple.

"Shit. Is she wearing a bra? Did I mention that?" Yesenia groaned as she kept typing. "Edit later." She adjusted the headband over her hair styled in two-stranded twists all over her head and hanging like ropes over her shoulders.

Tristan lowered his free hand down between her thick thighs.

Yesenia smiled. Voluptuous African-American women need love, too.

He slipped his hand inside her panties and located her clit.

Yesenia squirmed while she got into writing this section. Her wonderfully supportive husband had the enviable trait of leaving her alone to write and popping in to offer support, a drink and, on a couple of occasions, a piece of chocolate. The thought of the sweet treat broke Yesenia's attention from her laptop screen for a brief moment. She glanced at the bedroom door as though she could conjure her dear husband to be there with some dark chocolate-covered almonds, her favorite.

"Concentrate, girl. You're on a deadline."

Tristan leaned forward and buried his head next to hers to kiss her neck. Aya accommodated him by leaning her head to the side to give him a larger surface to use his incredible mouth. Then he—

"Wait. Fuck. Can he massage her tit, play with her clitoris, and nibble her neck at the same time?" Yesenia hovered her hands over her keyboard, contemplating her next move.

Keep writing or mull over the logistics of a sex scene?

She put her hands back on the keyboard, brushing her index fingers over the raised ridges on the F and J keys before eventually springing from her bed and marching to the family room, where she knew her husband was occupying himself with some mindless entertainment on TV.

Lloyd glanced at Yesenia and smiled. "Finished writing?"

Yesenia pulled Lloyd's hand to get him to rise from his velvety recliner. "I need you."

Lloyd widened his sky-blue eyes. "Oh. Okay." He stood in his bare feet, towering over his wife. His black shorts hung baggy on his hips and showed off his long legs. He picked up the remote long enough to silence the TV to give Yesenia his full attention. "What? You need me to get something off a high shelf?" He smirked before puffing out a chuckle.

"Cute. No, I'm working on a scene and I need to see if it makes sense." Before explaining further, she placed one of his hands on her breast.

Without instruction, Lloyd massaged her until her nipples hardened even more. "Okay. I like where this is going." His smile widened when she pulled the elastic of her shorts away from her waist and eased his other hand down into her panties. "And you say this is research? Should I be doing something with this hand?"

Before she could answer, Lloyd brushed the pads of his index and middle fingers over her clit, making it throb. This man knew her body. Yesenia needed that feeling, that familiarity, between her characters.

"That's nice. And totally appropriate for the scene." Yesenia closed her eyes. Her head automatically tilted to the side as she gyrated her hips, enjoying his delicate yet commanding ministrations.

Relief washed over her in that moment. No matter what she had on her plate, Lloyd made her life easier like he had always done since they'd met during their freshman year of college. He knew how to play with her body to get her to reach the heights of ecstasy. Fifteen years later, he kept her laughing and excited in every way.

She gasped when she felt his lips connect to the sensitive flesh on the side of her neck. At that moment, she forgot about writing. When she felt the distinctive bulge under Lloyd's shorts, she knew he must have forgotten his duty to help her in her research. Thank God he wasn't stopping where she had ended her scene.

Lloyd pulled her panties down her legs at the same time as she pulled down his shorts and boxers. "Don't know if this is part of your research, but you can't say I'm not thorough."

"Let's see how good you are." Yesenia held her husband's shoulders and pushed him down on the couch. She pulled off her shirt as he ripped off his. "For research."

He held her hips. She held the base of his shaft as she impaled herself. He filled her completely. Yesenia connected her gaze to his as she undulated her hips, moving him in and out of her.

She pressed her lips against his firm, full set, which made him grip her hips even more, guiding her motions by pulling her back and forth . . . just like those alpha-male heroes from the stories she wrote.

His pulsating cock rubbed against her inner walls, making the hairs stand up on her arms and the back of her neck. Lloyd raised his hips and dug his fingers into her flesh. She moved her body faster until she felt her stomach tighten. Yesenia drew her thighs against his body.

Lloyd wrapped his arms around her and pulled her against his chest. As soon as he nibbled on her earlobe, she shattered. Every muscle in her body constricted, including and especially, the slick inner walls of her vagina that gripped his hard shaft. Her heart pounded hard enough that she thought it would explode, the same feeling she had every time she and Lloyd had sex. If she'd survived all these years with him blowing her mind, another sensational orgasm wouldn't kill her.

She released a long, low moan that shook her body and made her pussy quiver. This closeness, the heart-pounding intensity, the absolute connection to her man—Yesenia wanted those sensations for her characters, too. She would have to remember this feeling in her writing.

Lloyd gripped her tighter and growled as he came deep in her. Through a panting breath, he said, "I love it when you write sex scenes."

Yesenia laughed. "Thank you for helping me in my research."

He kissed her forehead. "Anytime. And I do mean anytime."

ANONYMOUS

Jodie Griffin

Marina had no idea where she was. That was part of the rules, part of the agreement she had set up with Gavin, her next-door neighbor and unexpected ally. Some might call him a pimp for what he brokered, but she called him an angel. Maybe a fallen one, but an angel nonetheless. No money changed hands, even though he arranged for people to fuck her. She'd once asked him what he got out of it, but all he'd given her was one of those devilish grins of his, and the words "Trust me, I get plenty."

As per the agreement she'd more than willingly signed, she was stripped of sight and sound—and clothing—and bound to something. It was different each time, and her imagination always gave her ideas, but the *what* and the *where* and even the *who* never mattered.

All she had asked was that she be anonymously fucked into oblivion. No names. No speaking.

She craved orgasms. Not always with this clawing, desperate need, and not even on a regular schedule. Oh, it had started out that way in her mid-thirties, when it could be predicted by the calendar. Now, at nearly fifty, the frequency of the cravings had slowed, but the intensity had grown. She had no problem getting herself off, but when she got like this, with a nearly constant ache between her legs that she couldn't keep up with, she told Gavin.

And he arranged it all.

She had no idea where she was. Her house, a cabin in the woods, on a stage in front of a thousand people, or in the town square. She didn't care, but she loved thinking about it. Need might claw at her body, but her mind had to be seduced, too, before release was possible. The not knowing was a big part of the thrill. These encounters had become a choose-your-own-adventure of the sexual kind, with a thousand potential twists and turns leading to multiple orgasms for her.

Relief was almost here.

Anticipation and excitement zinged around her brain, making her twitch in her bindings. Today, she was flat on her back, a pillow beneath her head, her knees bent and her thighs wide open. When something touched her, she jolted, her pulse starting to race. As though the person who'd done it to her understood, a palm moved against her leg in long, soothing strokes until she relaxed again.

The touch became warm and slick, and fingers kneaded at muscles in her calf. Two hands then, one on each leg. Up and down, gliding smoothly and then tightening, moving past her knees to her thighs, and then back down again. The scent of coconut teased her nose. A soft sigh left her mouth, and she sank back onto the table.

The hands on her thighs moved closer and closer to the aching spot between her legs, thumbs brushing against the curls there. She jolted when that touch was joined by hands cupping her breasts, pinching her nipples. Different hands, one soft, one callused. A person on each side, working in synchronicity? Three people touching her at once?

Her imagination took over, and her body responded, her first orgasm cresting as fingers fucked into her body. Hands continued to stroke her, inside and out, drawing out the pleasure for her, but as the orgasm eased, so did the touches, until she was alone again.

That was the agreement. Once she came, the person touching her was done.

It wasn't long before her need started to build again. She shifted in her bindings. She was on a bed, or maybe a padded table. It vibrated a bit, and her legs were opened wider. The touch was impersonal this time; she felt a textured dildo slide inside her. Her body fluttered around it, a remnant of her last orgasm, but it would take a lot more than that to get her off again.

It always did.

It was pulled out of her body, and then slowly

pushed in. Once, twice, three times, twenty times. Slow and steady, until it wasn't. The movement sped up, her breathing hitching as she was brought closer and closer to the edge by the relentless pounding.

But the person fucking her with the dildo was just getting started. They slowed again, moving just enough to keep her aroused and not enough to send her over. Instead of steady and measured, though, now the movements were random. In. Out. Three beats before another stroke. In. Out. Ten beats. In. Out. One beat. In and holding. Back out again.

Her teeth clenched as frustration rose, as tension built inside her, wanting that dildo back inside her, fucking her. A hand landed on her stomach, fingers splayed wide. Just resting there, not touching her anywhere in a sexual way. Warm. Heavy. Controlled.

And then the fucking started up again, the pace slow but constant, inexorably driving her toward a peak that remained just outside her grasp.

Until it stopped again.

When it started for a third time, it was relentless. Hard, and deep, and fast, coiling the tension inside her until she went supernova, her release exploding through her and taking her breath away.

She wasn't sure how long she was out of it, but she'd felt that hand pressed on her belly, steady, supportive, as she came back into herself. Someone raised her head, gave her some water, which she drank gratefully through parched lips.

As she leaned back against the table, the hand on her stomach disappeared.

Time had no meaning right now. She lost track of how many orgasms she had, but each one was delicious.

A tongue between her legs, licking at her and sipping at her as soft hands held her hips down. A gentle orgasm, a release on a shuddered breath, an encounter that ended with a fleeting kiss to her mound.

A lube-slickened ass-fucking with a wand pressed against her clit that sent her back into the stratosphere. It didn't always happen, but the owner of that dick spent themselves inside her, and she felt their release trickle down between her cheeks.

A person between her legs, their long, thick dick reaching a place she hadn't believed existed, the coarse hair of their thighs rubbing against her smooth ones. They were relentless, driving her to a point where all she could do was thrash her head back and forth. Her orgasm burst forth and drenched her, and it took a long while for her breathing to settle back down.

She was, *finally*, exhausted and sated and so very satisfied. But before she could signal that, she was given another massage, this one stroking her lightly, inside and out. Two hands, gentle ones, and she came on a sigh, her mind floating away as her bindings were released.

Gavin got her home and into bed and kissed her forehead, pulling the covers up over her. The fire inside her had been quenched, at least in the short-term. He had come through for her again, to make sure she had all the orgasms she needed. And he'd be there for her the next time.

She just wished she knew why.

FEELING HIMSELF

Kendel Davi

Justin swallows hard. Excitement mixed with fear ravages his body. It's not like they haven't done this before, but what's going to be used on him tonight has his anxiety peaking.

"Are you ready, sweetie?" Rania calls out.

Her thick Manchester accent flows. After twenty-five years of marriage he knows when Rania returns to her native tongue she's completely uninhibited.

"I'm ready." He gulps.

Rania sashays into the bedroom in a ruby silk robe. Streaks of gray pepper her shoulder-length black hair. The robe embraces her full sensual curves as its shade brings out the honey color of her skin. Justin marvels at his wife's beauty but soon his focus drops to the healthy-size bulge at her midsection. Rania opens the robe with a flourish and delivers a playful, "Ta-dah!"

Justin's mouth drops.

"That was my same reaction when I first saw it." She chuckles as mischief beams from her eyes.

She isn't talking about the dildo hanging from her harness. It's a reference to the first time she saw his cock. Now a perfectly molded silicone replica swings between her legs. He'd laughed this off as an improbability when she'd first broached the subject, but now, as his eyes focus on the mocha representation of his cock, for the first time in his life he wished he wasn't, as Rania loves to say, blessed.

"It looks real," he whispers and takes a deep breath to calm his fluttering stomach.

"I tested it on myself. It feels real too." She takes a step back and stands with arms akimbo. "Now, come over here and suck your dick."

He clinches hard on his butt plug before moving his burly frame to the floor. She strokes the dildo in the same way Justin tugs on his dick when he jerks off. The movement brings a smile to his face as he crawls to her. Then he closes his eyes and slowly opens his mouth.

"We'll have none of that. I want your eyes open when you're sucking it."

Justin's heart races as he extends the tip of his tongue. His body shivers when he makes contact. Has his mind created a symbiotic link to this length of silicone? He swears he can feel it in his cock and moves further down the shaft just to be sure. This time there's no denying it and soon he's giving himself the fellatio of his dreams.

"You're such a handsome little cocksucker," Rania mutters as she strokes her fingers through his salt-and-pepper hair.

Justin watches her body react. It's as if she's feeling what he's doing with his mouth as well. She caresses his cheek gently before hooking her hand underneath his chin. He's given Rania this nonverbal cue numerous times. He knows what she wants and pushes the dildo as far as he can down his throat.

"Now I see why you love this so much." He struggles to hold the dildo in his throat. "Breathe through your nose, Justin. It helps," Rania suggests.

He closes his eyes to focus on his breath and dives further down the shaft. He feels he's reached his limit but the aroma of his wife's arousal pushes him beyond what he thought possible.

"That's so fucking hot," Rania coos before she bends over and delivers a short thrust into his throat. The heft of her breasts presses against his shoulders as she clasps her hands on his butt for leverage. His wife is using his throat for her pleasure, much like he's done to her over the years. He's determined to take this for as long as possible, but the feeling of Rania grabbing the base of the butt plug forces him to eject the dildo from his gullet.

"It's not as easy as it looks," she says. Justin nods his head in agreement. "Now, give me a gentle push, sweetie."

She softly twists the butt plug. Justin contracts and

it glides out of his well-lubed hole. The hollowness of his vacant cavity consumes him. He scurries to the bed and leans over, praying Rania will stuff his agony, but instead she gives him a soft peck on the cheek.

"Turn around. I want to see your face when I enter you."

Justin rolls onto his back. His eagerness has his body trembling, but Rania takes her time. She drips lube on the dildo and works it through with her hand as her gaze drifts between her husband's urgent expression and his puckering hole. Her delay has Justin's anxiety lathering in his vulnerability. He strokes his cock at the same pace that Rania lubes the dildo to stave off his nervousness.

"Don't worry. I'll be gentle," she promises.

The sweetness in her voice soothes him but his need has him jerking his cock at a furious rate.

Rania places the head of the dildo between his ass cheeks before slapping his hand away.

"Let me handle that," she says.

She teases his opening. His breath staggers with want. She holds the dildo steady as her other hand takes a firm grip of his cock. As she enters her husband, Rania squeezes his dick in her hand to match her journey into his ass.

"Oh, fuck," he squalls.

The sensation of being filled by his wife devours him as her tight grip on his cock has him clinging to reality.

"You feel that, babe? It's almost like you're fucking yourself."

With the dildo firmly inside him, Rania places her free hand on his chest. His heart pounds with every inch she drives into him.

"I can't believe I'm fucking your ass with this. How does it feel having your dick inside you the way you've had it inside me?"

She delivers another short, quick thrust into him, which renders him speechless. The only way he can let his wife know the strength of his satisfaction is to relax and allow her to take him in the way she's craved all these months.

Rania focuses on her husband's face with each stroke, breaking through whatever tension he has left. He takes a deep breath. She senses his need and fills him to the hilt as she slides her hand down his cock with the firmest grip she can possibly give. It's all too much and Justin cries out as the force of his orgasm ejects a flow of semen from his body.

"I'm sorry," he groans as his body twitches. "I thought I could last longer."

"You did wonderful," Rania chimes. She gently removes the dildo from his ass before giving him a loving kiss. Then she stares at his still hard cock. "And it looks like you saved some for me." She frees herself from the harness and climbs on top of Justin. "God, you're so good to me," she mumbles and drives his cock deep into her pussy.

Justin watches in awe as Rania pushes herself toward much-deserved relief. He now knows that getting fucked

by his wife, with a replica of his own dick, is something
he could really get used to.

VIBRATIONS

Angela Addams

After twenty years of marriage, you know me to my skeleton. To the marrow in my bones and the blood in my veins.

A lifetime of togetherness.

The fights. Stripping me raw.

The forgiveness. Balm to my wounds.

The compromise. Gluing us together.

The smiles, adventures, and laughter.

Whispered conversations late at night. Swift and silent fucking. Urgent desire, unbridled moaning, orgasms that shoot me to outer space.

You've had so much time to hone your skill.

"Hop up on the speaker," you say. "It's steady."

Stolen time fills my stomach with wild butter-flies, fluttering madly. The threat of getting caught is deliciously tantalizing. I climb onto the biggest speaker you've got.

"Check, check." Your voice vibrates up my spine, pinging along my nerve endings, tickling my brain.

I settle myself, fanning my box pleat skirt around me, adjusting so that my bare ass cheeks spread wide and my pussy presses into the faux leather of the speaker.

"Earplugs?" Your voice reverberates against my skin. My pussy shivers. "Blindfold?"

"Check, check." It comes out gravelly so I clear my throat. "I have them." I pull the earplugs along with the blindfold out of the little pocket in my skirt.

"We don't have much time, love."

Urgency is my catalyst. My pussy jolts, spasming with anticipatory need.

I put the earplugs in. Tie the blindfold on.

The world is dark. Sound muffled. I brace myself, spread my legs wider, then lean forward so that my clit rubs along the top of the speaker.

"Remember, no hands," you say. Your voice is both a distant sound and a rumble against my thighs. My nipples pebble, turning into hard buds underneath the silk fabric of my blouse. Without a bra, the sensation is immediate. I sway forward, rocking myself to get a tiny taste—

"Kess," you warn, your voice a small earthquake under my ass.

I stop. We have rules. No hands. No self-stimulation. No cheating.

You hum into the mic just to remind me. A steady ripple that travels through the speaker, teasing me with the barest of vibrations. You know it's not enough. "Kess, my love. My everything." Your voice is a deep baritone. Smooth and rich. "Cannnn you feeeeeeel me?"

The speaker shakes. I brace myself. Hands on the sides, fingers hooked if only to keep from touching myself.

I nod because I'm ready and time is slipping away from us. The band will be here soon. Then the small collection of fans. This is our moment. Our stolen minutes to test our love.

You quickly strum A, D, G. Your bass is an extension of your hands. I've seen you play so many times that I'm envisioning your fingers flying along the strings. Each time you pluck a note, it's a gentle touch against my clit.

My body coils.

I'm so ready.

When you stroke low E, it reverberates like a lightning strike.

Pleasure shoots through the speaker, against my pussy, beating along my clit. I arch my back and my tits brush the fabric of my blouse. You've hit the right note so you do it again . . . and again . . . then you start to sing.

Our song. The one about how we met. How we fell in love. An eternity in a song.

The earplugs suppress the sound of your voice but I know the words by heart.

My Kess. My love. My eeeeeverythingggggg.
You're my queen and I'm your kinnnnngggg.

I see you in my mind. Strong fingers caressing your bass. Blue eyes caressing me. I sway side to side so that my tits rub ever so gently, teasing my nipples along the silk. I grind my clit into the sound that throbs through the speaker.

Your voice touches me, plucking my clit, resonating over my pussy lips.

Your guitar solo crests like a wave full of heavy beats. It's loud enough to obliterate the dulling effect of the earplugs. It's insistent enough to send shockwaves to my core. My pussy clenches, gripping onto the sound, pulling it closer, rubbing along my sensitive flesh. I bow my back. My tits strain against my blouse, my nipples so hard they should pierce the fabric.

You strum harder. Louder. Intense tremors slide from the speakers into me, tendrils of deep bass filling me, pumping me full of sound.

My pussy quivers. My nipples quake.

My climax mounts with every vibration. And you keep singing. You keep strumming. Relentless tremors of your love.

Don't stop. Don't stop. Don't stop.

I moan. I gasp. Both sounds echo in my head along with your words.

My Kess. My love. My eeeeeverythingggggg.
I'm on my knees, so take my rinnngggg.

Your words lick my pussy. Circle my clit. Latch onto

my heart. We reach the crescendo together. Your fingers make music. Your voice sings love.

My body torques.

My pussy shudders.

My clit sparks.

I've reached the peak of pleasure and roll over the pinnacle until I'm freefalling. Every sensation only intensifies the shaking, spasming, earth-obliterating orgasm. Lightning flashes against the darkness of the blindfold, shooting sparks to my nipples so that I climax again . . . and again . . . one continuous string of pure bliss.

The sound stops pulsating but I don't.

Your energy is a magnetic force. Your hands slide up my legs. You grip my hips and pull me to the edge of the speaker. You press your lips to my throat and glide your cock deep inside so that my pussy stretches and my body shudders all over again.

This is what twenty years looks like. So comfortable that risks aren't as risky. So sure of one another that pleasure is a game.

You pull one earplug out. You sing the chorus again.

My Kess. My love. My eeeeeverythingggggg.

You're my queen and I'm your kinnnngggg.

A whisper against my ear.

Your cock is a piston. You drive me to the summit. We both fly off the peak.

BETTER
WITH TIME

Meka James

Time stopped as she lay naked, anticipating Marcus's arrival. When the bed dipped, Amari squeezed her eyes and bit her lip. She jumped when he touched her leg. He trailed his fingertips from the back of her knee, over the curve of her ass, to her lower back. Twenty years of marriage and their attraction was stronger than ever. More since they'd decided to get more adventurous with their sex life.

He pressed his lips to her shoulder as he opened the nightstand drawer. "Nervous?"

"Yes." Her voice, a breathy whisper. "But in the best kind of way." Amari let her eyes flutter open in time to see Marcus set the vibrating butt plug and bottle of lube on the top of the nightstand. Her mouth went dry, excitement pooled in her belly, and arousal rushed between her legs.

He shifted, straddling her on all fours. She wanted to turn over, to lock her lips with his and beg him to make love to her, but she waited. A new side of him had surfaced since they'd begun their journey. A quiet control . . . a dominance which excited her in ways she'd never imagined.

He moved her hair to the side and kissed the back of her neck. While running his tongue down the length of her back, he slid his hands down her sides. She gripped the covers, willing herself to be still and not push her hips back for him. When he got to her ass, she sucked in a breath. A kiss to one cheek and then the other before pressing his thumb against her tight hole. A reminder of what was in store for the night. Amari clenched on contact. He stroked until she relaxed. Only then did he continue his journey to where she wanted him most, widening her legs to give him more access.

"Oh, baby, so wet. So eager."

Amari gyrated her hips against his slow-moving fingers and let out a strangled moan when he eased two inside her pussy. She pushed back, needing more contact. Just as she was about to climax he withdrew and left her panting. Longing, aching for the release he'd denied her, she started grinding against the bed, but a gentle smack to her ass stopped her.

Marcus made a tsking sound. "Not yet."

He slid his slick fingers between her ass cheeks

and rubbed across her opening. She held her breath in anticipation. Marcus moved at a torturously slow pace, while Amari buried her face in the pillow, groaning from the sensation.

His hand eased down, again stroking her aching sex, recoating his digits, before returning to fondle her ass. She curled her toes and held onto the pillow for dear life, trying not to bring herself to orgasm; she thought she'd surely die from the effort. But with Marcus's exquisite control over her body this would be a great way to go.

"This might be a little cold," he warned.

Seconds later, the cool liquid hit her flesh. He circled his fingers around the puckered hole she'd always believed would be off limits. Now, she could barely contain the need to have her husband fill her. The tight muscles gave slight resistance as he eased in the toy, and she let out a throaty moan as it settled into place.

He pressed his lips to her shoulder. "Undress me."

Amari lifted her head, blinking to clear the stars from the change of light. She loosened her grip on the covers and let blood return to her fingers. When she moved, she clenched her ass around the silicone plug. Marcus stood with a sexy smile and helped her off the bed.

As his darkened gaze held hers, she swallowed the dryness in her mouth. With shaky hands, she eased up his shirt, revealing more of his warm brown skin. She let her fingers explore his toned abdomen and chest. He pulled the garment the rest of the way off and tossed it to the floor.

Amari kept her gaze on her husband as she reached for the waistband of his pants. Her eyes remained locked with his as she unbuttoned his jeans and slid the zipper down. When she took ahold of his hard dick, he groaned and gripped her hips. Pride rolled through her. As much as he made her body sing, knowing she had the same effect on him sent her heart into a tailspin.

She loved him. Marcus was her protector. Her lover. Her friend. She stroked his beautiful cock, circling the tip with her thumb. She sucked the digit into her mouth, licking off the pre-come. His eyes became mere slits. She smiled, a new warmth of desire flooding her. Marcus crashed his lips to hers. All she wanted in that moment was for her husband to ravish her body in the most glorious ways.

Marcus picked her up and gently laid her on the bed. Kicking his pants free, he settled between her legs, poised at her wet and eager pussy. He kissed her again as he eased forward. With a devilish smirk, he picked up the remote, then pressed a button.

Amari sucked in a breath as a low pulse radiated from the plug. He waited, giving them both time to get used to the sensation before he started to move, slowly at first. Marcus tangled his fingers with hers, pinning her arms above her head.

Between the vibrations of the plug, plus the tightness of having both it and her husband filling her in such a glorious way, Amari's release scratched just beneath the surface.

"Marcus, please," she whined.

He pulled out and pushed back in with more force. "Is this what you wanted?"

"Yes!"

Marcus thrust forward again and Amari squeezed her eyes shut as her orgasm tore through her.

"Look at me."

She popped her eyes open at his gruff command. Her husband loomed above her, pure lust in his brown eyes as her body trembled around him. Amari couldn't catch her breath before she was flipped onto her stomach. Marcus removed the plug and positioned his dick between her ass cheeks.

"You ready?"

Unable to speak, she nodded her consent. He inched in slowly and she breathed through the intrusion. The slow pumps in and out of her ass stole her ability to think. She focused on the sensations. His huffed breaths. And the way he kneaded and massaged her ass while he fucked her.

Marcus snaked a hand between her legs, teasing and stroking her clit. Her eyes rolled back and she gripped the blanket. She curled her toes and arched her back. Marcus continued his slow pace, and let out a deep grumble. He kept stroking her clit until he sent her over the edge again, pulling a strangled cry of ecstasy from her lips.

He thrust forward once more then stilled, spilling his release into her tight ass. Her entire body trembled, and her knees gave out. He jerked forward before slumping against her back. He kissed her shoulder, and then eased out of her.

She felt around until she found his hand and interlaced their fingers. "I love you."

He pulled her close. "Love you, too."

SOMEONE TO WATCH OVER ME

A.J. Harris

G ia ducked her head into her apartment's monitor
room as I plugged myself into the security station.
Tonight, she wore a deep green dress—low cut around
the shoulder and cleavage, high and tight around the
thighs. Working clothes. She asked how things were
going. Her first customer was due around seven thirty.
I was set. The mini-drones were online. The hidden
cameras were transmitting. Then she said: "Dylan?
Thank you. I mean it. You're the only one I can trust
these days."

"You're welcome." I stumbled over my words. Gia
wasn't usually this chatty before a job. I adjusted my
neural link cable's transmitters; signal strength was
good. "I appreciate it."

"I know you do." She hugged me. I froze, and

returned it. Gia never hugged *anyone* in the business—
not that I'd seen. And I'd seen everything. It was my job.
Gia setting my VR glasses on my nose, and brushing her
thumb against my cheek, raised alarms.

"Is everything okay?"

Gia smiled. "Everything's fine."

The smile persisted as her workspace reformatted
into a replica diner, with miniature counter, red vinyl
stools, and a single booth. She stocked it with props
and supplies. I closed my eyes and became every camera
in the smart room, every Taser drone in its charging
station. I was her guardian in every sense.

The client was an aggressively bland corporate
drone. He stripped right after confirming payment.
His cock, half-erect, perked up as he pulled down Gia's
dress and bared her dark brown nipples. The client
tweaked her tits between his knuckles. Gia gave him a
theatrical moan. I heard her voice, heavy and deep, over
the mics. She encouraged his nipple tweaking with one
hand while lifting her skirt with the other.

Gia licked her fingers and worked the spit into her
shaved folds. She told him she wanted his cock, his come.
When the client told her to bend over, she reached for
one of the sugar trays in the booth. It carried flavored
polyurethane condoms. After wrapping his engorged
dick, she bent against the counter, begging and pleading.
"C'mon. Slam it into me. I need you!"

The client obliged. His condom-covered length
plunged into her open pussy. She held onto the counter,

but her eyes focused on one of the cameras. As he fucked her, she looked at me and kept smiling. The telepresence nodes put me right there—right in front of her as he fucked Gia, slapping his thighs against her ass.

Declaring he was almost there, the client pulled free. Gia stripped away the condom. She stroked him, then she sucked his purpled head, slurping when it popped free of her lips. Her thumb pressed the underside of his shaft, milking him. She mashed her breasts together with one hand, begging, "It's okay, babe. Come on me. Come on my tits. I need your come. So warm . . ."

And he came—all over her clavicle and breasts. She caught the jizz on her breasts, and in her cleavage. When the last spurt hit, Gia reached into the booth seat and withdrew a petri dish. She scraped the liquid off of her skin with the dish's edge, cleaned it with the napkin on the table, and sealed it for the customer. She then presented her glistening breasts. "Cleanup in booth three?"

I held my breath, and checked the Taser charges on the drones. Clients could get violent and break contract at any time. But the worst ones were afterward. Disappointed with their performance, they'd take it out on her. Or try, until the drones hit.

But this client was content with the session, and his souvenir dish of come. He licked her clean, dressed, and left without complaint. I tracked him to his car, verified his departure, and archived his session for safekeeping.

I pulled my VR glasses off as the cameras showed Gia knock open the monitor room's door.

"Please." I spun in my chair. Her eyes locked on me. She stroked her still wet pussy, her fingers kneading rough circles around her clit and lips. I'd seen her many ways, but never so hungry. Gia dove at me, kissed me. Her fingers smelled of strawberry and salt. Each kiss was punctuated with a "Please." She ran her fingers over my telepresence nodes. "I need to let go. I can't with them. Want to stop acting for once. Please? Say yes."

I breathed in and said, "Yes."

Gia pulled me out of my chair and took my place. She leaned the seat back and propped her legs up on the armrests. Her toes curled. She licked her lips, ravenous. Spreading her pussy open, she whispered, "Eat me, Dylan. Please. You know what I like. You've seen me."

I knelt between her legs and kissed her thighs. The salty strawberry scent guided me. Slow and steady, I tongued her open. Any wetness from the client doubled when I brushed her clit. I circled her, mirroring her fingers all the times clients made her masturbate until she came and squirted. Gia moaned, almost snarled, and ran her fingers through my hair. She cupped the interface ports at the nape of my neck, guiding me like a kitten nudged to fresh food.

Sucking her clit sent shivers and shockwaves along her belly. "Fuckkkk!" She squirmed, sweat dappling the faux leather chair and sticking to her skin. When she adjusted to give me better access, the chair complained with a farting sound.

We laughed for a moment, and kept doing so as I

rested my forehead against her mons, breathing her in. But laughs could wait. She couldn't. I slid two fingers inside her, pressing against the roof of her pussy while still sucking her clit. She swelled around me, tightening, demanding more. I pleasured her until juice dripped down my hand.

Gia howled when she came. I'd never heard her like that with a client. The fantasy and cyber-age theater of her job fell away. All that remained was a deep, feral orgasm. I rested my head against her thigh. She combed my hair, and circled me with her legs.

"Did you come?" I looked up.

"Did I come?" She laughed. "Fuck. Yeah. Thank you."

"Happy to help." For a moment, she cradled me, playing with my hair, enjoying the moment. I broke it by asking, "Why?"

"Why?" Gia lifted me up and kissed me. Not a client kiss. Not the hungry kiss. A soft, yearning kiss, asking for more in the future. "Because you're the only one I can trust anymore. And I love you for it."

That made sense. In the end, what do we really want? Beyond our kinks and physical needs? Connection. Not with a machine, but a person. Someone we can trust at our backs. Someone to watch over us. I'm happy to watch over her for as long as she wants.

PAINTING RUBY

Tess Danesi

J anie looked in the mirror as she dressed. Pulling
her black panties up her legs and over her hips, she
touched the little roll of flesh where a nice taut belly
had once been. Her formerly perky breasts were sadly
a thing of the past. Still, the pretty, lacy pushup bra
helped.

*I guess I'm not half-bad for the ripe old age of fifty-
nine,* she thought.

Janie applied some eyeliner and mascara, something
she wouldn't normally do when going to her studio. But
today, a fledgling artist was coming by to assist with a
large painting. Janie had to admit she was hot for her.
She was glad she'd chosen her prettiest undies because
wearing them brought back memories of when she
never left the house without beautiful undergarments.

They had made her feel sexy and desirable—even when no one else knew they were there.

She had always felt alluring and seductive in her youth; men and women would flirt with her regularly. But each passing year was making her feel more and more invisible. In the past, Janie and her husband, Steve, had had an understanding about her being able to sleep with women. She was bi and she needed to be able to express that side of her sexuality. It wasn't an issue for Steve; what made her happy also made him happy. But once children had come, time was devoted to them, her marriage, and her career. Frankly, she hadn't had the energy to pursue more.

Four years ago, Janie had retired early to pursue her love of painting. She had acquired a studio and found a moderate degree of success. She was proud to have her paintings displayed in several local galleries, including some as far away as Washington, DC.

Janie met Ruby at the opening of one of her DC shows. She was shocked that Ruby had been following her work, even declaring herself a fan. She found Ruby, just pushing thirty, stunning. Born to a Japanese father and African-American mother, Ruby's caramel skin glowed from within. It was Ruby who was coming to the studio today to work with Janie and Janie was feeling intimidated by her attraction to this younger woman.

Arriving early, she changed into her overalls and Crocs and set about getting everything prepped. Her studio, a cavernous space in an abandoned warehouse, had been completely renovated. It now had a decadent bathroom she had splurged on, so she could clean up and come home paint-free.

Nervous, she jumped when she heard a knock at the door. It was hard to contain her excitement at seeing Ruby looking radiant even in her comfy sweats. A pulsation surged through Janie's clit. Feeling like a dirty old woman, she promptly made herself stop and get down to business.

As Ruby helped her get the large tarp spread out over the floor, Janie's gaze lingered on Ruby's taut bottom. It made her smile to think of rubbing her hands all over that luscious round ass but it also brought a wistfulness for her own younger body that made her sigh out loud.

"Is everything okay, Janie? Is this good?" asked Ruby.

"It's perfect. I just got momentarily lost in my thoughts," said Janie.

"Oh, I know that feeling." Ruby laughed.

"Can you grab the bucket of crimson, Ruby?"

"Sure thing."

But as Ruby was carrying the bucket of paint, her foot caught on the tarp and she tripped, landing on her butt with a solid thud.

"Oh, my God, are you all right? Here," she said, extending a hand to a paint-covered Ruby, "let me help you up."

But Ruby shook her head, looking like she was about to cry. She apologized repeatedly for her clumsiness. It broke Janie's heart to see Ruby berate herself.

Janie reached for the nearest bucket of paint, smiling as she poured the violet liquid over herself and Ruby. The paints mixed and swirled as she reached for Ruby, the women falling on each other. Now, both drenched in paint and laughing, they rolled around on the tarp, making art with their bodies. Their playfulness turned heated. Ruby pulled Janie near until she was close enough to kiss.

Their lips touched, Ruby's tongue probing past Janie's lips as she gently coaxed Janie's tongue to meet her own. Ruby slid her hands down Janie's body, cupping her breasts, her own nipples hardening. She deftly unhooked Janie's overalls and pushed them down until they pooled at Janie's waist. Then she lifted Janie's T-shirt over her head to reveal her lacy bra.

"You're so beautiful, Janie. Now I want you to see me," she said, pulling off her own tank top.

Janie was wetter than she'd been in years, her pussy getting warm and slick. She was grateful her aging body hadn't failed her.

Janie dipped her finger into the paint and started making circles around Ruby's nipples, steadily trailing her fingers down her belly to the waistband of her sweatpants. Ruby encouraged her by standing to remove her pants and panties. She stood there, bare in the perfect light that flooded the studio, looking every inch the goddess of Janie's fantasies. Janie suddenly knew what her next painting would be.

Ruby laid Janie down on the tarp and slowly removed

Janie's clothes. Janie felt ready to come before the fabric slid past her ankles. Ruby noticed her tension and gently shook her head no.

As Ruby's fingers softly stroked around her clit, Janie's breathing became shallow and raspy. She hadn't been touched by a woman in years and everything about it felt like heaven: Ruby's soft, smooth skin, the scent of jasmine that enveloped her, the tenderness of her touch, the plushness of her lips, and the way she innately knew her way around Janie's body.

Ruby's touch felt magical. She kept her eyes fixed on Janie's, constantly evaluating her reaction. When she bent to let her lips lightly graze Janie's clit, she whispered, "I want you to come for me, Janie. I want you to surrender, baby. Let go."

And Janie did. She let go of everything—her fear, her self-consciousness. Her fucking mind that would never turn off suddenly did as her body was overcome with an intensity that made her muscles go taut and relax over and over. Ruby slid her fingers inside Janie, curving them to hit her G-spot. The sensation was immediate and electric, a bolt of lightning that made her gasp as she felt herself squirt.

Janie pulled Ruby up to meet her face, kissing her lips, tasting the unique tang of her own sex.

She stared into Ruby's eyes for a long moment before she spoke. "Thank you for giving me that. I believe I owe you something in return. How about a hot shower first?"

"Woman, do not dare thank me. Ever since I saw your art, I felt connected to you. Then I met you and you were more than I could have dreamed. So do not thank me. Now, about this owing me something . . . I believe I will allow that," Ruby said. "Now, which way is that shower?"

ALL THE WEATHER EVENTS

Ash Orlando

I want to call you but I can't call you.

I want to call you because I remember when I kneeled down before you and you made me take off your boots, one at a time. I was naked and you made me pull them free from your feet and you smiled at me, and told me I was good.

I want to hear your voice, the way it deepens when I fuck you a little harder than you are sure you can take. The way you urge me on, the way you trust me, the fact you let me fill you and taste your surrender.

We both know how to give, how to let go. Our bodies talk a language that is my first language, the language of bodies that are undefined. Bodies that are not female, not male. I had everything with you.

I remember how we would start and you would say to me, gently, are you are boy or a girl today? And I would tune into myself in a way I never had before and tell you. Some days, I am a girl. You can call me a girl's name today. Some days, I am a boy and I am your boy and I will always be your boy. Other days, I don't know but I want you to do me like this. Touch me here. Give me this. Now, harder.

I was demanding. I was fearless in a way that shocked me, that uncovered me. My vulnerability like a nuclear event, clearing me free of every misconception and everything I thought I was. I was nothing like any of it. I rewrote myself, in a heady rush of heartache and need and loss and want.

I told you all my fantasies. I said, I want all of these things. I said, go shopping and come back with this, and this, and two of these, and then let's play. Your bank account would empty but I rewarded you each time. I wore men's overalls with lacy panties. I dressed you up in uniforms. I let you spank me till there were marks and then said, one more. One more, please. After I bought the biggest cock I could find, you twisted your hands through my hair and pushed my willing lips open. We used ropes and ties and more. We pushed limits each time, and laughed.

You were a drug to me. I was so gone.

The first time we fucked, I bled. I bled because my body was ready to, and I said, "Oh, God, I'm sorry. I didn't know I was still bleeding. I started like a week ago, and I thought my cycle had finished."

You laughed, languid, and wiped your hands on the sheets. You didn't care. "Bodies are bodies," you said. Then you flipped me and held me down and I let all my air leave my body in release.

I had brought my best strap-on to our first date and you said, okay sure, and wore it for me like a king. I remember being on top of you and sinking down and saying, "Please," like I was begging, and I was. I had been begging for years for your strong, sure hands, but how did it take you so long to find me? I was here the whole time, shouting into a void, my body nothing but a shout: Please! Where are you?

I said to you that night, "Sometimes I don't come when I fuck," and you said, "I rarely do." We smiled and let go of expectations, but both of us came so hard, and so simply. Your body said to my body, *I am ready for this.*

I shouted with pleasure when you came. You were loud like thunder. All the other lovers in your past had lain back and took what you offered, but not me. I topped you, with a firm hand, directed the electricity of you, mapped all your pathways and knelt over you with certainty. "Come for me," I instructed. "I'm telling you to. Give me what I want. Let go."

That's how I took you.

It was October but still cold. I had found a place with a fire and the fire burned low. I remember the ice feeling of the air, sharp against my skin. The tiny shower that warmed me, the immediacy of the air outside that shook me. Hot and cold, hot and cold. Extremes of things. All of us, all the weather events, the extremes.

I want to call you so bad, it's like a weaponized need. It's a full heart of need.

Can I call you?

I can't call you.

And if I called you, what would be said? Come over, I would say, come over. Come over here. Be here with me, please.

Open your mouth and speak my new name, in the language only you and I know.

Please. Come.

A PERFECT MATCH

Natasha Moore

He loves to watch.

Sometimes through their bedroom window. Other times he could be anywhere, thanks to the webcam pointed at their king-size bed. Most often he's in the room with them. She likes that best. His musky scent. His ragged, eager gasps. She can always hear him, even over another man's heavy breathing.

Often Declan's naked. Stroking his cock. Giving directions in that commanding way she loves. "Play with her nipples, she loves that." "Pound her harder, make her body dance." "Make her come so hard she screams."

Or he might sit silently, fully dressed, sipping on whisky while he watches. The ice rattles against the glass, rattling her nerves. Sometimes Kerry still gets edgy when she's in bed with someone else.

Tonight, Declan's at the head of the bed, atop the soft puffy white duvet she only brings out on nights like this. She's naked on her back, her head in his lap. His hard-on presses against her cheek through his soft boxer briefs. His familiar scent makes her mouth water. A part of her wants to take him in her arms right now.

But another man's on top of her, pressing her into the mattress. Large hands run over her. Heating her. Turning her body pliant and needy. He suckles one of her nipples, then the other. Nips them with his teeth. She closes her eyes and writhes from the exquisite bites of pain. Declan strokes her hair. "Open your eyes," he whispers. "Look at *him*. Don't pretend he's me."

Her pussy clenches. She needs the reminder. Sometimes she does pretend. He knows it'll be better if she doesn't.

Her eyes fly open. All the lights are on in the room. No hiding in the shadows. He has a craggy face, this man who's touching her body, but not her heart. There's no mistaking him for Declan. He's bigger. Darker. Broader, with a shaved head.

His calloused fingers lightly trace her ribs. Sharp sensations prickle her skin. Her breath catches while his lips skim, tease. Tingles gather between her thighs. She can't help but whimper and wriggle beneath him.

His fingers slip between her legs to slide along her folds. She's already slick and ready. But still she hesitates to let him in. She gives a frustrated moan. It makes no sense. She wants this as much as he does. As much as both of the men she's with right now. But knowing in the back of her mind that she *shouldn't* want this often makes her freeze.

"Open your legs, Kerry." Declan's lips brush her ear as his deep voice urges her on. "This is what we've been waiting for. Open wide for him."

They've been doing this for years, but she still feels better hearing him say he's okay with it. She bends her knees and spreads wide. The air hits her slick flesh and she almost comes. *Not yet. Not yet.*

The best is still ahead.

The big man smiles when he slides two fingers into her body, testing, teasing. She takes a shaky breath at the penetration. Then he draws his fingers out and drags them up to her clit, spreading the lubrication in lazy circles. Oh, God, the sensitive bud's already pulsing but there's not enough friction now. She rocks her hips, desperately riding the hand of a man she's never met before. She doesn't even know his name.

She turns her head and looks at Declan. Her mouth is dry from panting. She swallows. "Are you watching? Can you see?"

"I can see everything." His dark eyes spark, his voice rough. "You're going to come for him."

I'm going to come for you. "Yes."

He pinches her chin. "Look at him. Not me." Declan's smile is deliciously wicked before she turns away. "He's going to take you. And I'm going to watch him fuck . . . my . . . wife." She moans at the twisted promise. The stranger's already rolled on a condom. Thick fingers spread her sensitive pussy. He plunges in with one long thrust. The momentum pushes her back against Declan.

Kerry forces her eyes to stay open. His big body looms over her. Her body buzzes, a million tiny bee-stings along her skin. Her hips rock again, seeking more. His fingers bite into her hips as he drives his cock in and out. In and out. The fluttering is back. Faster. Stronger.

Hands too big. Scent too spicy. But his angle is just right. What they're doing might be wrong but it's what she needs. Declan knows it, too. It's what they both need. She keeps her eyes on the man using her for his pleasure. But aren't they using him?

Her blood pounds in her ears. She's breathing so fast, so hard, she feels as if she's going to hyperventilate. Intense sensations spiral through her. Anticipation wars with desperation until she can't think anymore. She curls her fingers into the bedcovers, but it doesn't help anchor her in the moment.

When the orgasm bursts through her, she arches her back and bucks the mattress. Lights flash behind her eyelids. She doesn't exactly scream, but the wild moans are pretty spectacular. Declan's strong hands grasp her shoulders. He's her anchor. "Open your eyes, Kerry."

She didn't realize she'd closed them again. "Sorry." She's coming down from that erotic high she craves. But not too far down, she hopes.

The stranger still holds her hips and after a few more thrusts he grunts and throws back his head as he comes. He smiles down at her then. After a moment he pulls out, brushes his lips along her cheek, and heads for the bathroom.

Declan kisses the top of her head. "Beautiful. You're so beautiful when you come." Still shaky from her climax, she eagerly crawls onto his lap. All this has been foreplay. Now it's Declan's turn. Now he's the one who's desperate. She squirms against his erection, teasing him, teasing herself. The flutters start once more. It won't be long until she's flying again.

Kerry loves to *be* watched. Not only does she crave the sense of power it gives her, but she gets the best damned orgasms that way.

GARMENT

Jeremy Edwards

"Would you like being tickled to an orgasm? I mean, tickled only? Tickled all over, until you orgasmed from the tickling alone?"

Lynne loved the precision of the things Gérard asked in bed. Or, in this case, at the self-checkout at the library. The crystal clarity of the present questions sent a tickle downward from her nape, which dissolved into the small of her back like finely crushed ice on a summer tongue.

Once outside, she met his eyes. "Hmm . . ." was her response. She trusted him to recognize this particular *hmm* as a *hmm* with potential. A *hmm* with a *tell me more* cocooned inside.

He did. "I keep thinking about what you do with my hands when you ride me. How you splay my fingers around your breasts, so I can make you giggle. And when I'm on top, and you get my hands under your bottom so I can tease the crack . . ."

She chuckled lasciviously and reached over to squeeze his butt, though she had to juggle an armload of books to do so.

"And the way you offer your underarms right before you come. All those little tickles you adore—it seems like maybe it's your favorite part."

Maybe it was.

"I took the liberty of preparing a *garment*," Gérard explained, after Lynne had undressed. He gave the *n* in the word full value, as in *moment*. She could practically feel the point of Gérard's tongue as it nudged the back of his teeth. "In case it turned out you were interested." He opened a drawer and unfurled his creation.

It was a long-sleeved, sheer fishnet body stocking, into which a shrewd array of customized gaps had been cut, then lovingly hemmed.

"Gaps one and two: your naked armpits. Gaps three and four: your aching nipples."

Lynne inhaled huskily.

"Well, I said your nipples—but, as you can see, we'll have access to most of your breast. All that warm, round flesh." His voice melted on the last few words.

She swallowed greedily before prompting him. "Continuing . . ."

"Continuing . . . Five and six: ovals above your

waist, like where I'd grab you for a quick tickle under
your ribs. Seven: your spreading pussy. Eight . . . um,
what I'd call a miniature moon of derriere, centered on
the sweetest stretch of your ass cleft."

Lynne squeaked.

"Bare feet, of course. Bare soles. Bare toes. Bare
crevices *between* the toes." He laid the garment on the
bed. "There were body stockings sort of like this online,
but I wanted it to be perfect for you. I mean, there's that
specific strip of your ass cleft we like so much. I was
afraid a store-bought ass-cleft gap wouldn't fall in quite
the right place."

Lynne took another deep breath and raised a forefinger: *I have an idea*. She hopped off the bed and
opened a different drawer, producing a small, hexag-
onal box, from which she lifted an assortment of two-
inch feathers in various colors. "From when I worked at
that hat shop," she noted, placing the box in Gérard's
palm.

Gérard undid his Oxford shirt, presenting a long,
spare swath of torso above his jeans, framed for her in
a way he knew made her mouth water. Then he helped
Lynne into the body stocking, pulling and shifting and
smoothing until she was situated just so: buttocks crack
beautifully centered, bare breasts popped forward,
underarms gaping hungrily.

She sprawled supine on the mattress. Gérard had
selected a plum purple feather, speckled with ivory
dots—like little giggles, Lynne thought—and sugges-

tively fluffy looking. When he crouched beside the bed
and ran it lightly down the sole of her foot, she felt a
twang of sensuality in her throat, like the pluck of a
violin string.

She flexed her toes in invitation, and he dabbed
between them. She luxuriated, purring, and he favored
one of the exposed ovals of her midriff with a short,
tickly visit from his fingers. Her hands flitted toward
her crotch, but she didn't touch. Her "oh, *yes*" was
composed of giggles.

"Oh, yes, indeed," he answered, eyes keen with
excitement.

She raised her arms, arching up to draw his focus to
her tingling breasts and wide-open pits. Gérard knelt by
her and circled her left nipple with the feather, tracing
orbits on her flesh, coaxing her into a cozy idle of lazy
chuckles that were punctuated with soft moans, and
cradled in the rocking motion that her body had found.

When the feather jumped from breast to armpit,
she squealed with approval, then shouted with laughter
while he tickled, then stopped, then tickled. As she
grooved into a sultry pleasure dance, the feather moved
nimbly from locus to locus—to a nipple, to the midriff,
to an underarm, back to a jiggling breast—always gentle
but insistent, quick but piquant in its doses of titillation.
Lynne's dance became wilder and wetter, and when they
paused for a breather, she kept wriggling with arousal.

She rolled onto her belly now, shimmying her hips and
pointing her toes toward Gérard's fingertips. He took

the hint, and deftly used fingers and feather to reawaken both feet. Soon her giggles blossomed into a randy, staccato motorboat cackle until, in an orgy of tickled glee, she was clawing at the sheet and pummeling the pillow with her fists. When, after another brief pause, he graced her middle with a playful volley of tickles at left and at right, she laughed loud and hard, her joy resounding in their friendly little bedroom.

And—oh!—there it was. The feather's kiss between her ass cheeks. "The best spot, the best . . ." she crooned, before losing her enunciation in wanton howls, while her bottom bounced roundly under Gérard's ministrations. And here was the narrow edge of Gérard's forefinger, skimming shallowly along the crevice, wiggling just enough to tickle like holy fuck.

She was in paradise, her sensitive behind delirious with bliss, too turned on to last. Her inner nerves sizzled as her pussy anticipated the feathery touch, wetting her upper thighs and the yawning crotch hem of the body stocking. Frantically she flipped over, speaking through a throaty chortle as she hooked her hands under her knees: "Make me come, make me cuh-huh-ha-ha-hummmm!"

Her thigh muscles were taut with eagerness as she spread for him, already imagining the fluff of the feather before, at last, it arrived on the delicate skin next to her lips . . . whispering itself inward, so tickly, so delicious. Then came the tiniest brushing over her clit—light as a breeze, but she felt it all the way to her nipples. Her squirming became a shuddering, and her arpeggiated laughter an aria. She'd never been this horny and stimulated, this overwhelmed with sensory delight. She was a network of tickles, all those exposed receptors pulsing to each other and into her core.

Unlike other orgasms, this orgasm wasn't one big, bursting bubble. This orgasm was the popping of countless bite-size bubbles at once—a giddy, effervescent ecstasy.

As she came, she saw that Gérard was trembling, too.

THIS IS IT

Adriana Anders

I roll over and, for once, he's here. Warm and solid next to me. And quiet. Well, almost. There's a little drag and grunt every time he breathes.

He's asleep. Just the way I like him.

Eyes shut, I imagine how I used to feel beside him, excited at the prospect of touching all that skin. Now I'm relieved that he doesn't want anything.

But his presence makes me itchy. I should get up and sleep on the sofa.

I almost do. Almost.

He turns onto his back and flops his arm over me. It's heavy and warm and it smells just like him. Like how he used to smell, before everything got in the way.

Now, though, I'm trapped under that heavy arm and I can't move. Well, I could, but I like the idea that I can't. This isn't my choice. If I shift, just the tiniest bit, that arm skims my breast in just the right way.

Forcing a fake sleep sound, I shift and shimmy and then it's more than just an errant breast-nudging, it's full-on spooning. Accidental, of course. With a snuffled sound, he moves in to meet me and the scent changes into a close smell—musk, lined with mint and soap.

He's still damp from a nighttime shower. Why? To hose off some other woman's stink? Is that what this distance is about?

I push his arm off and slide away, grab my pillow, ready for another restless night on the sofa.

"Stop." His voice is rough, his hand tight on my shoulder. "Don't go."

"Can't sleep with you here." I pause, stupid brain not letting it go. "Like *this*."

"Like what?"

"Smelling like a shower."

"You're leaving because I'm clean?"

"I'm leaving because you've—" I pull at my arm.

"Can I lick you?" He sounds anxious. "I've been thinking about licking your cunt all day. I had to . . ."

His voice shuts down and I want to kick the next words out of him. "You had to what?"

"I had to jerk off in the shower. So I wouldn't, you know."

"Wouldn't what?" Why do I sound so breathless?

"So I wouldn't jump on you in your sleep. Like I . . . We . . ."

Like we used to do, he means. Because, yes, that's who we were. He'd get into bed and reach for me and I'd flow into his arms and he'd pour himself into my body, like we were meant to be there. I loved waking up with him inside me.

I don't know what to say to him anymore. How do you react when there's nothing left? When all those hours away have turned into days and months and then kids make sex improbable, uncomfortable, impossible. The daily mess of our lives makes just the idea of fucking a far-off memory.

He used to spread honey on me and lick it off. Our sheets were sticky. I loved the messes we made with our bodies. Messes were sexy.

Nothing sexy to see here.

"Can I?" I wish he wouldn't fucking ask. Asking means that I have to make one more goddamn decision.

Does he have *any* idea how many decisions I make in the course of a day? *Mommy, can I . . . ? Baby, would you . . . ? Ma'am, which one do you . . . ?*

I'm grinding my teeth again, even with the stupid night guard in: the one that cost a fortune. I pull it out so I can speak clearly, instead of mumbling like a toothless, ninety-year-old version of myself.

"C'mere." The hand that returns to my shoulder and urges me back to bed is stronger than I remember. Bigger. He's been working out. When does he have time for that? I've gained thirty pounds and he's got a gym body.

"C'mere," he whispers again, bypassing my face entirely. Which is probably wise, since I'm not sure I could stand to kiss right now. I'd probably bite.

I'm on my back, my long, ratty nightgown up around my neck and he's there, between my legs and I pull at him. "No, no, no, nooooooo," I wail, because he smells like shampoo and soap and mint, but I can't even remember when I last showered and whatever's down there, it's not even close to a good, clean, gym sweat. It's chasing-baby-broccoli-sweet-potato-frustration sweat. It's two-glasses-of-wine-just-so-I-can-sleep sweat. This body hasn't seen a razor in two years.

"Please."

My "*Yeah*," slides out, despite myself.

I'm forty and my husband is hot and I'm not. I'm just *not* anymore. But he's licking me and it feels a little bit good. Just a little. So I let him.

A tongue swipe up takes me all in. I worry about the last time I shaved, which was ages ago. But he knows me. He knows my hair, my smell. Knows how it all looked when the babies came out.

He groans, like maybe he's missed this, and I relax, just the tiniest bit. Another lick, sucking on my lips.

An "*Ooooh*," escapes me—oozing out into the room, ripe with the pleasure of taking it.

His lips close around my clit, which he knows so well. His hands tug hard at my thighs and I hear little things, words that I only slightly believe. "I've missed this, baby. Look at all these curves. You taste good.

So fucking good." Can I believe him? Should I? If he just—

My body's hauled up and over him and he's under me now, pulling at my ass until my cunt's pressed firmly onto his face and he's eating. A starving man, devouring me, making me wet with his saliva and my juices. I brace myself on the wall at the head of our bed, and grind hard against his teeth and lips. *Take it.* I force-feed him this new body he's given me.

He laps it up. All of it: my resentment, my animalistic grunts, the thrust of my hips. One big hand moves to my breast and, although I miss its hold on my ass, I enjoy the pinch. This nipple that's been used for other things for so long, it's sore and leaky, but he gets it just right. My belly tightens, I'm aching and empty for him.

His other hand roves up my body and ends up plastered over my mouth, holding in the hoarse shouts as his finger slides in and his teeth send me over.

Oh, Christ, it's good, this orgasm. Short and sharp and bright. It wakes up dormant nerve endings, reminds me that I'm alive.

I remain still through the aftershocks, smothering him in my pleasure, before rolling off and onto my side.

I'll rest. Just for a second before the monitor lights up with sound.

He wraps himself around me, conforming to my back, erection hot against my ass. Should I turn over and—

"Shhhhhhh, baby. Sleep." His familiar voice is

warm against my ear and I imagine us back in our first place—that tiny apartment where everything was possible.

"I've got the monitor. I love you. Sleep."

PHANTOM PAINS

Leandra Vane

M arcy groaned, and the sound echoed off her tall bedroom ceiling. This would have been thrilling if the groan had been in the throes of ecstasy rather than an intonation of frustration.

They don't tell you this on those remodel-your-dream-home TV shows, but even buying the Victorian-era Gothic Revival you've been craving your entire life will not soothe the sleepless nights when you haven't had a proper orgasm in months.

And now, though her days were filled with resto-ration projects and historically accurate wallpaper swatches, her nights were nothing but agonizing.

Marcy had toys. Marcy had a detachable shower-head. Marcy had a whole bookcase of ladies' literature. But the submissive in her was begging for more. Her regular play partner had moved to the coast so it had now been half a year since her last satisfying scene. She could cuff her own wrists to the headboard but there was no way she could give herself a satisfying spanking.

Marcy had dipped her toes into a light scene with a new play partner recently. But after he commanded she bend down, the only thing Marcy could think about were how ugly his shoes were. In such a position, the last thing on a sub's mind should be the dom's ugly-ass shoes.

Tossing such thoughts aside, Marcy drifted into an uneasy sleep. When she awoke, the moonlight was cast in swirling shapes over the ceiling, filtering in through sheer lace curtains. She was instantly awake, eyes wide, muscles tensed into action. She couldn't tell if it had been a snippet of a dream or if she had really heard the creak of opening door hinges.

Marcy glanced over and saw her bedroom door was still closed. But the thud in her chest from her startled heartbeat was very real. Marcy took a deep breath and settled back down, burying her head under the covers. Still, she had a strange feeling—intrusive, like someone was watching her.

Marcy wiggled out of the blankets. The bedroom door was indeed still closed. A chill crept across her bare arm and a shadow appeared in the corner of her vision.

Marcy sat straight up in bed. A figure loomed in the corner of the room.

She bolted for the bedroom door but the metal of the doorknob froze in her grasp. She rattled the knob hard but it wouldn't turn.

A snap sounded above her head and the light bulb illuminated from the high ceiling. Marcy's gaze crawled across the Victorian wallpaper to the modern switch, the lever firmly slanted down toward *off*.

"Going somewhere?" a man's voice asked, tone condescending.

The edges of Marcy's fear bristled with anger. She spun around to confront the possibility of an unruly intruder. But what she found was even more unexpected than imagined: a tall man in a white, high-collared dress shirt and sharply pleated black pants.

Everything from his haircut to the soft sheen of his leather shoes looked like he'd stepped out of a history book. The iridescence of the mother-of-pearl buttons on his shirt shimmered in the modern lighting.

"Is this what I've been reduced to?" He took a solid step forward. "Coming home to discover a wife adorned in nothing but the color of a harlot?"

Marcy glanced down at her silky red nightgown. When her gaze re-met his, she saw the smoldering mix of lust and control that was so rare to find in its natural state.

Either her imagination had conjured up the perfect dominant for her dream abode or this ghost was her soul mate. The fear that had been coursing cold through Marcy's veins heated instantly into arousal.

The brat in her spat out, "It's not *my* fault if you *like* it."

He closed the distance and grabbed for Marcy's wrist. He pulled her toward him, so close the fabric of his dress shirt crinkled in Marcy's ear. She pushed back, but instead of resisting he too took a step back, making Marcy stumble. He caught her, her hip resting on his thigh, his grip holding her arm tight and immobile.

"I ought to teach you a lesson," sounded his graveled voice from above.

"Sure," Marcy said, tossing an exaggeratedly bored stare at the mulberry wallpaper. "Go ahead."

When the man pulled back his free arm, she felt all his energy lift away for a moment. A breath. A beat.

Oh.

As his hand slapped her firmly across the ass, Marcy let out a shriek. Before she could breathe in he popped her again with a clean smack on her bottom.

"I intend you won't forget it."

The third stroke rang out in the cold air.

The heat rose from Marcy's body, a sweat breaking against her brow. She was too surprised to recover. The man took advantage of this fact, pivoting her to face the bed. Wasting no time, he wrenched her arm behind her back and pushed her facedown onto the bed.

Marcy wriggled against his hold, shoving blankets out of the way with her free hand, twisting against his grip on her wrist. She kicked her bare feet, her toes barely glancing the hardwood floor.

Her resistance did little to help her. The man lifted the bottom of her nightgown, baring her fully to him.

He's spanking me . . . He's seriously spanking *me.* The edge of this realization glittered with anticipation.

He spanked her with an open palm with full, underhanded strokes. Each whip of pain sent a surge of excitement up Marcy's spine. *One . . . Two . . . Three . . . Four . . .*

Marcy's struggling feet found the floor and she pressed her tiptoes against it so her ass was wedged just a little bit higher. She wiggled her cheeks just a little bit, too.

Thus the next slap he delivered was even harder than the blows before. The whole bed shook. Marcy was starting to shake.

"I'm not going to stop until the lesson is full in that mind of yours."

Not like Marcy had asked him to stop.

"Have you learned your lesson?"

Silence. Smack.

"I asked you a question."

Marcy bit her lip, forcing her voice to stay silent.

He delivered two more weighted spanks.

One more, raced Marcy's mind. *Please just one more.*

"Well?"

Marcy held her breath, squeezed the twisted sheet in her trembling grasp.

The final stroke exploded on her tender flesh, the tail of pain igniting her orgasm.

She cried out, not even caring to stifle her outburst in the crumpled sheets.

As the last sparks fizzled from the corners of her vision, the light above clicked off.

Marcy jumped up and clawed across the wall until she found the light switch. She gave a wild look around the room. There was nothing but the shambles that had become of her bedsheets and the lingering burn over her backside.

Marcy turned out the light and guided her trembling steps back into bed. She fell into it, feeling more comfortable in her body than she had in months.

Blissful sleep set in. Tomorrow night Marcy would ask his name so she could moan it out and hear its delicious echo from the tall ceiling.

KEYWORD SEARCH

Shayna York

How could the meaning of a word change so much from one generation to the next? Margie Kent shook her head, remembering the conversation she'd overheard at the coffee shop that morning. Two women in their early thirties had giggled about last evening's intimate pursuits, with no care to who might overhear.

One word had caught Margie's attention, and she struggled to understand how it fit within their kinky exploits. Holding her mind captive all day, it underlined her obvious lack of sexual knowledge. Now, in front of her home computer, she stared at the search engine, embarrassed to type those seven fateful letters.

At fifty-two, Margie had remained single since splitting from her husband three years ago. Their careers came with conflicting schedules and they'd developed individual interests. One cloudy Saturday morning over coffee, they'd looked up and realized they were strangers.

After one painful and frightening conversation, they'd worked together to divide up their life. She valued their continued friendship, but her bed, body, and heart were empty of passion and human touch.

"Damn it, type," Margie scolded out loud. Her fingers cooperated, and before she could delete the search she hit enter.

"What the hell! Oh, my God . . ." Her voice trailed off as a list of sexually graphic video clips popped up. These scenes were as far as you could get from her interpretation of the word.

She thought back to her school years—jocks posturing in front of giggling girls, issuing threats to lesser males. Pegging someone meant targeting them during dodgeball, or during the coach's baseball games, not a hint of these kinky sex scenes.

She pressed play.

A handsome, naked man climbed onto a bench, settling on all fours. A gorgeous woman approached him from behind, a large, glistening black dildo harnessed around her hips. Margie's cheeks flushed. Unable to look away, she bit her lip as the woman slid the phallus into the man's anus, while he whimpered in ecstasy. His cries grew as she pounded deep into his ass. With a final cry, he came. His lover stepped away, the dildo slipping out with an audible pop.

No, wait, Margie thought, *it was too soon.* Scrolling through the list of videos, she found a compilation of pegging scenes. She cranked the volume, leaning in to see every detail, and hear each moan and whimper.

The minutes passed, raunch and kink playing out in graphic detail. Margie grew restless, fidgeting. Her body tightened and her nipples firmed into sensitive peaks. She realized she was aroused, embarrassingly so. These erotic scenes, something she had never seen, jumpstarted a part of her ignored too long.

A sharp slap, followed by a trembling groan, drew her attention to the current scene. An Amazon, a curvaceous woman with cascades of dark brown hair, stood tall behind a prime example of a human male. His firm muscles, lighter brown body hair, and strong features were paired with green eyes and a hint of stubble. Naked and chained to a frame, he knelt on a bench, knees spread out. A gag, nipple clamps, and a blindfold left him at her mercy.

With a delicate paddle, she covered the flesh of his buttocks with strokes until they were dark red. The color was so enticing Margie wanted to smooth her hand over the abused flesh, to feel the heat rising from his bound body.

The camera focused on the panting man. Margie licked her lips as sweat raced down his neck and across his pecs. Tracking to show his engorged penis, the camera zoomed in on strands of pre-come glistening in the studio lights. His generous shaft twitched as he fought to calm his breathing. Margie watched as his heartbeat seemed to pulse right to the tip.

As the video panned out, Margie's jaw dropped at the massive dildo now strapped to the Amazon's hips. The tool glistened with lube, the head full and wide. The camera captured the pair from the side. Margie panted, waiting to see his reaction the very instant the fake cock breached his rear hole.

His eyes widened at the intrusion, and he pulled against the restraints as if to escape the anal assault. The Amazon pulsed her generous hips, his whimpering cries and ragged breathing evidence of his sweet agony. An unchecked moan stuttered from her throat as Margie saw his cock flex, evidence of his arousal flowing smoothly from the slit. She felt an answering liquid slickness between her thighs.

The sensory overload took its toll on Margie, just as the powerful thrusts were overwhelming the chained male. Rivers of sweat ran down his face and torso as he thrashed in his bonds, his cries primal. Margie wanted him. She wanted to shove him to his back, mount his hips, and impale herself on his swollen cock, riding him until she came, screaming her pleasure into the air.

Deeper and deeper the Amazon worked the entire length into her powerless partner. She set a pace that Margie could feel in her blood, in her now swollen clit.

Easing a hand into her leggings, Margie slipped fingers through folds soaking with her own juices. She couldn't remember ever being so turned on. Stroking her swollen flesh, she rubbed the pad of her thumb over her clit, moving faster, pressing harder.

Her cries matched his, as if they were joined in some way. When he shouted around the ball gag, Margie gasped, pinching her sensitive flesh. She was getting closer, but she needed to wait for him.

With the paddle, the Amazon reached around his torso, snagging the chain that connected the nipple clamps. Her captive bucked and screamed, his dick so swollen and red Margie was sure it would split. But still the powerful woman thrust in and out, taking him to his limit and beyond. Margie followed willingly.

It was no longer enough to finger her clit and play with her folds. Margie slipped two fingers into her aching channel, then another. Pumping her hand into her pussy, her body tightened. But she couldn't fly free yet.

A latex-gloved hand slid over his hip, the Amazon grasping his cock tightly. He bucked against the added pressure. Margie tried to breathe. She had to wait, to come with him.

Then it happened; his body tensed, head thrown back as ropes of thick, creamy come shot from his cock. Margie's muscles clamped down, fingers moving deep in her pussy. His glazed eyes seemed to lock onto hers. His tortured shout filled the air in chorus with her cries of ecstasy. His shaft continued to spurt, as Margie's body pulsed in pleasure.

She slumped back into her chair. On the screen, the

Amazon walked away, leaving her victim to hang, spent and exhausted.

It was well past the end of the video when Margie finally pulled herself together. Stumbling into her room, she fell onto the bed, dragging the covers over her numb body.

Her eyes closed, but a final thought had her lips turning up into a smile. Tomorrow she needed a new keyword to explore.

BEST IN SHOW

Rien Gray

Most girls wouldn't want their boyfriends to be called dogs. Madeline didn't mind so much.

Gabriel looked incredible as a pup. She loved his mask the most, with its sculpted leather ears and broad brow, tapering down to a muzzle with a plush black nose. Clever cutouts revealed Gabriel's warm brown eyes and the very bottom of his chin, where dark stubble grew in devil-may-care patches.

Just below was his collar, decorated with blue piping that Madeline added in dozens of careful stitches. The polished steel tag hanging from Gabriel's neck proudly declared his title as Pup G.

His leather harness was a web of straps framing his collarbones and shoulders, connected to tight cuffs that added an extra bulge to his biceps. Another strap flattened Gabriel's chest, but that was for comfort, not aesthetics.

Whenever he bent over, the slender whip of Gabriel's silicone tail came into view, wiggling with excitement. In Madeline's mind, puppy play was where "cute" met "scorching hot," because the tail was attached to a thick plug buried deep in Gabriel's ass.

Everything seemed to be in place, but she leaned in with a perfectionist's eye and brushed a stray hair off the muzzle. With a fresh polish before tomorrow evening, Gabriel would have the finest gear in the house—she'd make sure of it.

"How do I look?" he asked, settling onto all fours. The knuckles of his padded gloves squished against the carpet, knees and elbows relaxed. Tensing up on the floor meant sore joints for days.

"You look great, baby." Madeline smiled. "Now tell me, what are we going to do?"

Gabriel's head rose, high and determined. "We're going to win the Best Scene contest at the club tomorrow night."

She rewarded him with a tender stroke under the muzzle. "And why are we doing it?"

"To win the prize money so I can get rid of *these*." Gabriel's hands came up off the floor and gripped his chest tight. A hint of both nipples slipped past the strap, taped over with black Xs keep the public decency cops quiet.

"Exactly." Madeline's hand fell to her side. "We'll

show them what a good dog you are. Every leather mommy and daddy is going to be desperate to hold your leash by the time it's over. But who owns you, G?"

He dropped to all fours again. "You do, mistress."

With that word, the playful spark of dominance glowing in Madeline's chest cooled, sharpening to steel. She was exacting but not cruel, a firm and educating hand. As a man, Gabriel was the shining soul that kissed her thigh after every estrogen injection; as a dog, he had instincts in need of taming.

"Sit, boy."

Gabriel leaned back on his haunches in one smooth motion, spine erect. His eyes flickered upward, awaiting her next command.

That part was important. They'd practiced this scene a dozen times—it was for a performance, after all—but if they reacted too early on stage, the magic would evaporate. There was a fine, trembling line between perfect and organic.

"Very good." Madeline's fingers retreated to the zipper of her skirt, caressing its steel tongue and teeth. "I have a special toy for you to play with tonight."

With one firm pull, the skirt slipped down her thighs like a cocoon of leather, landing at her heels in a circle of dark fabric. She was bare underneath, save for the silicone ring around the base of her shaft. Gabriel's jaw slackened as he started to pant. It took everything Madeline had not to crack a smile.

After years on E, getting hard on command was

basically impossible, but it was easier—and very hot—to make Gabriel do the work for her. "Open up, puppy."

He obeyed immediately, and Madeline took herself in a light grip, guiding the head to Gabriel's lips. His tongue flicked out, tasting the hint of wetness at her slit before Gabriel's mouth slid like silk down every soft inch of her. Madeline gripped the back of his head, stroking the dark hair there, damp with sweat.

"Swallow," she commanded.

Gabriel gulped audibly around her length, face pressed against the gentle curve of her stomach. His throat quivered, but after a quick breath through his nose, Gabriel relaxed again, starting to suck and offering even more hot, slick friction. Madeline slowly rocked her hips, stealing and surrendering that last inch until she started to swell in his mouth.

"That's a good dog," Madeline said, keeping her voice steady. "You like to play, don't you, G?"

Holding his head tighter for balance, Madeline wedged one of her heels between Gabriel's legs. A hint of pressure spread him open, slick arousal smeared across the leather like fresh polish. An inch higher, he was already hard, his cock peeking out from its hood.

He whined around her as the vibration sent shocks of bliss up Madeline's spine. It would have been easy to lose herself fucking his mouth, but any amateur domme could demonstrate that. Showing off a true simultaneous orgasm onstage? Now that would knock the jock off even the most grumpy, hardcore leatherman.

Working out the timing had taken ages. Reading Gabriel's body language was key since he couldn't speak. "Ride me."

Her heel was drenched with the first roll of his hips, dragging his cock against the top of her shoe. Madeline felt Gabriel gag and pulled back enough for a full breath, marveling at the sticky threads of saliva clinging to the muzzle before she pushed into his mouth again, making him groan.

That was a good sign. She was getting closer too, pleasure blooming in the pit of her stomach with every thrust. A ripple of Velcro betrayed Gabriel's gloved hands clenching into tight fists, so she angled her shoe up even higher.

He groaned again, louder than before. His thighs quivered when they pressed in against her calf, making Madeline's length ache against the silicone ring. She was right on the edge, riding the line between oversensitive and eager to burst, but Gabriel wasn't there—not quite yet.

Full and wet, Madeline pumped her hips harder, digging her nails into Gabriel's scalp. That jolt of pain did the trick. He gasped, throat clenching tight, and Madeline braced her heels hard against the floor, ensuring Gabriel could take the friction he needed without toppling both of them over.

Orgasm was a hot, heady rush as she spilled into his mouth, the ring drawing out her release until there was nothing but white, relentless heat. Gabriel echoed her pleasure with needy jerks of his hips, coming so hard his eyes rolled back.

She pulled out slowly and left Gabriel panting, lips swollen and red with effort. Madeline shifted her imperious gaze out toward the imaginary crowd, then relaxed with a shaky breath. "Fuck. We did it."

Gabriel shivered. "How'd I do? You think it's enough?"

Subspace cast a glaze over his eyes, but if he was still verbal, that changed her aftercare plans. Madeline dropped onto her knees and ruffled Gabriel's hair, tilting up the muzzle to kiss him.

"You'll be best in show, baby," Madeline whispered.

In her heart, he already was.

THE DRESSAGE MASTER

Jordan Monroe

Sighing, Wulfe gathered his supplies. Black bridles and saddles hung on the walls, shining despite the dust. The daily polish was considered the most tedious of chores, but not to Wulfe.

This was his secret joy.

Today, he started in the left corner, glancing at the brass label. The name "Primevero" gleamed back at him. Wulfe smiled. All Lipizzaner stallions were magnificent, but Primevero was of a different caliber. He was the school's current master of the capriole, the most difficult maneuver. Wulfe couldn't count how many times he'd watched in awe as the beast leapt from the ground, kicked out his hind legs, and landed squarely on all four hooves, only to eagerly turn his large white head to his rider, who would present a sugar cube from the back pocket of his tailcoat.

Wulfe pulled the saddle off the rack and lowered the stirrups. As he cleaned, the scent flooded his nostrils. Something deep within his blood sharpened whenever he performed this task. The odor of commingled perspiration and tanned hides evoked something ancient and powerful.

The door opened and a rich baritone voice broke the silence. "There you are."

Wulfe didn't turn his head. Of all the riders to sneak into the tack room, it had to be Maximilian. And, of course, this pompous prick was Primevero's rider.

He continued his work, doing his best to ignore Maximilian. The man was too grand for his own good and was unfortunately as beautiful as the steed he rode. Tall, blond, and possessing eyes as blue as the Danube on a summer's day, Maximilian looked like he'd stepped from the pages of a Teutonic chronicle. Wulfe vigorously scrubbed the leather, ignoring the blush rising to his cheeks.

"Did you hear me?" Maximilian asked.

Wulfe heard deliberate steps on the stone floor. Before he could stop himself, Wulfe replied, "Don't schoolmasters have better things to do than skulk around the *Sattelkammer?*"

"Ordinarily, yes."

Wulfe was surprised the man didn't acknowledge his rudeness. "Then why are you here?"

Maximilian cleared his throat and answered, "I knew you'd be here."

That gave Wulfe pause. He wiped the rag over the smooth saddle and turned to face the interloper.

Don't stare, he admonished himself.

The afternoon sunlight illuminated Maximilian as though he were an angel—seraphim, not cherub. The brown tailcoat, white breeches, and black top boots fit him to perfection. Had he carried his whip, Wulfe could have easily mistaken him for an archangel.

"Why did you need to find me?"

"Two reasons. The first is that the headmaster has decided you'll start longe training next week."

Wulfe's grip on the rag and sponge loosened as his heart leapt.

Maximilian continued. "You'll be without stirrups or reins while on the longe. Without these aids, you'll learn the subtle muscles in your seat and legs. Yes, you'll fall off a great deal. The trick is to land on your ass."

"What's the second reason?" Wulfe was dazed. This was the opportunity of a lifetime.

Maximilian stepped closer to him. "You'll need to learn to trust me, as I've trusted you with my tack. I'll teach you our methods."

Wulfe dropped his supplies. He bent to pick them up but—

"Ignore them."

When he raised his eyes, the gleaming black tips of Maximilian's boots were before him. Slowly, Wulfe rose and studied the other man: leather-encased strong calves yielding to powerful thighs barely contained in white buckskin. Ascending brass buttons sat snugly on a flat, wide belly, followed by a bleached-white cravat. From this vantage, Wulfe noticed that even Maximilian's lips seemed to have been formed from Michelangelo's masterful hands.

Without thinking, Wulfe pressed his mouth to those perfect lips.

When the other man froze, Wulfe panicked. He tried to pull away, but he couldn't because Maximilian's lips responded to his. Unsure, Wulfe kissed more firmly. Their movements were clumsy, their bodies asking questions their souls could not.

Wulfe clung to Maximilian's thick arms for balance and groaned as Maximilian's tongue eased its way into his mouth, filling him with the subtle flavors of mint and cane sugar.

With that, he pulled his head back. Maximilian stared back at him with eyes clouded with desire. "Is this what you want?"

Wulfe heard hesitation in the other man's voice. This mighty figure in his arms needed his protection. Caressing Maximilian's face, he whispered, "Yes."

Maximilian sighed and covered Wulfe's lips with his own. Their kisses became more urgent, more deliberate. Hot breath covered Wulfe's upper lip and the two men pulled each other closer. In seconds, Wulfe was pinned to the brick wall. He tilted his hips forward and looked down the other man's body. The brutal shape of

Maximilian's cock was clearly visible beneath the buckskin. Wulfe's mouth watered.

"You'll get it in good time," Maximilian whispered and gently nipped Wulfe's earlobe.

Before Wulfe could respond, Maximilian kissed and licked his neck while his large hands traversed his body. Wulfe surrendered, softly groaning when those hands, skilled with rein and whip, reached his hips.

Nimble fingers quickly unbuttoned the fly at his trousers. Wulfe hissed through his teeth as Maximilian rubbed his cock, which was nearly bursting through the thin fabric of his smallclothes. He rocked his hips further forward, desperately reaching for more contact, more warmth, more—

"Maximilian," he couldn't help but moan.

There was a brief kiss on his mouth. "Call me Max."

The man knelt before him, the silver points of his spurs glinting in the sunlight. Those splendid fingers moved languidly as Max pulled Wulfe's engorged organ from his smallclothes. His knees buckled as Max rubbed his thumb over the tip, spreading the pearl of fluid. Soul-piercing blue eyes never left his as Max placed his thumb between his lips.

Without warning, Max closed his mouth over Wulfe's length, his thick tongue coating him. Wulfe asked breathlessly, "Can I touch you? My hands are dirty."

Max didn't let him go as he reached for one of Wulfe's wrists and guided his hand to the top of his head. Wulfe cradled the back of Max's neck while he let him do as he wished. His ministrations were varied and complex, with moments of delicate teasing followed by his entire mouth engulfing Wulfe's cock. With each descent further toward Wulfe's body, Max grunted.

Glorious tingling sensations coursed through Wulfe; rather than restrain them, he further surrendered, letting the pressure build. He whispered, "Can I come?"

Max didn't pause; rather, he pressed the meaty part of his tongue against the frenulum and rolled his tongue against it. Wulfe's toes curled in his boots and, with a few deliberate thrusts, he emptied himself. Max's tongue swept over his swollen head until Wulfe cried out and gently pushed him away. He opened his eyes to find the most beautiful man he'd ever encountered smiling up at him. Overwhelmed, Wulfe caressed his cheek and then helped him rise to his feet.

Maximilian reached out and returned the caress. With that, he walked to the door. Over his shoulder, he said to Wulfe, "Be ready for next week. The stallion will be hard on you, as will I."

THE THIN VEIL

Heather Lin

A delaide was angry. She was angry that her father, rather than choosing from one of *three* interested suitors, had given in to peasant unrest and chosen her to be this year's sacrifice to the dragon.

She was lovely, with amber eyes and smooth brown skin—and she was, of course, a virgin. The dragon would quite literally eat her alive and enjoy every moment. But what choice did she have? If she refused to go and her father sent a peasant in her stead, there would be a revolt. If he refused to send anyone at all, the dragon would burn the kingdom.

So she went, and the eunuch that accompanied her bore the brunt of her mood. His name was Alexei. He was a handsome, dark-haired emissary of the queen.

Adelaide imagined he would have been quite the

catch before his manhood had been cut off. In fact, that was the reason it had been removed, according to her maid. He'd fucked the wrong married woman. Now he was unable to molest another soul.

He was dull and unfriendly, and their journey along the narrow, muddy path was silent except for the sucking sound of mud beneath the horses' hooves. Adelaide was cold, saddle sore, and caked with dirt. Alexei would never agree to stopping by the stream, so she didn't ask him. She simply stopped her horse and dismounted. He narrowed his eyes, his irritation obvious, but it wasn't as if he would wrestle her back onto the horse.

She'd get her way. It was the last shred of control she could claim before facing the fire.

Adelaide didn't ask him to follow her behind the waterside shrubs, but he did, ever the vigilant escort, and he looked just a shred shocked to find her stripped down to her chemise. He turned away, olive skin flushed, while she removed the last barrier between herself and the cool, cleansing water of the stream.

When she was hip-deep, she glanced back at him. "Will you join me?"

He looked at her then, only glancing at her exposed breasts and stomach. She couldn't decide whether he was impressed by what he saw or not. She felt a tight excitement deep in her belly, and her anger burned again. She'd never know what it was like to lie with a man. What was the use of feeling attracted to this one? If he was capable of feeling the same, he could do nothing about it.

"Men and women don't bathe together," he said.

"I'm aware of the rules."

"You're implying I'm not a man."

Adelaide smirked. She was in a cruel mood, but she couldn't bring herself to lash out directly. Subtle nicks and bruises. That was how the court ladies played. She turned and lowered herself into the water, swimming a few strokes and letting the water envelop her.

She was startled by a splashing noise, but before she could turn around, Alexei was behind her, naked. His chest was hard, muscular, and his strong arms wrapped around her waist. She could have escaped him if she wanted to, but she hesitated. Having him against her like that felt good somehow. Sensation flooded between her legs, making her tremble. The missing element didn't seem so important in that moment.

"I may lack the instrument needed to plant my seed in your belly, but I still climb into women's beds and find triumph in their pleasure."

Adelaide couldn't imagine what he meant, but she was curious. That curiosity held her, even as uncertainty tried to push her toward shore.

He waited a moment, and when she didn't pull away, he slid his palm down her abdomen, into the water, and between her legs. She gasped as his finger landed neatly on her clit and bucked as he put pressure on the sensitive place. She'd noticed that place before, rubbed her thighs together, pressed herself against a table corner experimentally. But she was a lady, and she'd never taken it further.

Sensation exploded as he moved his finger in a slow, gentle rhythm, moving his hips in the same way until she was fully caught in the intimate dance. The feeling rose until Adelaide's mind and body were lost to it. She felt so desperate—panicked—for what was coming, she thought she might die, but she didn't care.

He spread her legs, distracting her for a moment, and pulled his body back. She felt the loss of warmth keenly, even as his finger remained in place. Much to her chagrin, she whimpered. His other hand slid between her thighs from behind, and he introduced the tip of a finger between her folds, *inside* her.

She froze. "No," she gasped, and he stopped. "You can't break—"

"I'm aware of the rules," he mocked in a smooth voice.

Adelaide moaned again. She didn't want him to stop the movement on her clit, and she tried to press against him. He obliged, keeping the tip of his finger still inside of her while moving his opposite hand. Soon, she was bucking against him, trying to drive that dangerous finger deeper.

"Ah, ah, ah," he reminded her, clearly enjoying her torment. "You can't break the veil or all will be lost."

His own tenor voice was hitched and breathy. She wondered if he was deriving some physical pleasure, as well. She hoped so. She didn't want to be alone in this.

She reached down, grasping his wrist, feeling like she was about to rush off the edge of a waterfall and wanting to stay connected to him. He noticed the change. His finger picked up speed, and just when she was on the brink of orgasm, he pressed the thumb of his other hand against the pucker between her round cheeks.

Adelaide was lost. She couldn't say what noise she made or how her body behaved. She'd been turned into liquid and was melting, rushing away with the water around them.

Too soon, she returned to herself. She collapsed against Alexei, and once she'd caught her breath, he loosed his arms. She turned to him. His dark eyes were hard, his jaw tight. She wondered why and reached a hand up to touch his cheek. A muscle twitched.

"You needn't feel any obligation toward me, Lady Adelaide."

So that was it. How many times had he pleased a woman only to be rejected after? Perhaps she just didn't know enough to be disgusted by his condition, but she would never make the mistake of believing that the manhood made the man again.

Life was short, and hers would be shorter than most. She didn't have time for battling instinct, and her instinct now was to kiss him.

"I don't," she assured him softly before pressing her lips to his, catching him by surprise.

He smiled slightly against her mouth and wrapped his arms around her. She had a feeling the rest of their journey together would be a friendlier one.

FIRST DAY

Katrina Jackson

'm starting a new job today, and I'm nervous. I wake up early to exfoliate my entire body. I spend half an hour applying my makeup because a perfectly symmetrical winged liner takes patience. I carefully untwist my curls, so they frame my face. I pull on a thin camel cashmere sweater and tuck it into a pair of navy cigarette pants. I slip on sensible ballet flats and head for the door.

I want to look professional and sexy, but I decide to forgo a bra because . . . I don't want to answer that question, so I rush out of the apartment before my roommate can interrogate me.

It's a twenty-minute drive to work, which isn't enough time to calm my nerves. My interview to be the Peters's personal assistant was intense, to say the least, and I've spent the past three months thinking about it, masturbating to the memory of it, and waiting impatiently for the day when I could be theirs officially.

Their assistant, I mean.

I pull into the driveway and stop in front of the black iron gate and intercom. I roll down my window. Yes, my car has manual windows, so what? Anyway, I roll down my window and speak into the intercom.

"Um . . . hi. It's Kierra. Your new assistant." My voice squeaks. I'm met with an excruciatingly long silence before the gates finally part, and I pull my car into the driveway.

I check my smile and lipstick in the rearview mirror. They're perfect, naturally. I grab my purse and push my car door, only to yelp when someone pulls it all the way open.

When I look up into Lane Peters's face, I get lost for a second in cool blue eyes and a flirty grin. Nearly two months have passed since I interviewed with Lane and Monica, and apparently, I'd forgotten a few key things.

First, Lane's smile is flirty and filthy.

Second, that whole Southern gentleman thing he has going on makes my knees weak. He offers his hand to help me from the car, and I swallow hard when he grips mine tight.

Third, they're tall, and I have a bit of a height kink.

Fourth, Monica's stare is intense, like make-my-nipples-harden intense. That was a problem on the day of my interview and is a bigger problem now, what with my lack of bra.

And lastly, the combination of Monica's eyes boring a hole through me and Lane's relaxed stare swallowing me whole makes my pussy quiver in excitement.

"Hi," I squeak.

"Were you giving yourself a lil' pep talk?" Lane teases.

"No, sir."

I don't know why I call him "sir," but he likes it. He wraps his free arm around Monica's waist and pulls her close to his side. "Sir. I could get used to that."

I don't doubt he feels my body shiver through our clasped hands.

"Phone," Monica barks, holding out her hand to me. The sharp bite of her command zips down my spine in the best way. I hold my purse close to my chest to hide my nipples.

I step forward to drop my phone into Monica's hand. My fingers accidentally brush against her palm, and I jump back—not that a single step can erase the dirty fantasies that brief touch arouses. I imagine that palm smoothing over my hip before slapping my ass with a sharp sting.

Lane chuckles warmly.

"Follow me." Monica turns on her heel and walks toward the house.

"Y-yes, ma'am," I whisper eagerly.

Monica's steps falter briefly.

Lane's hand settles at the small of my back, and his soft, minty breath disturbs my curls. "Don't fret, sweet girl."

My sharp groan shocks me, but I don't regret it.

Inside the house, I try to take in their suburban mansion while Monica gives me a quick tour, but it's too much, and I'm too horny.

"And here's your office."

Distracted, I nearly collide with her. I jump back and bounce against the lean column of Lane's body.

His hands wrap around my arms to steady me, but he doesn't let go.

I swallow the groan this time, not that it matters. They're close enough to hear my gulp and the pounding of my heart against my chest. This is all so inappropriate. I know that, but I don't care. *This* is what I've been dreaming about every night while in bed with my favorite vibrator: shivering between Monica and Lane, overheated skin, hard nipples, and a wet, aching pussy.

"Where are your offices?"

Monica steps forward. Lane's thumbs stroke me. When I take a deep breath, my nipples brush Monica's chest, and I swear Lane pushes me forward as if they've done this before. As if he knows what I want or, maybe, what his wife needs.

Me. I want them to need me. Take me.

Monica winds one of my curls carefully around her index finger. Blood is pounding through my veins, swelling my clit. The moment slows and stretches, and I pray that it'll never end.

"We have offices upstairs," she breathes, stretching

my curl gently, letting it bounce free. "But we're not home often."

"Right," I say, remembering that they're busy diplomats. This isn't a full-time job. I'm only here for a few months to get them coffee and keep their calendars. None of this can last.

Monica's index finger moves under my chin. She tips my head back to rest on Lane's shoulder. I feel caged between them. A feeling of calm washes over me.

"An agency representative will call to begin your onboarding." Her finger moves down my neck and rims the neckline of my sweater. "After your call, we'll discuss your day-to-day responsibilities."

"Okay," I breathe. We pretend it wasn't a moan.

"And the dress code," Lane adds, his lips almost brushing the shell of my ear. I want him to move closer, speak softer, touch me harder.

Monica's finger dips just inside my sweater.

My entire body coils tight with desperate, shameless, begging need.

"Someone forgot an article of clothing this morning," he says.

"I didn't mean to." I accidentally smile at my lie.

"Yes, you did," she says. "But then you second-guessed yourself and tried to hide everything you wanted to expose." Monica's forehead creases in disappointment, and they move away from me.

I sway on unsteady feet without them holding me up.

"If you're going to work for us, you'll need to learn

to go with your instincts," Monica says. She brushes past me down the hall with Lane close on her heels.

"Wait." My voice is as shaky as my fluttering pulse.

When they turn back, their eyes move slowly over my body, drinking in everything I'd shamelessly put on display. I realize now that Monica's disappointed that I hadn't been *more* shameless.

I never make the same mistake twice.

"What's the dress code?"

"Anything you think we'd like," Lane says.

"Because we will like it." Monica's voice is thick with desire.

I feel some crucial but unknown part of myself break free. I might only be their assistant for a few months, but I know that working for Monica and Lane will change me.

It already has.

THE VELVET

Roxanna Cross

Belinda opens her walk-in closet and wonders what the fuck is appropriate to wear to a sex club. She decides on a simple black backless dress that hits her mid-thigh. Her best friend, Chad, had bought her this dress after her divorce as a feel-good-about-herself gift, but Belinda had never dared to wear it. It's formfitting and way out of her comfort zone. Totally perfect for tonight.

Belinda stands on the tips of her toes, reaching for a box hidden at the back of the shelf. Her fingers wiggle to get a better hold, but only manage to topple the box onto her head. "Son of a bitch," she curses, rubbing her abused temple. A pair of vintage lace-up stiletto boots are now spilled at her feet. She hasn't worn these in ages and can't remember if she can walk in them without breaking her neck. Belinda picks them up along with her courage and slips them on. With each tug on the lace, the more confident she becomes. *I can do this,* she thinks as she struts across the room.

The Velvet's parking lot is full when Belinda arrives. When the valet opens her car door, she doesn't miss the heated look he gives her, which travels through her like a flame, shooting her confidence sky-high. She gives him a soft smile in return and makes her way to the entrance.

The doorman offers her a polite smile. "Good evening, miss. Do you have your invitation?" She deflates. "Miss?" he prompts.

"I . . . I," Belinda stutters, unable to find her words.

"Everything okay, Hank?" She hears Chad's husband, Trevor, say, his voice traveling across the floor. She casts her eyes down. Clearly, she made a mistake coming here. Hank turns aside and whispers something to Trevor. Belinda wants the earth to open up and swallow her whole. No such luck. Trevor stands on the other side of the threshold with a stunned look on his face, but triumph in his eyes. This can only mean one thing: Chad and Trevor set a bet to see if she would show up!

"Hot damn, Bells. You look gorgeous." He pulls her into a hug and leads her inside. "Oh, my God, I can't believe you agreed to this. I'm so excited. What made you change your mind?"

"I guess I finally took Chad's advice."

"My advice?" Chad asks, walking up to them with a huge smile on his face.

"Yes. You told me to fuck that stupid eat-pray-love shit and what I needed was a good dose of pussy worship."

"Honey cakes, the room is über comfy. I'll secure your legs with cuffs, but those boots, they stay on!"

"Okay," she squeaks.

Chad gathers her in his arms, kissing her forehead. "Bells, you got this." He winks and exits the room, gyrating his pelvis.

Trevor opens a side door. "Get comfortable," he orders. She strips off her dress, settling on what looks like half a massage bed bolted to the wall. There are openings for her legs and pelvis. "I've got you," Trevor calls, and she feels his hands on her legs. "Let me know if this is comfortable." He's lifted her legs and tied cuffs to her ankles and calves. She finds she can still move, flex, and bend.

Holy shit. She's really doing this. "Bells, you good?" Trevor asks.

She swallows her nerves and answers him, "Yes." He squeezes her ass and leaves her there, exposed. Naked, pussy hanging out, waiting. It's scary and thrilling. So is the sound of his footsteps moving further away; with each echoing footfall, Belinda's heart rate climbs. She's unsure if it's from nervousness, fear, anticipation, or a mix of all three.

There's a charge in the air that makes her suck in her breath. Fingers part her swollen folds. Goosebumps form under her flesh, making her wonder if she's truly ready for this. *Is this a man touching me?* The finger feels broad and wide, but it doesn't mean the owner is male. The finger slowly pushes in. "So fucking tight." The grunt of appreciation is deep and male and acts like a balm. After years of celibacy and an ex-husband who preferred cozying up to his assistant, this pure male, near animalistic response soothes old wounds and has Belinda's inner diva doing cartwheels. Warm lips close over her clit, and a hungry tongue licks it.

Suppressed yearnings awaken, as if the hands of time have rewound the clock and she is no longer a thirty-seven-year-old divorcée, but rather a green, untouched virgin experiencing sex for the first time all over again. Only this time is so much better. This lover is skilled and patient; his tongue swipes over her clit, laves it and licks up her juice-slick pussy lips. Belinda loses herself in the feel of his mouth on her skin, his hot breath traveling through her system, large, agile fingers stretching her flesh. He sucks and penetrates her with his tongue. "You taste so good," he whispers against her skin. This unseen stranger makes her feel desired and sexy.

Belinda's throat is closing up with unshed tears; she feels silly and stupid and all the more grateful for the protection offered by the glory hole's walls. At least her mystery lover can't witness her falling apart at the seams by his ministrations. She's overwhelmed by the storm of sensations and not just the sexual pleasure. Each groan and grunt and moan of his feeds her self-esteem, builds up her confidence, as a sense of empowerment grows into each of her cells. Her inner diva is shining through.

Basking in the pleasure offered, she surrenders to the experience. She can hear others in the room groaning and moaning, and clothes ruffling. Belinda never thought she'd be into exhibitionism but her newfound desire to show off is thrilling. Belinda feels beautiful, for the first time in forever. This man touching her, tasting her, and these voyeurs taking pleasure from watching her lover pleasuring her, are making her feel like a queen. The swirl of his tongue deep in her channel heats her blood as she feels the orgasm build.

Belinda's toes curls and eyelids close, her eyes rolling in the back of her head, while her teeth bite down on her lip hard enough for her to taste blood. The wild beat of her heart is so loud it's a wonder it's not echoing in surround sound. She moans shamelessly to the rhythm of his tongue spearing her core. Belinda finally understands why Chad said her vibrator provided only cheap thrills. The pleasure gained by her battery-operated boyfriend pales in comparison to this hot-blooded ravenous male savoring her as if she's the most exquisite delicacy.

He's a worshipper, and her pussy is his altar. She finally offers him her release, digging her nails into her palms as the shudders overtake her body, giving her exactly what she's been looking for.

ALTER EGO

Remy Parker

Simon rang the masseur's doorbell.

Although he'd been there before, he was nervous as he waited. This time would be different because he and the masseur had made a rather specific plan. They'd emailed repeatedly, back and forth, before settling on it. He stared at his feet, feeling a delicious mix of anxiety and arousal coursing through his core. He had never done this before.

"Hi, Simon!" said the masseur, smiling, just like any other visit. Simon felt a little more relaxed.

"Hello, good to see you," he replied.

"Do you need the bathroom?"

"No thanks, I'm fine. All set."

"Okay, there's water by the table there. I'll give you a minute, make yourself comfortable."

Simon was left alone. He undressed and climbed onto the massage table, wriggled, facedown, until he found the right position. He closed his eyes and took several deep breaths; making himself unwind was hard. This was not his usual massage. This time, the masseur would push him to do something new. He knew he wanted this, but he was unsure if he would be able to go through with it. His *alter ego,* forming night-fantasies in his mind that he would not bring up in person, had emailed Michael, the masseur, and planned this experience. Simon had thought deeply about these fantasies and knew that reticence might prevent him from experiencing them. If Michael simply asked him if he wanted anything different today, he would have hesitated; he would probably have said nothing. His *alter ego* had devised a way to lull him into proceeding and agreed to ground rules in advance. Simon simply had to say "broccoli" and Michael would stop.

Simon licked his lips, perhaps in anticipation. He felt the air move, and the slight shift as Michael's weight settled onto the table. He felt Michael straddle his thighs, and the warm oil drip onto his back. He felt the long, firm strokes, and he finally began to relax, drifting into the delicious twilight that massage could bring. He was barely present, focusing only on the movement of hands across his body. Michael's hands flowed smoothly and firmly down Simon's torso across his buttocks and to his calves before shifting back upward, slowly over his inner thighs, glancing his cock as they passed. Each traversal moved Michael's hands closer, and he then took Simon's cock and caressed it gently, coaxing forth its full rigidity. Simon stayed in that haze of peaceful pleasure as Michael stroked his arousal yet higher.

Then, Simon felt his wrists being held, and heard a breathy voice whisper in his ear. "I am going to cuff your wrists now." Simon did not move or speak. For the experience he craved, that he was afraid of, that he had agreed to last night, he now only had to do nothing. He knew he was safe, but allowed himself the feeling of having no choice, of being completely at Michael's mercy. His *alter ego,* when confirming that he would be there on time, had anticipated that when aroused, Simon would just let things proceed. He had planned this very moment of silent decision. If he remained still, he'd take a one-way step. Stepping off a diving board, you cannot change your mind once in the air. Simon was almost breathless with excitement and anticipation.

"Once these cuffs are on, your choice is made," Michael said gently. Simon did not move or speak; he let things he knew, deep down, he wanted, happen. As he heard the cuffs click, his arousal spiked. He knew what was coming next; he had planned it for himself. It was now inevitable. He suddenly doubted he could do this. Surely he'd be overwhelmed?

"Get ready. You're going to swallow my cock now." Michael held Simon's head, tipped it back slightly, and spoke again. "Open up, we're getting started." Simon felt the soft spongy tip of Michael's hard cock press against his lips, pushing through.

"Mmmmm, that's good. So good that you're going to take it all," said Michael. "Not right away. I'm going to take my time, enjoy myself, but you're going to take it. All of it. You're going to deep throat this cock. And I am going to come across your tongue and push my load down your throat with it. *You made your choice.* This *is* going to happen." Uncertain, Simon licked at the cock as it passed further into his mouth. Michael eased back, paused, and then pushed his cock back in. And again, not yet going deep.

"Suck," he said. Simon did as he was told. "Lick, suck, and run your tongue on the underside of my cock." He did as he was told. The masseur withdrew, pushed back in, this time going a bit further. And again, a little bit deeper, touching the back of his mouth. When he resisted a little, the masseur grasped his head, holding it firmly for a few seconds. The cock withdrew again.

"Stick your tongue out," said Michael. "Try to touch your chin with it." Simon complied. Michael waited a few moments. Simon held still, his tongue out, a frisson of fear spiking with the erotic anticipation. He held still. The masseur waited too, slowly moving the tip of his cock across Simon's lips, using the top of his protruding tongue.

"This is what you need . . ." said Michael, and in a firm, smooth stroke, pushed his stiff cock down into Simon's throat.

Simon had never done this before. He tried to pull back but couldn't. His hands trapped behind him and his head held firmly, Simon felt a brief surge of something like panic yet also an awareness that his own cock was rock hard and that every inch of Michael's length felt incredible. Simon let himself feel out of control, he struggled against his arm restraints, relishing the sense of powerlessness, the feeling of being overwhelmed.

"Good . . ." said the masseur, and withdrew, then pushed back down. Again, and again, he withdrew and pushed back deep. Then Michael pulled out and coated his cock with lube, ready to pleasure himself with his own hand.

"God yes," he said, "getting close now." Michael pumped his cock, feeling the orgasm bubbling in his belly. "Open wide. Tongue out."

Michael moaned suddenly and loudly, pushing his cock back into Simon's mouth. Simon knew what was about to happen, and that knowledge made his cock twitch with arousal. A pulse of excitement ran fast through his body and then hot come shot across his tongue, filling his mouth with saltiness. He thought he might try to swallow it, but before he could, the masseur's cock was back deep in his throat, pushing the load down, and still coming. He felt the orgasmic pulsing of Michael's cock in his throat, a new sensation he knew instantly he would want again.

Simon was bursting now with need, breathless with excitement and the aftermath of the cock in his throat.

Michael savored the moment, gently moving, enjoying the final strokes, and slowly withdrew, sighing deeply.

"Thank you," he said. "That was wonderful. Now, let's get you turned over."

Simon smiled, wondering what Michael would do next.

CATCH ME

Gwendolyn J. Bean

Suddenly, she was there. She strained her hips forward, almost touching him, almost grinding against his fingers, feeling the warmth spread through her body. Fuck. She pushed harder. Again. He pressed on her clit with just as much urgency, sending her over the edge. She exploded in an impossible orgasm. When the spasms subsided, she collapsed to the ground. He fell to his knees beside her, his head resting over her back, his arms wrapped around her, holding her. They stayed in tableau like this, acutely aware of the audience, on their feet, cheering, in a standing ovation. And she was left wondering, how did she get here?

The room had been silent. The man had stood, mute, looking at her, asking in his way, as he had many times before. The woman raised a hand to her heart.

It was racing. The light shining on her was suddenly too bright, too hot. She swallowed. The sound seemed deafeningly loud and she was relieved to have the white face paint that hid her blushing. With a deep breath, she had nodded.

They hadn't rehearsed it, but had talked about it late at night, planned it, fantasized about it. The man smiled and slowly raised an arm. He twirled an imaginary rope over his head, circling three times, and tossed it around her with inevitable accuracy. The woman gasped silently, as she felt the lasso tighten and pull her toward him. She moved awkwardly, pulled from the waist, and stumbled to a stop only a foot away. He loosened the imaginary rope. They stood silently staring at each other. There were a few nervous giggles from the audience, feeling the electricity but unsure where the story was going.

She hadn't known either and it made her pause. She studied her partner. He looked so sexy in black and white, his tight black pants, striped shirt, and suspenders. His mannerisms perfectly exaggerated, his white gloves drawing attention to the most subtle of hand gestures. His face paint was a canvas of white and black. The white paint highlighted the black, his eyebrows painted as an accent, a question for her. He had asked this question many times, during each of the sixty-three performances since she'd first brought it up. Each time he asked, she had hesitated, stuffing down her desire and letting the question go unanswered, letting the scene end and the audience clap awkwardly, not sure the show was over. Each time he had smiled at her, understanding her hesitation. She had been struggling lately, struggling to feel her body, always overthinking. But this time when he asked, something shifted. Every tendon leaned in, every nerve jumped, aching with this new desire, and her whole body said yes.

By now, the audience was on the edge of their seats, wanting to know the question, to know what was coming, not understanding but feeling somehow that the rules had changed. She looked at him and gave another slight, almost imperceptible nod. In response, he raised his arm and, without touching her, brought her lips to his. Their lips stayed an inch apart, but they could feel the presence of the other, the heat of the kiss.

A few people in the audience had started to clap, thinking the kiss was the end, the climax of the show. But most people stayed focused, waiting, willing it to continue, not sure how far it would go.

When they finally took a step back, she stood facing him, out of breath, black lips smudged, clothes rumpled. He smoothed her shirt for her and tucked a loosened strand of hair behind her ear. She had reached out for his hand, nervous, trying to keep the audience from seeing that she was shaking. She felt electricity in the space between them, and again, she nodded, yes. He brushed his fingers gently along her sides. His hands roamed over her, as he watched her respond to his touch, as the audience watched her body move with his. He pressed his palms to the space in front of her breasts, making deliberate circles, teasing her. She was sure the audience could see her nipples hardening. Her breathing quickened and he shifted in time, matching his movements to the rise and fall of her breath.

Suddenly, it was too much. She panicked and swooned, falling into his arms. It was a dramatic pantomime she'd perfected years ago and used whenever their improv got out of control. Her hand went to her forehead and her body slowly twisted and crumpled down, freezing in an impossibly awkward tableau an inch above his reluctantly waiting arms. He always caught her.

This time, the audience laughed too loud, releasing the tension that had been building. But she could feel his impatience. He had not wanted to break the tension. He pulled her, roughly, back up to standing. She thought about putting herself in a box, shifting the scene to a game of hide and seek, knowing he would follow her lead. But instead she stayed facing him, her stomach in knots of nerves and desire, waiting for him to make the next move.

He started over. In one smooth motion, he shifted behind her, his arms circled her, grazing over every part of her for the audience to see. He was standing so close that she could feel his erection pressed into the space between them. When he was finished exploring her body, his hands stopped at her breasts, almost rolling her hard nipples between his fingers. Slowly, he moved down her stomach, pausing, and then continuing lower until she knew he could feel the heat from her pussy. He continued between her thighs, forcing her legs apart without touching her. She stood, legs spread in front of the audience, on full display. He stood behind her, one hand groping her breast and the other massaging her mound.

She pressed her hips back into his cock as he pulled her closer, pinning her to him. Despite the inch of space between them, she felt his hardness with every movement, insistently present. He slid his hands to her hips and hooked his fingers under the band of her pants. He paused, and then with a dramatic move, he gave a firm tug, as if pulling her pants to her knees. The audience gave a collective gasp, and she stood there, exposed.

The smell of sex, of her sex, filled the air in the small space. The spotlight blaringly hot. She was lost. She alternated, rocking back on his cock and then forward, pressing his palm to her clit. He moved lower, spreading her legs further so the audience could see him dip a finger into her hole, watching her shiver. She pressed, more urgently now, feeling herself building, getting close to an orgasm as he rubbed his fingers in exaggerated circles over her clit. Every member of the audience held their breath, anticipating, building with her. The pressure of his fingers beating on her pussy, the heat of the spotlight, the presence of the audience, all making her dizzy. There was no turning back now.

THE RITUAL

M.P. Clifton

My Thursday evening ritual begins with steam rising from the placid surface of the bathwater where bubbles float like miniature icebergs. Their fragrance suggests roses, violets, and jasmine. The workday has taken its toll. Thanks to the jagged edge of a desk, a pair of pantyhose, worn only once, is destined for the trash bin beneath the bathroom sink.

If only someone were here to help with the zipper. But they're not. So I contort my arms. The dress falls away. Thankfully, my bra unsnaps in front. There are red lines where the straps dug into my shoulders all day.

I push the useless pantyhose to the floor. The mirror offers a sterile view of my body. Buds, not blossoms for breasts. Curves, not chiseled planes. A line similar to the one left by the bra encircles my midriff.

On days when I wear those god-awful control top pantyhose, I opt for no underwear. My scent clings to the tuft of chestnut hair between my legs.

Standing naked, except for the black onyx ring—a gift from Carlos—I step into the tub, my place of intimate refuge. No telephones, no television, no text messages. My routine is predictable, comforting. Warm water, bath oil, a glass of Chablis, candles along the rim of the tub, and the classical music Carlos introduced me to on our decadent holiday in Portugal.

The Joly Braga Santos Symphony Number 2 begins. A small ripple propels an island of foam as I wait for the strings to swell. Water caresses my body. I lean back in the oversized soaking tub. Immense for one, it easily accommodates two. With an inflatable pillow supporting my neck, I drape a washcloth over my eyes. The outside world disappears and with it the day's stress.

The pastorale evokes woodland scenes. I imagine couples frolicking around haystacks while grasping voluminous petticoats and loosened shirttails. Then, they swim naked in tranquil pools beneath low-hanging boughs. Each vision offers something unexpected, yet satisfying.

"Enjoying the bath?"

Startled, I open my eyes to see Carlos sitting atop the wicker clothes hamper. "When did you get here?" I say.

"Just now. May I watch?" he asks. The devilish smile, which caught my eye in that Lisbon airport bar years ago, flashes again.

"I'd rather you join me," I tease.

"I might. But for now, let me just sit here."

Using the washcloth, I drizzle water over my arms and shoulders in slow, gentle strokes, each a self-indulgent massage of tired muscle. Only my shoulders and the slight swell of my breasts are above the waterline.

Candle flames sway in small drafts caused by my movements. When I squint, those flames become distant stars. The bath oil, the aroma of his sandalwood cologne, and the fragrant Chablis create an intoxicating bouquet.

"I think I will join you," Carlos says.

I watch him undress. Though not burly, his shoulders are broad in the sleeveless undershirt. Without breaking our gaze, he unbuckles his jeans and pushes them to the floor before stepping from his briefs. He turns to grab a towel. When he does, I study his buttocks. Tight, muscular, and dimpled. I want to take hold and kiss him while wrapping my arms around his waist.

"I'll slip in next to you," he says while easing into the water and looping his arm over my shoulder. I rest my head in the crook of that arm. Heat rises from his body. I kiss his bicep and slide my hand along his thigh. When it approaches the point where it joins his torso, I look into his eyes, smile, but go no farther.

Tonight, ours will be a deliberately slow ballet.

Carlos kisses my neck, then nuzzles my ear. He caresses my body delicately, reminding me of our scuba diving in the Azores when schools of fish swam around us, their tiny fins tickling our arms and legs.

His fingers dance over me, yet make no attempt to find the spots that would hasten our lovemaking. He times his strokes to the music. Although he knows exactly what I like and where, each of our intimate interludes is a unique lascivious adventure.

I sip some wine. Its effervescence awakens my tongue. My hand rests on one of my thighs, while his inches up my other.

He whispers the words I long to hear, *"Amo-te."*

"I love you too," I echo.

Carlos traces my cheek, my forehead, around my ear. I am still astonished at the power of his slender fingers. As though electrified, they send sensuous messages my body cannot ignore. Seeking the focus of my desire, my hand climbs his leg. He is ready.

Though rigid, underwater he feels silken, smooth. My hand glides up and down, spiraling with each stroke. All the while his hand's journey continues. It moves from my face, down my neck, skips across my shoulder, then teases my nipple before settling between my legs. I react instantly. A soft moan escapes my lips. Our mouths meet. Our tongues dance.

Carlos whispers in my ear, "I want to love you," then slips behind me. With his legs on either side, he encircles me. He strums my body like it is one of those delicate stringed instruments playing in the background. I shudder at his touch. His erection presses against my back.

"I want you," I sigh.

"Turn around, *meu amor*," he murmurs.

I straddle him and kiss his chest. Our bodies shift, searching for the perfect fit of male and female. The warmth of the bath eases muscles, making his entry smooth. We do not seek quick climax but instead begin a lingering relaxed rhythm that will last until we collapse, exhausted.

His fingers work my back, paying particular attention to my spine. Somehow, he can soothe and excite all in the same touch. His powerful legs lift me. I grasp the rim of the tub. Candles on either side of his head cast a golden aura. Haloed, he is now a mythical god of hedonism. I throw my head back, offering him my arched body.

Carlos leans forward and feasts on my breasts. My nipples are tender strawberries atop modest pale mounds that he savors with his tongue.

Our bodies rock. We push against one another. Carlos cradles my ass in his hands, guiding me up and down. I cover his jaw with kisses. My heart pounds.

I embrace Carlos as he thrusts deep. The music approaches its crescendo just as we do. One final lunge and we dissolve into a wonderful orgasm. Drained and satisfied, I close my eyes to prolong the moment.

I wait all week for Thursday evening because Carlos always quenches my every carnal wish, whether spoken or not.

My eyes open to an empty bathroom where candles have melted, the water has cooled, and that open bottle of men's cologne stands exactly where I had placed it. Tomorrow night's imaginary lover will likely be Henrik from Berlin.

Not surprisingly, he prefers Handel's *Water Music*.

TOY WITH ME

Flora Rae

My phone rang suddenly, cutting off my best friend Oli's voice on the other line. A name flashed on the screen—Quinn Jacobs. I felt something swell in my throat, an anticipation that built in my chest and then surged. My fingers hovered, the distance between imagination and reality like the distance before a kiss, the barrier of the unknown begging to be dissolved.

"Hey, Oli, I have to go," I said. "Quinn's here."

"Oooh." His teasing lilt echoed my enthusiasm. "Have fun."

"Stop. We both know she's just a friend." I pressed *end call* and wondered if that curt, default answer could really be true. I hadn't seen Quinn in a year, not since she moved to New York City for her mysterious engineering job. Now, she sat in the lobby of my downtown

St. Louis apartment. The surroundings that I knew so well—the purple velvet loveseat, the twinkling lights shining through the windows—looked enlivened with Quinn posed against them, the yoga pants she usually wore traded in for a sleek, maroon wrap dress. I imagined tugging its thin string, effortlessly unveiling the woman at once so familiar and so distinctly changed.

The unspoken weight of our last encounter played on her face, tugging her lips into a half smile and softening her brown eyes into a hazy, downturned stare. After I'd driven her to the airport a year ago, she'd lingered in my Mini Cooper. The memories it carried enveloped us and wove us together. It was hard not to recall the times we'd pulled out of drive-throughs, laughing at the milkshake slicked across each other's upper lips, fingers gently reaching out to wipe it away. Or the times we'd changed in the backseat before a night out, memorizing each other's bra clasps, zippers, and errant strands of hair. I remembered blasting Shakira, her hand seizing my wrist in excitement. *Our favorite song.* Had there been more than just friendship in those small gestures?

I'll visit you. I love you, Liza. We ended most conversations this way: the sacred, ever-present vow of girls at a sleepover, about to divulge their biggest secrets. But something in her tone suggested the secret might be bigger than we thought—that we might have been keeping the same secret from each other. Her voice shook, a foundation buckling under new development. She had kissed me, then left me, all in the same suspended minute.

And she'd returned to me, too, fulfilling the promise. "Hi. I brought you a present." She smiled, extending a small, nondescript gift sack. "Wait until we get upstairs to open it."

The flirtation in her voice showed me she hadn't forgotten, or wanted to forget, that maybe our kiss had buoyed her while we'd been apart, like it had for me. As I pressed a button on the elevator, she pressed her hand into the small of my back, two twin gestures echoing each other.

"Are we really going to hook up in the elevator like Dan and Blair on *Gossip Girl*?" I referenced the shared fabric of our teenaged years strategically. This way I could say I was joking. I could say I'd just been bingeing our favorite show and it'd been in the back of my mind, in case . . .

Following the cue I didn't know I'd just given, Quinn crashed against me like we were two hot actresses on the CW. Her tongue parted my lips, replicating the first kiss we'd shared and taking it to an intensified level. Being entangled felt natural, so much so that when the door slid open and I removed my hand from her curls, it found an easy fit against her palm. Somehow, even holding hands felt charged, like a suggestion of what would happen later.

As we made our way through my apartment door, we continued our exploration, hands resting against body parts they'd only grazed before, rubbing and gripping with intentions that were impossible to mistake. I tugged the string that had mesmerized me earlier, Quinn's dress falling in a swirl of vibrant satin. Her newly bare legs pressed against mine through the ripped denim at my knees, so much heat transported up my entire body through just inches of skin. Quinn undid the button and zipper nimbly, her hand caressing me through my underwear as I groaned and desperately slid my pants off.

"Open your present," she murmured, a wet command an inch from my ear. I bristled, my clitoris throbbing under her precise, insistent touch. Couldn't she feel my yearning through my underwear, the fact that I wanted her more than some souvenir?

I reached into the sack out of obligation, surprised when something cool and contoured buzzed in my hand.

"The start-up in New York? We've been making sex toys," Quinn explained breathlessly, sounding like the most magnetic career fair presenter I'd ever heard. "I said I'd test this one on you, since, well"—her voice demurred to a lower, rumbly octave,—" . . . you were kind of the inspiration. Meet The Liza."

Never before had I been so turned on by my own name, or by the confidence and innovative genius of the woman who'd uttered it. "Wait," I gasped, recognizing the toy as Quinn's capable hands edged me onto the bar, its marble surface thrillingly cold and steady beneath my thighs. "That whole campaign about how women's

orgasms should be taken just as seriously as men's . . .
that was you?" I flashed back to a billboard featuring an
open mouth and legs spread beneath a short skirt. *The
Liza: Introducing the name everyone will be screaming.*

"We could talk about orgasm equality," Quinn
mused, a devious smirk curling across her face, "or I
could show you."

She brought the small toy to my clitoris, shocking
me with its unbridled power. I felt my legs tense as the
pulses began slowly, like a heartbeat, then grew into an
unrelenting echo that threatened to overtake me. As I
moaned through the waves of pleasure, Quinn tapped
the toy and its buzzes became more sure, its pattern
memorizing my hardened, dripping clit and its greedy
thrusts. I grinded against the rhythm, wanting no space
between my body and this intoxicating voltage.

Though it seemed impossible to direct my attention anywhere else but the stiffening button that now
felt like the center of my being, the aching sensation
doubled when Quinn moved her fingers inside me. The
walls of my vagina strained, gripping her and pushing
her deeper.

"Look into my eyes when I fuck you," she growled.
I obeyed and locked my gaze with hers, observing her
fierceness and pride as I fell apart in her hands. I felt
myself gush against the twisting, frantic prodding of her
curved fingers, my clitoris giving in to a spasm that shivered with a relief so strong it was almost painful. Quinn
pulled her fingers from me leisurely, extending the last

of my lingering chills. She cupped my face to kiss me and my own sticky release traced my lips.

I sighed, then heard a buzz as she opened her legs and directed my hand. "Orgasm equality, remember?" She rubbed my fingers against her with each playful, chiding syllable. "We're not done yet."

THIRD TIME'S THE CHARM

Ryley Banks

The first time it happened was between my legs in downward dog.

I was in my usual spot—last row, right-hand corner in front of the yoga studio's walls of mirrors—when my eyes met those of the woman next to me in the tight pink capris. Between *her* legs. In the mirror. A flush heated my body, and I glanced away. She's gorgeous. No way did she look at me like *that*. I adjusted my mat where it had bunched up and a small part of me wondered— would it happen again?

The second time, it was in cobra. The instructor had us hold the pose, shaking our heads gently left and right. Our eyes locked, neither of us moving. Hers were a stunning sapphire, somehow fitting with her tied-up long blonde hair.

She wore a light blue top with a built-in bra—I couldn't see lines. What I could see, though, were tight, eager nipples pushing shamelessly against the fabric. I turned in the other direction and caught the image of my own achy breasts in a mirror. Even after a few years, my silhouette still surprised me. Worth every penny.

I rotated back and hot yoga neighbor's eyes skipped down to my chest. Straight white teeth sank into her juicy bottom lip, and I wanted nothing more than for it to be *my* teeth instead. Warm arousal pooled low in my belly. The instructor changed poses, and I wanted to yell in frustration.

The third time—standing forward fold. Legs spread, hands clasped behind my back, bent at the waist. Her gaze greeted mine in the mirror, upside down between her toned, pink-clad thighs. *Please* let my ass look as good as hers.

Her lips mouthed: "Wait for me."

My breath caught, tight in my chest—was I reading her right? Still upside down, I nodded, my stomach clenched with anticipation. We straightened, standing upright in mountain pose, and I had to shake my long chestnut ponytail from my face. I snuck a glance to my left, pleased when the corners of her mouth quirked up. Lovely.

I barely noticed the rest of the moves, following along like a robot while fantasizing. But at the end, hot yoga neighbor walked away to talk to the instructor.

Wait. What if . . .

I took a few deep, centering breaths. I couldn't

control what happened. If she changed her mind, there was nothing I could do.

I rolled my mat and drank from my water bottle, adjusted my flowy tank top, packed and repacked my tote just to have something for my hands to do, to keep them from trembling.

As I watched, hot yoga neighbor nodded to the instructor and returned to her mat. She tilted her chin up, tongue briefly peeking from between her lips. Now that we stood next to each other, I towered over her by several inches, even barefoot.

"Hi," she said, her smile growing to a grin as she extended a hand. "I'm Megan."

"Jamie." I took her hand. Her skin was soft, her fingers long, elegant. "I've seen you here before. You're . . . busy."

"You could say that. I'm one of the co-owners of the studio." Megan did that lip-biting thing that had turned me inside out before. "I observe the classes and do one-on-ones. In fact"—she reached out, settling a warm hand on my bicep—"I usually have one now. But my student cancelled."

"That's too bad."

Megan tipped her head to the side. "Not really." The hand on my bicep—holy shit, she hadn't let go— squeezed.

"So . . . you have . . . free time?" Was my voice shaky?

Her blue eyes bored into my dark brown ones. "Would you like to see where we do private sessions?"

My skin ignited and my clit fattened, thickening a little with each heartbeat. I nodded.

In what felt like slow motion, Megan's sapphire eyes traveled from my face down my chest to where my loose top ended at my upper thighs and my clit pressed against my yoga pants, twitching as she stared.

Time stopped. Megan licked her lips. "Come with me."

I followed her down a short hall, desperately trying not to overthink this. I hadn't exactly been—involved? intimate?—with many people since my transition.

Before I could say anything, Megan led me through a wooden door with a nearly opaque, frosted glass inset that glowed in the soft lighting. The room smelled faintly of sandalwood, the floor covered with black gym mats.

We stopped in the middle of the room.

Close. So close.

The blue of her eyes was nearly swallowed by black pupils, and her breath came in little pants between parted lips. One of her hands returned to my bicep and the other mirrored it, thumbs caressing my smooth skin. I broke out in goosebumps.

"Is this okay?" she whispered.

"Yes."

The kiss was a frantic crash of lips, as much tongue and teeth as it was tender. I wove a hand around her ponytail, drawing her up on her tiptoes, while she grabbed the hair at the nape of my neck, gasping into my mouth.

We sank to the floor. Kneeling, pressed tightly front to front, there was nowhere to hide.

Slowly, confidently, her hand slipped between us, sliding along the full length of my clit, thumbing the tip. Coiled tension broke when she didn't back away.

"You're so wet," she said against my lips. "How do you want . . ."

I moved, sitting upright, drawing her in to straddle my lap. Then I leaned back a little, bracing myself on my arms. She pushed herself flush against me, her yoga pants warm and damp where she pressed her pussy to mine. Megan trembled as she used my ponytail to tilt my head. I cried into her mouth as she executed a filthy, full-body roll.

The musky scent of our arousal and frantic grunts as we rutted together filled the room. I ground up, pumping my hips, our bodies sliding with the slippery material between us. My fingers clawed the mat, desperately trying to hold onto my last shred of control.

Megan jerked my top down to reveal one of my tits, then pinched the plump nipple. The sharp, sudden sensation shot down my spine and I tugged her lower lip between my teeth as I came, shaking and wetting the slick fabric. She threw her head back, mouth slack, groaning as she rode me, her hips stuttering against the ridge of my clit.

We caught our breath, gently kissing. My hands found their way to her waist, nudging under her shirt to find the silky skin there. Megan stroked her hand down my front, tracing the wet spot on my pants. I shivered.

"I've been wanting to have a private lesson with you for a while," she said, laughing. "Your ass in these . . ."

"I've . . . wanted you, too. Coffee?"

She playfully cocked an eyebrow. "Shower first."

"Are there private showers?"

Megan nodded.

"Then lead the way."

OUTCALL

Elle Stanger

"*Did you bring the wipes?*" She crunched a mint between her teeth and dug through her purse. I had the wipes, the condoms, the strap, the lube, the gloves, and the Chapstick. I was nervous, but not because I was doing shows again.

We'd met in the strip club in our twenties and she was the best hustler I ever saw. She didn't talk about her personal life, didn't date or fuck the other staff or strippers, and always focused on her hustle. I liked the wild spark in her eyes that shone when she was popping out pole tricks or when leading a client to the dance rooms. We'd both worked in the strip club and nightlife industries for years, and eventually I saw her very rarely.

I need a break from the clubs! she exclaimed over text-message one night. *It's killing my knees and my soul. How do you feel about doing private shows with me?*

My heart pounded, I sat up to tap and respond, *I'd love to.* My pussy clenched as I hit send. I dug under my bed to retrieve my strongest vibrator.

I was breathing hard into my pillow while pushing the vibrator onto my pubic mound, thinking of touching her.

"Are you sure he's gonna like me?"

"He's gonna *love* you," she said as she tossed her hair up and checked the car mirror. "You're mysterious and striking and what's more important is that I like you, and that he can tell you're into me." *Does she know?* My heart was pounding harder now, my pussy clenching and twitching again.

"Just remember," she added, "it's all for fantasy and he can't tell you're nervous, because he's nervous."

I sniffed my armpits and nodded. We were ready.

"Timer set?"

"Got it, thirty-five minutes."

"I'll make sure we get paid first."

"Got it. You said he's chill though?"

"Yep, never had a problem so far. He thinks there's a bouncer waiting in the car anyway."

God, I loved her.

Mike was rather unremarkable looking, seemingly a nice-enough client with a few quirks and decent hygiene.

"Wow, you ladies just look wonderful." He rubbed his hand over his knee, smoothing his pants. "Something to drink? I have all the libations." Ah yes, this client type: the affable nerd, I thought to myself. She cultivates the best clients.

"Hi." I told him my work name, extending my hand and stepping gently toward him. "Angela and I really get along well, thanks for having us." The words felt stupid upon leaving my lips. Get along well? *Like, I'm dying to have her cunt on my face, thanks for the occasion, Mike.*

Angela laughed and picked up the envelope. "I'm going to freshen up. Why don't you remind Mike about the agreements?" She headed down a hallway while thumbing through the cash.

"Angela has filled me in on the call you had. We agree to a half hour of live entertainment for your pleasure. You are allowed to touch yourself but please do not touch us, okay, Mike?"

"Yes, mistress." He nodded, wincing and blushing.

I leaned in a little. "Angela has specified that you like to be . . . humiliated verbally?"

"For extra!" she shouted down the hallway. "Thanks for the gratuity, Mikey-boy." She was patting her damp hands on her skirt. She had washed her hands. I loved her even more. "Shall we begin?" She unrolled her blanket on the clean carpet, and we opened our purses of supplies.

Angela took my hand, running her long pointed

fingernail down my palm, which I knew Mike couldn't see. An electric shock ran up my throat. I swallowed hard.

"I bet you wish you were able to make women come." Her tone was hard, taunting.

Mike gasped out, "Yes, mistress." I giggled, suddenly feeling out of control. *Work. Move!* I told myself. I wrapped my arms around her waist, felt the curve of her spine. As my fingertips arrived at the nape of her neck, I moaned sweetly, "Ohhh, are you gonna make me come?" The client's chest was rising and falling as he sat in his chair. One hand rose from his lap and moved to his waist.

"*Sit on your hands!*" Angela barked. Her client, her lead. I said nothing, fascinated. "You can touch yourself when I tell you," she affirmed. Her eyes glowed, and they turned back to meet mine. *I'm gonna make you come*, she mouthed slowly, then her lips twisted into a devious smile.

I responded by peeling down the straps of her top and meeting my thumbs to her nipples while cupping her big breasts and bringing my lips to kiss them. As we sank to the blanket on the floor, I felt the softness under our knees, and I straddled her thigh without hesitation. "Oh!" My warm wetness slid hard upon her thigh, as I kissed her sweet, minty mouth.

"Hand me my bag, cuck," Angela snipped suddenly.

He eagerly complied, and seated back down, rocking excitedly. "Please, mistress . . ." he begged.

"Not yet, cuck. I want you to watch women pleasure themselves in a way you'll never understand."

"Yes, mistresses."

She snapped on a black nitrile glove, size small. Her long pointed finger claws were softened by it, yet still pointed right to me. My cunt throbbed, and I sucked on her nipples even more, tangled up in her legs. She brushed hair out of my eyes. "Lean back," she whispered and we moved like water together into another dimension of balance. I lifted my skirt and opened my legs obediently, and she cupped at my bulging pussy with her gloved hand before running her nails along the lacy sides of my black thong.

"You may touch your pathetic dick now."

"Thank you mistress," our client said, clearly overjoyed and breathless as he began frantically rubbing the crease of his pants, unzipping them. I saw the pinkness of his cock spring forward and then he was squeezing at the base of it, and at his balls.

"Ohhhh!" I gasped as the client unwittingly ejaculated, gasped, and sighed. Silence. My pussy and mouth gaped aghast as we realized our scene was coming to an end.

"Erm. Thank you, mistress."

Angela stared, stunned. "That was . . . faster than usual this time, cuck." She chuckled. "That's okay, glad to be of service." Angela handed him a wipe as her eyes flashed at the floor, partly triumphant, partly annoyed.

* * *

Street bulbs glared down as we drove quietly through the neighborhood. I rolled down the window after lighting a joint as we approached the freeway, heading back into the city.

"Well . . . that was an easy gig," Angela said smoothly.

"Yeah."

"It almost didn't even feel like work . . ." I passed the joint to Angela. She inhaled, coughed, laughed, and inhaled again.

"Yes, you were a good partner . . . let's work together again. We can book an hour next time, or maybe just give me directions to your place now and we can get in bed together."

"Sounds expensive." I giggled.

"Show me that you know how to help a woman come," she said, her eyes flashing in the dark. And I did.

OUR FRAGILE MOUTHS

Ruby Barrett

It's not that she has a food kink. It's his mouth. His lips purse after a sip of coffee, glistening and wet. His tongue chases the juice from a strawberry across his chin the same way he used to chase a bead of sweat from her navel. It's the sharp edge of his jaw as he chews, his throat working as he swallows.

Ben hasn't made her come since she lost the baby. Not with his hands, his cock. Not with his mouth.

The only way he uses his mouth on her at all is to press chaste kisses to her forehead.

She's a pop bottle, shaken up. Fizzing. She's all bubbles inside, ready to burst and one touch of his lips around the rim will set her off.

The loss never goes away. A never-healing tenderness around her hips that she keeps bumping against. A catch in her back that tweaks at just the right moment and sends her to the floor. It's that this is there too:

The memory of his mouth wrapped around her nipple.

His tongue flat against her pussy.

"Alice," he says.

She blinks away from his lips, turned in a funny sort of way, resembling the question mark in his gaze. "Can you pass the butter?"

She slides it across the table.

His knife slices through the fat. Easy. The same way he could slide his thumb through her cunt right now. If he wanted to. If he'd bother to touch her.

This isn't a food kink. Right now she's butter desperate for a knife.

The old wood floors creak beneath her as she pushes back from the table and stumbles to their tiny apartment bathroom.

She pictures his mouth when he says her favorite words: *couche* and *bise* and *miel*, as she slides her fingers into her pants and finds her clit swollen and begging. She grips the cold porcelain sink to keep from falling. Grits her teeth as she comes from the short hard pressure of her middle finger. But it's not enough, never enough. She's left angry with him, unfairly.

The oblivion is missing, that feeling of losing herself. Of pleasure so good it could be pain. It could be dying and she wouldn't care. She's lost without his beard rough between her legs, his nose nudging her clit.

The grief arrives on this slick slide of an unsatisfying climax. For the baby they lost and the ones before that. For the marriage they had before them. For the way he touched her before he believed her body was fragile.

He finds her on her knees on the wet bath mat with the tears of so many miscarried moments on her cheeks. He holds her because that's what Ben does. He pulls her into his lap, his arms wrapped tight around her. He kisses her fucking forehead.

"We'll try again," he whispers.

She wants to know when.

She wants to scream, *God no*. She doesn't want to try for anything. She wants to go back to a time when her forehead wasn't the only place on her body imprinted with his lips, when he whispered obscene words in her ear.

He sends her texts throughout the day with pictures of the sites he visits around Montreal. Working from home has perks but not when she's new to her husband's hometown and already lonely. Usually she texts him back with a picture of her lunch or the neighbor's cat cleaning its paws outside their window. Today she stabs at the screen until they disappear. She boils chicken and steams broccoli for dinner. A boring meal to punish his neglectful mouth.

"*Merci*," he murmurs as she sets down his plate. "You're upset with me."

She leans her hip so hard into the counter it hurts.

Pushing back from the table and standing behind her, his heat warms her from the outside in, reaching even the coldest part of her.

"Yes."

Ben brushes the hair back from her shoulder, placing a gentle kiss to her bare skin.

She gasps. "You haven't kissed me in so long."

"Of course I have." He sounds insouciant.

She turns to face him, grabbing his hand and placing it between her legs, cupping her cunt. "You haven't," she insists. "Not here."

He takes a step back, like she's shocked him. "*Non,*" he says and she watches the calculations across his face as he realizes how long it's been.

He drops to his knees and without pause, pulls her pants and panties down. He bites his lip as he takes in the V between her legs, the tight curls. His hand is a brand on her thigh as he spreads her legs wider and slides his thumb through her lips. She melts against the counter, in danger of falling to the ground until he is there.

His mouth. His beautiful mouth, his soft tongue, and warm breath. He swears against her lips while he fucks her with his mouth. Running his hand up the back of her leg, he slides one finger into her. She cries out and it mingles with the wet sounds of sex, the grunts, the slap of his hand against her ass.

Her hands are in his hair, pushing and pulling at him as he tongues her clit.

"*S'il vous plait*," he repeats over and over against her, the shock of his voice penetrating as deep as his finger does until blessedly, as she white-knuckles the countertop, she comes on his face, gushing her pleasure over him. Finally, the oblivion. The pleasure so good it hurts. It hurts so much it feels like dying and now she knows why every time before, without him, wasn't enough. Each shockwave of her orgasm is another little death.

The mother she wants to be, the marriage she wants back so desperately. She dies and dies again and again until she is nothing but fractals of herself. So many small pieces shattered on their linoleum floor. Ripped apart but put back together stronger.

Alice looks down at him and realizes he's coming apart too. His glasses askew, his face wet. His mouth trembling.

"My love." She crashes to the floor beside him, her hand on his hard cock before she can register the pain in her knees. His hands shake and flutter over her as she strokes him, spits into her palm, and strokes him again.

He is heat in her hand. The swollen head red, his cock dripping with his pre-come. But where her other palm is pressed to his chest, his heart can't find a rhythm. His eyes tear up even as they roll back in satisfaction.

With sudden clarity she knows he wasn't touching her like *she* was fragile. He wasn't touching her because *he* was.

He's breaking apart beneath her.

"Alice," he begs.

So she shows him, pardons him with her mouth around his cockhead as the first streamer of come jets into her throat. She coaxes from him the simple truth with her own mouth: it's okay to let yourself die this little bit, if it means coming back together.

SOFT

Sprocket J. Rydyr

It isn't precisely a secret. It's just an embarrassing habit and one Ash doesn't think that Toya would understand, so it's a habit they really only indulge in when she's not around. Like when Toya's at work or out with friends, or now when she's out picking up something from the hardware store that Ash has no opinions about (Toya's always got opinions when it comes to tools). Toya knows about the jockstrap, knows about the soft packer, even knows about the occasional indulgence in gay-for-pay porn, but she doesn't know how they all come together.

Toya's got a soft packer of her own for days when she's feeling a bit ballsy, days when she wants to strut around with "the confidence of a mediocre white man" as she puts it even though she's none of those things.

It's a bit of light drag for her, maybe an illicit thrill as she walks down the streets with a secret in the front pocket of her briefs, but it isn't like *this* for her. Toya's the bold one, the one who talks about these things instead of letting them molder in the back of the closet or the bottom of a drawer; if it felt like this for Toya she would've mentioned it by now.

Ash adjusts their bulge in the mirror with careful hands, savoring the feel of the flaccid cyberskin cock tucked into the pouch of their jockstrap: the anatomical details they can just feel through the sturdy fabric, the soft fullness of it fleshing out their crotch in the mirror, the way it sits pressed up against their body. It feels cool at first, but between arousal and body heat it'll warm up quickly.

Sometimes Ash walks around like this all day while Toya's at work. They'll put on their booty shorts or some butch gym shorts and just walk around the apartment with a bulge at their crotch, comfortable and reassuring as they go about the mundane minutiae of their day. Washing the dishes. Working in their home office. Feeling good and just a little bit sexy all day. Some days it's not even about feeling sexy; some days it just feels right.

But Toya's not at work; she's only at the hardware store. And although she could be there for hours, she could just as easily find exactly what she needs right away and be back within forty minutes, so Ash doesn't have all day to savor this feeling. Besides, they've been pent up for days. Their period ended not that long ago and they're still cruising on that hormonal high since Ash and Toya have both been too busy this week to get down to business—and they need a quick release.

Well, relatively quick. They need some buildup first or else it's totally unsatisfying.

So Ash fondles themself through their jockstrap and watches the display in the mirror and lets the heat build slowly. They trace the ridge of their glans, so clearly defined through the fabric of their jock. They cup the full bulk of their flaccid cock in one palm and squeeze. They press and rub and stroke until their face goes red and their skin dampens with sweat. They reach into their pouch and adjust, flipping the packer up into a soft erection. They run their fingers along the ridge from balls to glans then down again, rubbing back and forth, locking eyes with their reflection in the mirror.

It's ridiculous; it's silly. If anybody saw the spectacle, they'd laugh; but it's also hot as hell and it's got Ash panting.

How long has Toya been out, now? Ten minutes? Twenty?

Ash reaches back into their pouch and jerks themself off slowly, pressing their balls against their mons through the mesh pocket of the jock in a grinding motion, stirring hot friction between their legs. It only catches their clit slightly through the cushion of pubic hair, but that's enough to drag a heated grunt from their lips. They come like this, standing before the mirror and trembling just slightly, a gentle explosion that only makes their eyelids flutter for five seconds before they're back and thirsting for more.

To the bed, then. Soft packer grinding into the mattress, sweat dripping down to the small of their back and pooling there. Phone on: straight men making out in loud sucks and pops on the tiny screen, stiffening cocks rubbing together through designer boxer briefs. Toes braced against the mattress, bedsprings creaking, hamstrings and calves starting to burn because they forgot to stretch first. Arousal searing through their clit as they thrust against the yielding fleshiness of their prick. The men on-screen moan into each other's mouths, boxer briefs hitting the floor, obscene sucking sounds moving south.

The second orgasm is stronger than the first—a lightning bolt rather than a distant rumble of thunder—but their clit is still ablaze, begging for more friction, more, harder, faster, so they keep grinding. Muscles burning almost as fiercely as their arousal, sweat pouring, breath heaving; a slight change of angle and *there*, a third hot on the heels of the second, body still singing for a fourth.

The straight guys still haven't come once for the camera and Ash is on their fourth, their fifth—body greedy and desperate, hot flesh against hot cyberskin, grinding past exhaustion, grinding till their eyelashes are dotted with tears of exertion—their sixth and it's still good, it's still *so good* but their body is exhausted. They need a break and if they keep feeding this fire they're going to burn out every muscle in their body before they're sated.

"I'm gonna come," one of the guys promises right before he finally bursts, and Ash wants a seventh to time perfectly with his first but you can't have everything. As their breath slows and their body cools and the second straight guy pops his cork, Ash becomes aware of another breath in the room. They lift their head with some effort and look to the bedroom door where Toya stands frozen with her hand still on the knob, looking flushed and in awe. Toya blinks rapidly—caught in the act of catching Ash in the act—and closes her gaping mouth before opening it again.

"H-hey," Ash says unsteadily, almost too fucked out to be embarrassed.

"Hey," Toya says. "I didn't mean to interrupt, I just . . ." She chuckles, dazed. "That was *so* fucking hot," she admits. "I just, I heard you groaning and I wanted to make sure you were okay, and then you were obviously *beyond* okay, and I just—"

"It's fine," Ash says, and it is. It's embarrassing, sure, but Toya's clearly turned on rather than making fun, so it's fine.

" . . . Can I touch you?"

And even though Ash is a boneless, sweaty mess on the bed and their exhausted muscles are screaming for respite, they really want to be touched right now. "Yeah," Ash says. "Fuck yeah. You can touch."

ALL-NIGHTER

Ella Dawson

H e kisses you like he loves you. The memory of it will keep you awake for weeks after this. His breath shivers against your mouth as he pulls away to steady himself.

It is dark in this section of the library. The dusty fluorescent light flickers with exhaustion in the next row over. His face is mostly in shadow but you can still read the awe and tension in his features. His eyes have long since shuddered closed. A calloused hand is tight at your thigh, bracing you against a shelf; your fingers tangle in his hair and hold on for dear life. You dimly wonder in that lust-addled way if you will knock over the metal structure, if it can even *be* knocked over. But then his hips rock forward and dusty spines dig into your back and you groan and stop wondering about the shelves or the noise or the thirty pages due at the end of the week because his fingers are delving under the hem of the skirt rucked up around your waist. You want him to fuck you finally, *finally*.

It took seven weeks. Seven weeks of poorly concealed glances over the divider between your desks. Seven weeks of increasingly intentional games of footsie under the table. Seven weeks of chatting about "these damn all-nighters, am I right?" He is in your major but somehow you never met him before the library gods assigned you attached open carrels. You became fixated on the hard slope of his broad shoulders as he dropped his backpack to the dirty carpet each night.

"Sam," he introduced himself at some point in February when working here became a ritual. His handshake was firm and warm, his eyes clear as he leaned over the divider. By April a sooty layer of scruff overtook his previously clean-shaven jaw and you began to concoct stress-induced schemes of seduction between paragraphs. *Hey can you help me reach this book I need from the top shelf I can't quite get it and I—*

In the end he was the one who invented some bullshit excuse about needing help carrying books from the far end of the stacks. You didn't bother pointing out that he had long since finished the research portion of his thesis. It wasn't long before you were crushed up against his chest, his hand cupping your chin to find your lips in the half-light. It does not surprise you how quickly it escalates.

What does surprise you is how tender his touch is as he drags your sleeve down your shoulder to press a kiss against your skin, not with hunger but with reverence. Your head falls back against the shelf and you are grateful to be pinned between him and the sturdy weight of the library when your knees threaten to give out. He kisses you like he loves you and it scares you more than the risk of getting caught.

He buries his face in your neck, breathes hard as you fumble with the button of his jeans. The fabric gives under your shaking fingers and he hisses as you curve your hand around the hard length of him. Inane thoughts flit through your mind while you familiarize yourself with the smooth texture of his cock: *I never do things like this I don't know your last name I have wanted this for months.* You vocalize only the last, somehow finding breath to stammer, "I, I want—" before your voice cracks and the pad of his thumb traces the slick silk of your underwear.

There is a muted crinkle as he tears open the condom wrapper but you are not paying attention, focused instead on how you can feel the blood rushing along your lifeline when you clench your fist, fingertips pressed to palm. Or maybe that's your love line etched deep into your skin, supposed futures written across your hand. Then he hitches your leg around his waist and the air leaves your lungs as he guides himself into you, torturously slow.

Your teeth shred into your lower lip as you swallow

the moan building in your throat. He stills once he is thrust to the hilt inside of you, giving you both an opportunity to breathe and adjust. But then he hisses, strain written into his shoulders as he tries not to move until you're ready. You turn your head to find his lips with your own. The kiss is barely more than a brush because then he is moving, your back grinding against the shelves with each drawn out movement. One of your hands gets lost under his T-shirt and he covers your mouth to catch the whimpered cries you cannot rein in.

As much as you had thought of this happening, you never imagined it would taste so sweet, ache so much. A quick fuck in the stacks maybe, rushed and rough, but not borderline intimate, not with his lips humming against your neck, voice breaking as he stammers something about how good you feel, how gorgeous you are. You knew you wanted him, you just didn't know you wanted him like this.

He is kissing you again when you are close and you cry out against his mouth, every muscle in your body tensing like a stretched spring. You wish you could yell out his name and announce to the whole library that you are coming because of him. Then you release, fall and shudder and melt between his body and the bookshelf. Your mind is nothing, nothing beyond divine silence and the soft dust of the stacks.

And then there are details again—his forehead creased, a hand trembling as he hoists you up the shelf. You nip at his lower lip and he growls. Sweat drips from his hair onto your nose. Little details that make up a human, a whole person you've never known and will never forget. His sturdy weight writes you into the stacks as he breaks.

A KNIGHT'S VIRTUE

Madrigal Geist

"I can stay only three days," said Sir Gawain to Lord Bertilak de Hautdesert. "Then I must continue on to the Green Chapel, and the Green Knight who awaits me there."

"My wife Brisolais and I will consider ourselves blessed to have a knight of the Round Table stay with us, even for only three days," Bertilak said. "And such a blessing! I would offer you a game, sir knight, a small entertainment. A bargain: I go hunting tomorrow. My winnings are yours when I return, if in exchange you will give me whatever *you* should earn while I am away."

"I am not certain what you expect me to find in your own castle," Gawain said. "But if it pleases my lord—very well. I accept your bargain."

* * *

The first trade was easy. Lord Bertilak returned with a deer slung over his broad shoulders, its antlers skewing his silhouette. He breathed easily even under the weight. Bertilak knelt in the great hall to present his prize to Gawain, then looked up with a sly smile on his weathered face. Still kneeling, he asked what Gawain had in return.

Gawain said nothing, only leaned over Bertilak, smoothed his hair out of the way, and pressed a kiss to his forehead. It would have been almost chaste if not for how Gawain lingered. The castle looked on in silence until Gawain pulled away, his breath harsh even as Bertilak's was calm.

Bertilak was still smiling, gentler now. "I hunt again tomorrow. Will you make the same bargain?"

"I will," Gawain said, turning away. "Tonight the castle should dine on venison. This is too much of a bounty for me alone." Bertilak did not ask who had given Gawain the kiss, and Gawain did not tell him.

Bertilak returned the next evening with a mighty boar. Gawain smiled to see it, and smiled more to see his host unhurt, though his body was sheened with sweat even in the midwinter air. "Today this boar is my gift to you," Bertilak said, kneeling again. "What do you have for me?"

Gawain lifted Bertilak's bearded chin and kissed him, mouth open, and when Bertilak parted his lips Gawain slid his tongue into Bertilak's mouth, tangled his hands in Bertilak's curly hair, tasted Bertilak's breath. Kept his eyes closed tight against Bertilak's grass-green gaze.

When they parted, Gawain saw Lady Brisolais Hautdesert seated behind them at the high table, licking her lips. She winked; he looked away.

"You have one more day with us," Lord Bertilak said, "and then you leave for the Green Chapel. God willing you shall return to us the day after, but God makes no promises to creatures such as we. I ask you for a promise between men: one more day, and one more bargain."

"I so promise," Gawain said.

On the third day Bertilak returned carrying only a fox. "It is a small and ragged prize," he said in the hall, "and it shames me to present it to you. It is unfit that my court should see what little I can offer, compared to the great gifts you must surely have in return."

Gawain shook his head. "What I have for you, I would not give in sight of your court. Let us dine first, and I shall give you your gift alone."

Bertilak dined with Gawain seated at his right shoulder and Brisolais at his left. Wife and husband laughed together as they ate, and she kissed his cheek, and whispered in his ear, and draped herself upon his shoulder, stretching one hand behind his back, close enough for Gawain to touch. After dinner she kissed Bertilak again before leaving—to do her embroidery, she said, her green eyes sparkling. Gawain led Lord Bertilak alone to his chambers.

"Now, what could this gift be," Bertilak said, smiling, "that you would wish to give it to me in private?"

"Not a gift I've given before, my lord," Gawain said. "And not one I think I will have much skill in giving, but I will endeavor to do my best."

"How virtuous, for a knight to strive against difficulty."

"Not difficult, but—" Gawain gestured clumsily. "My lord, could you sit down? On the edge of your bed."

Bertilak did so, and Gawain knelt between his spread knees, reached for the laces holding up his hose. Palmed the hardness of him through his breeches, tugged down his garments. Bertilak took a breath but said nothing.

Gawain leaned forward as Bertilak's cock came free of his clothes. He kissed the tip, already slick, and took Bertilak's cock into his mouth. He bobbed his head tentatively as he closed his eyes in concentration, trying to remember what Brisolais had done earlier that day, the clever motions of her mouth that had brought Gawain to shuddering climax. He worked his tongue—

A calloused hand, gentle against his cheek. "Sir Gawain," Bertilak said.

Gawain let Bertilak's cock fall from his mouth. "My lord?" he asked.

"I would look into your eyes, if you would have me."

Gawain nodded and returned to his ministrations. He knew he was being clumsy, felt Bertilak flinch when Gawain grazed teeth along his shaft, but Gawain kept his gaze locked on those green eyes, almost luminous, as Bertilak tangled fingers in his hair, gasped, and lost himself. Gawain closed his eyes then, as Bertilak's seed filled his mouth, and Bertilak murmured with pleasure as Gawain swallowed.

"I have no hunt planned for tomorrow," Bertilak said. "I can make you no exchanges. Will you stay even so?"

"I cannot," Gawain said, resting his forehead against Bertilak's knee. "My three days are over. The Green Chapel awaits."

"So dutiful." Bertilak took a deep breath. "My wife will return soon." Gawain tensed, but Bertilak continued. "Tomorrow you go to the Green Chapel, but for tonight, Gawain, will you stay with us?"

"With—with both of you?"

"Yes. Or do you prefer us singly?"

Gawain worried the hem of Bertilak's sheets. "Then you know," he said. "Then—my lord, I am ruined, I have—"

Bertilak put a finger to Gawain's lips. "You've ruined nothing. Not even my wife's dress, though she says she asked you to."

Gawain still flushed. "I have acted in a manner unbecoming of a knight."

"Hmm." Bertilak rubbed his chin. "The creature

you swore to meet at the Green Chapel—he may kill you. Your knighthood may be your death."

"My honor is worth death."

"Then we could offer you a little death here. You could do it: discard your honor, your knighthood, forget about the Chapel and the monster within. Stay at Castle Hautdesert, unbound by bargains or games. You'll lose the company of the Round Table, but my wife and I will be companionship enough, I'm sure."

Gawain sighed, kissed the inside of Bertilak's thigh. "I cannot, my lord," he said, and stood.

Bertilak nodded. "Very well, my knight. The Green Chapel awaits. But know that when your duties are done, I too will wait for you."

"A knight's duty does not end."

"Then I must be very patient indeed. I've waited three days—I can wait a lifetime more."

MARS ABUZZ

Rose Caraway

Marta guided the *Hatidže* over its designated docking port, next to her brand new lab—Mars's very first Bee Enclosure Module. The schematics she'd seen hadn't done the building justice, and her eyes opened wide as her ship touched ground. A spread of thirty gravity-assisted greenhouses sat beyond the BEM, similarly made but measuring one square mile *each*. The site was an audacious spectacle against the Martian mountain-scape, and Marta's eyes brimmed with tears at the breathtaking view.

She'd been commissioned by Mars's Apis ONE project for pollination services so that colonists would have consistently grown fresh produce and to solidify the idea that the big red planet was indeed their home. Freeze-dried meals traveled well, but fresh-grown, farmto-fork food could never be replaced. *Just like with sex,* Marta thought. *Nothing can replace real skin-against-skin fucking.* Her inner biologist was honored to make history today; however, another sort of excitement warmed her pussy. After eighteen long months, she'd finally get to feel Jack's strong arms wrapped around her body again.

Marta got her computer to communicate with the BEM, and, trusting that nothing mechanical would malfunction, she raced down to the ship's hold while the accordion-style umbilical slowly extended and attached itself to her ship.

Marta stripped out of her flight suit, including her bra and underwear, not wanting to wear too many layers while working in the greenhouses. The scent of her own arousal filled the small space, and lewd thoughts blossomed in her mind as she stepped into her beekeeper's suit. She zipped up her veil and then hit the inner cargo hatch release. The heavy door slid open, and balmy, propolis-scented air whooshed against her face like a salve. She tapped into her beekeeper's log, studying the infrared readings to verify that her queens were still viable. Across the board, all thirty brood clusters shone like bright little suns. Satisfied, she climbed into the vehicle and entered GAG#30's coordinates. The loader softly lurched into gear.

The pressure to finish quickly and go meet up with Jack was difficult to ignore, but Marta reminded herself that Mars wasn't paying her for hasty workmanship.

Besides, putting the mission unnecessarily at risk just because she wanted her husband's cock inside her was unacceptable. Once inside the greenhouse, Marta stepped out of the loader and hefted COLONY_30 onto its waiting hive-stand. Then she opened the hive's bottom entrance and stood back. Forager bees emerged and began their very first orientation flights on Mars.

It was exciting, sweaty work, but before Marta knew it, she was back at the BEM installing her last colony. She placed the hive on its stand, then headed back to the loader. Between the two front seats, sunlight glinted off the rim of a pint-size glass jar. She couldn't help but think about Jack and her sexy plans for him later. Marta's nipples scratched against the inside of her suit, and she quickly snatched up the jar, then grabbed her folding table and tools. When she was ready, she opened COLONY_1's top cover and pulled out a frame.

Bees buzzed around her veil as she whispered the old beekeeper's mantra, "Half for me. Half for you."

She cut out a section of ripe honeycomb and, one-handed, slid the frame back into the hive and replaced the lid. Marta was holding the honeycomb up to the sunlight when a soft, mechanical *zwoosh!* sounded behind her. She glanced over her shoulder and saw Jack standing in the lab's entrance. Honeycomb still in hand, Marta rushed to his outstretched arms. She cried, kissing him through her veil's scratchy screen.

"I tried to get here sooner," Jack whispered between kisses while fumbling for the veil's zipper.

"It doesn't matter." Marta sniffled. One-handed, she expertly unzipped her veil, and then Jack's warm lips fell against hers. Their shared urgency quickly became a groping, sticky set of actions. Jack tugged off his shirt while Marta undid the front of his pants. Jack busied himself divesting Marta of her bee suit next, but then he halted, seemingly in awe of her unexpected nudity underneath. Jack embraced Marta once more, pressing kisses against her neck. Eventually, his big hands slid and cupped the weight of her breasts. Slowly, he moved his kisses downward, over her sweaty abdomen, until he rested on his knees. He pressed his nose deep into her bushy pubic hair and issued a low, possessive growl. Jack said, "Just like this . . . this is what home feels like."

Marta swallowed and replied, "I know, baby. I know."

When Jack slid his tongue between her folds, slowly tasting, Marta gripped the back of her husband's head and nearly squished the honeycomb in her other hand. Back on Earth, she'd felt so alone, so unexpectedly homesick. But now, Mars wasn't between them anymore. Now, Mars was theirs. She tightened her grip on Jack's moppy, black hair and pulled until his mouth released her pussy with an audible *smack*. "There'll be time for pussy-worship later."

Jack looked up. His gaze slid toward the honeycomb.

"You want to give me a proper homecoming?" Marta purred.

Without hesitation, Jack nodded, his thick hair

tugging rhythmically in her tight grip. "Yes, ma'am, I definitely do."

"Assume the position, then," she said, releasing him.

Jack lay on the red-dirt path, supine, his palms up, his lean muscles relaxed. The sight of her husband's nude body, his cock made available for her use—reassured Marta that, though they'd been apart for so long, his submissive instincts hadn't abandoned him.

She straddled his thighs and raised the honeycomb.

"I want to feel your body against mine, Jack. I need your skin to stick to mine." Marta squeezed the honeycomb, trailing honey over her husband's brawny left nipple and then his right. She shimmied up a little more, until his swollen shaft pressed against her hairy cunt. She said, "I'm going to *take* that big, sweet cock of yours, Jack. I'm going to fill myself up with it."

Jack sucked in a breath as Marta drizzled the warm honey over his erection. Slathering the remaining sticky substance over her tits, she rose onto her knees and lowered herself down. Her head fell back as she very slowly took him in. She reveled in the sticky grip of her now honey-coated cunt hairs, labia, and clit as they all tried to cling to the base of her husband's cock as she rocked her hips.

It wasn't long before Marta urgently pitched forward, however. The hard-packed red dirt was rough against her knees but Marta didn't care. Her pussy-pounding efforts distracted her from any pain and pushed her toward a fast-approaching orgasm. She gripped Jack's hands, shoved them back over his head, and then she took his lips in hers. Their teeth clashed as Marta possessed him completely. As the slow, cunt-gripping wave of orgasm tightened in her middle, she ordered, "Give it all to me, Jack, now."

Arms still pinned, Jack tightened his abdomen and bucked up into her. Marta rode her husband until the long, pulsing waves of sticky ecstasy finally brought her home.

SAFE

Alain Bell

The torture has gone on for hours. Relentless. Unending. She only ever asks one question. The one query I refuse to answer. Why won't she ask something else? Something I can answer? Something that won't make me feel a failure.

Mistress promises it's not a failure. And I know that it's a necessary answer. One that ensures I'll come to no harm. A simple word that'll stop everything.

But I'm stubborn.

Sweat drips from my skin while a more intimate fluid trickles from my core, scenting the air with the pungent aroma of sex and perspiration. I'm force field bound to a diabolical chair-like contraption that allows her to put me in nearly any position she likes. The force fields that bind me to the chair by my forearms and shins are comfortable and never chafe.

"Say the word and I'll carry you into a warm, relaxing bath." She strokes a nail down my sensitized skin from breast to a millimeter above my hard, straining, and swollen clit. A trail of goosebumps follows the digit as another shock of sensation flows through my exhausted body.

I can't give in. I want to please her. I want to worship her. I want to show her.

Show her I can be her good pet.

Show her I can accept her devotion.

Show her I can love her with all I am.

She asks again. "Will you say your safeword?"

I shake my head, trying for vigorous, but exhaustion limits my motion to a feeble side-to-side. The safeword is about love and care, not lack of endurance. Not an inability to take the pain. Not a lack of devotion. I know it's there because she wants the experience to always be within my limits. To avoid scaring me. To make the experience great for us both.

But I want to rise to the challenge.

Her eyes twinkle with a gleam some would call evil, but I call sexy. That look promises a night of pain, pleasure, and passion. Even after hours of play, she maintains that expression, keeping me aroused and expecting what will come.

"Repeat the count, pet." She strokes her red-painted nail in a mirror of the path she did a moment ago.

"S-sixty-eight, mistress."

She started with my small, sensitive breasts. Gentle

caresses over the undersides that drove me to the precipice, then a sharp tweak to a nipple that tossed me over the edge. Her treatment of my tits became rougher through successive orgasms to culminate in her use of a short-tailed kurt until both globes glowed red and a sixth orgasm overcame me.

My love for her is a flower garden that feeds my soul with its beauty, but a fresh bloom grows as the redness increased on my chest. My adoration isn't because of the BDSM, but because she seemed to always know my wants and desires, loves and hates, comforts and kinks. Her eager acceptance and participation in my darker desires is the thick just-right-sweetness frosting I adore on the delicious, moist, and rich chocolate cake of our relationship.

Her caution while whipping me nourishes this latest budding of affection. I enjoy her dominance and control and some minor pain, but not bruising and scarring. She learned my limits in our first session and never strayed. She's a master—well, mistress—at the perfect application of the flogger to give me a warm flush that drenches my core like Niagara Falls.

For the next six orgasms, she concentrated on my clit until I was squirming away from her touch as much as my bonds would allow. She followed that with attention to my G-spot. She started with her fingers and graduated to a vibrating massager that made my toes tingle when I came. Warmth suffused me and the chemical mishmash from my brain reinforced my undying love for her.

She says she wants to break our record of fifty. I'm multiorgasmic, but after a while the contractions become painful, yet still gloriously pleasurable. But she doesn't stop. My longest break was sixteen minutes to use the restroom. Had she not needed to replace a burned-out focusing crystal on an ankle force band, my respite would have been shorter.

Over the next few hours, she used direct nerve stimulation. Usually she considers artificial stimulation cheating, but she has a goal, and only my safeword would stop it. Throughout it all she checked in, made sure I drank water, and even liquid nutrition.

Without my safeword, she would never stop.

She says, "Enough rest, pet. You can do this for me. You can withstand. But if you do not, I will still cherish you, still love you, still adore you."

A warm flush, not of another orgasm but of contentment and joy, flows through me. Throughout our years together she has protected me, cared for me, and given me all I could hope for. She is my everything.

She places bulky yet light clamps over my nipples. I'm confused because they are not exerting the pressure she knows makes me oh-so-wet. She doesn't pause as she slides our right-size vibrating G-spot stimulating dildo into my sopping core. The stimulation quakes through my tired body. At the same instance, as if something links them, my nipples feel like a warm, soft mouth is sucking and licking them with oh-so-perfect attention.

She keeps me there, stroking and adoring my body

while I rise higher and higher. Until now, she's seemed eager to bring me to orgasm quickly. Not this time. Instead, as I approach the precipice, she reduces the setting on the devious machines tormenting me. Over and over I approach the edge, and time and time again she stops me.

I beg and plead until my senses are so scrambled, I barely know where I am. Then, she does something she hasn't done the entire sixty-eight other times. She licks my clit with her wonderful, warm, wet tongue.

Multicolored sparks erupt from my center as my orgasm overtakes me. Heat flows through every cell of me from the tips of my toes to the very ends of my hair follicles. My pleasure overwhelms the cramps from my core at their continued punishment. The rainbow of light behind my eyelids turns white and I fade into a blissful sleep.

When I wake, my wife cuddled behind me stroking my thigh, I'm no longer in the chair. My body aches in a sublime, used way that I cherish. I let out a sigh and push into my mistress.

Her lips tickle my lobe, and she whispers in my ear. "Sixty-nine. I'm proud of you, love. My pillow princess."

I mumble, "I didn't say it."

She snuggles into my hair. "No, you didn't, love. Rest. Tomorrow you can prove me wrong."

Happy serotonin surges through my body as I fade back into sleep, protected by the love of my life.

MASTURBATING PREGNANT DANCING FEMALE SEEKS HERSELF

Endionajones

I t took the course of nine months for her identity of thirty years to be overthrown. In such a short amount of time, her new role seemed to dominate all others. Expecting. Glowing. She was now just a person growing another person. The Maiden had become the Mother, all praise. Her friends and family could not talk to her about anything else but mothering and the baby to come. She needed to feel that she was something more than a breeder. So, at the end of her pregnancy, she finally started dancing.

To her, dance was an act of explosive expression, something a shy introvert like herself would never do. Luckily, she was about to give birth during a pandemic. A new, deadly virus had caused a worldwide strict shutdown of in-person activities to reduce the spread. Like most businesses, the belly dance studio she religiously followed on social media had to close, but began virtual lessons.

Before the restrictions, she had ached to attend courses they held, but never had the courage to actually go. Now, she could dance from the privacy of her own home; it was the perfect event to see what else her body was capable of. A pressing endeavor, for the creature inside her was coming and soon would limit her time and energy even more. This was her chance to begin again, on her own terms, and it seemed like an act of delicious rebellion.

The first day was incredibly awkward. Rhythm was not in the vocabulary of her limbs, and even less so now that her torso was at max capacity. Her hips were stiff and she had a hard time isolating them to follow the movements. She did not feel very sexy and knew she did not look like the charismatic dancers she envied. Never mind that she was nine months pregnant. It was hard to shut off her brain, to let go . . . and impossible not to get quickly disappointed and frustrated. But, as she participated in each session, she felt a tiny bit transformed: looser and less serious. Each new motion watered the seeds of confidence that were buried deep inside of her, bursting to sprout. As the days went on, she actually had fun! In the movements, she started to feel powerful and playful. She had control. Even her parasitic hitchhiker could not judge her in that moment. She drowned in the sacredness of it and wanted to feel that way forever. She desperately needed to know how to continue to tap into that feeling. This new unexpected sensation of mastery and confidence.

Belly dance gets the baby in, belly dance gets the baby out, she remembered someone saying. Now she could feel why. As she jiggled each hip up and down, she could envision the entire female anatomy dancing with her, truly being a part of her. The cervix, vagina, perineum, and vulva all joined in on the investigation of her truest self finally being studied. Toward the end of the last dance class, the mystery of her undercarriage sang its siren call. The gyration of her hips in time with tribal drums elicited primitive cravings. The shimmying relaxed all of her lips.

Dripping with sweat and inspiration, her hand went south, circumventing the globe of her stretched torso, an expedition to better know her sex. Lying down and stretching legs wider on the floor, she found better access. Fingers reached hungrily and found their feast of layered flesh. One at a time, she parted her lips with a single finger. Surprisingly wet already, her fingertips made small timid strokes as far as they could reach. Each one found a new fold and with it a new texture. Index and middle finger plummeted inside, burning wet and sending sparks down her legs and warmth up her spine as they discovered ridges, hills, valleys, and canyons drenched in *yes . . . more.* She realized that she couldn't reach far enough inside to mimic penetration from another like she was used to. This was her territory but she was a foreign explorer. Her diligent digits worked their way north, moist and ready for the magic beanstalk. There they found the small rod under squishy flesh, swollen with attention, and moved steadily faster against it. She made her own music as her hips now moved fluidly and danced to the fresh flesh drumbeat. They melted. Every centimeter of her body became soaked with warm primal lubricant of lust. Buzzing from the inside out, pressure mounted against pelvic bones and she had to remind herself to breathe. When she did, moaning and coyote howls crawled out from deep within her center.

The organism dwelling inside her was not immune to the newly found liberation. It purred as the surrounding warm liquid vibrated and bathed it with oxytocin.

Her motions became mechanical, robotic in their purpose. It did not matter that her wrist was twisted awkwardly and starting to cramp from the unpracticed and unfamiliar motion. She would not stop until the experiment was completed. The conclusion to the ultimate hypothesis . . . an eruption of self and sanity! Stars glistened in her mind's eye and all was lost and found. Waves of warmth, achievement, and satisfaction came and went. The mechanism for feeling in control of who she was was with her all along. She could now add Goddess to her identities.

She closed her eyes and breathed deeply, taking in the smell of her dance sweat, the plants around her, and her bravery. With a soft smile, she slowly opened her eyes. She felt like she had been gone for years. Time had stood still, and it took several moments for her eyes to adjust to the room. Her hands lingered on her hips underneath her loose linen pants, feeling the pulse of pleasure on her skin. Sensations began to slowly dissipate, leaving her to face reality once again. She scanned her surroundings, looking at every piece of furniture, trinket, or painting in the room as if for the first time. Eventually her gaze met her desk, and paused at her open laptop.

She sat up abruptly, closed her legs, and brought both her hands to her mouth. It took several moments to believe what she saw. The computer had been left on. The live group meeting still running! How could she forget that her laptop was still open!?

Luckily, she had habitually turned off her camera at the last minute before the class began and the dance class had not watched her entire somatic voyage.

She slowly stood up, embarrassed, but slightly proud of herself. She imagined an orgasm ovation coming from the individual little boxes on the screen. She sighed in relief and, as with any great performance, all that was left to do was bow. The Masturbating Mama did a clumsy curtsy, smiled, and couldn't wait to dance again.

GOOD
FOR YOU

Imogen Markwell-Tweed

With his eyes screwed shut, Max laid on the bed. He was doing his best not to tremble, but the crackling fire across the room barely did anything to warm his naked body as he waited.

Noah was in the room somewhere, but behind the satin blindfold, Max had no idea *where*. He fought against the urge to call out for him or reach out, knowing that his boyfriend wanted him to be still and wait.

It was a new dynamic for them, this teasing. And he did like it. He liked when the waiting ended—he *really* liked that. But as he squirmed against the bed, chills running down his body, and his half-hard cock bobbing against his belly, he very much wanted to be done waiting.

Max took a deep breath, trying to center himself and listen to what Noah had asked of him. Without his sight, without being able to touch anything except the soft sheets underneath his body, he felt like he could come apart with just a thought.

"Very good," Noah said, voice closer than Max expected. He jolted, a low whine coming from his throat accidentally, and Noah rewarded him with a gentle touch down his stomach. His knuckles grazed Max's sensitive, cool skin, making his partner shiver.

"I—" He cut himself off when Noah's hand flattened against his lower belly, fingers digging in a little from the pressure. It didn't hurt—not even close. But it was a warning all the same, and Max bit hard on his bottom lip to keep himself from speaking.

"You're so good to me, Max," Noah praised. Max trembled and nodded eagerly.

The mattress dipped as Noah climbed on top of it. Max held his muscles tight and still as Noah straddled his hips, hovering over him. The thick material of his denim jeans dragged over Max's sensitive thighs, and he lost control of his muscles, trembling, even as the disappointment that his boyfriend was still clothed faintly floated into his thoughts.

"So pretty like this," Noah said, voice rough as he flattened both hands on Max's chest. He dragged them down, thumbs catching on his hard nipples. Max couldn't help the hiss that he let out. It was followed by a whimper when Noah pinched them.

"I'm going to help you," Noah promised. "Just keep being a good boy for me."

Then Noah grabbed his chin and kissed him. It was a bit too sloppy, Max stretching his neck up to meet Noah's teasing lips. He kept drawing away before dipping closer again; Max wiggled beneath his thighs as he tried to get closer. Noah's laugh ghosted over his lips and he bit a bruising kiss against his throat, smiling into it when Max let out a helpless groan.

The blindfold was starting to slip a little off his brow, not half as tight as it usually was. Max made sure to squeeze his eyes shut before the whole thing fell off.

Noah's fingers slid beneath the satin material, gently running the pads of his fingertips along the curve of his cheekbone, before he pulled it away.

"Do you want to look?" he asked, and if Max hadn't known him inside and out, he wouldn't have heard how *wrecked* Noah already was. Max nodded fast. "You're so good to me, sweetheart. Open your eyes."

Max opened them quickly, drinking in the sight before him.

Noah hovered over him. In the dim, flame-licked light of their bedroom, his eyes were pupil-blown and dark, hungry. The set of his mouth in a parted smirk had Max scrambling closer in seconds. Noah reached out, hand against his chest, and held him against the bed.

"No," he said sharply, and Max forced himself to stop struggling. Noah's eyes flashed and he rewarded Max's submission with a long, deep kiss. When they parted, Max's lungs were wild with the need to breathe. His lips were tender, like a bruise.

"So good," Noah breathed out, and this time, Max got to see the delight on his face, the lust-blown awe in his eyes. It had his eyes screwing closed, biting hard on his lip to keep his hips flat against the bed. His cock twitched, helpless and desperate, against his belly.

So badly Max wanted to thrust up, to feel *anything,* hard denim or not, against his aching cock. He was almost dizzy with it. When his eyes opened, Noah crawled slowly down his body. Max pushed himself up on his elbows, eyelids drooping as he watched Noah move.

"You've been waiting for me here so good," Noah murmured against his hipbone, placing a kiss there. Max couldn't help but cry out, twisting beneath the firm hands holding him steady.

"I—" He stopped again, unsure if he could speak. He sent a pleading glance toward Noah. Noah watched him from beneath his eyelashes, slowly toying with his jutting hipbone with his tongue and teeth. He bit, just a little, and grinned when Max cried out again.

"You have something to say?" Noah asked, voice somehow light even as it dragged rough and low.

Max nodded eagerly before realizing he could reply. "Please, Noah," was all he managed to get out. Noah smiled at him, sweetly, and then dipped his chin, parting his lips, taking all of Max's throbbing cock into his mouth.

Max moaned, hands flying into Noah's hair. He scraped hard at his scalp, back arching as the most intense pleasure Max had ever felt rocketed through him, hot as the fire in the corner.

"Oh, fuck, oh, fuck, Noah, *please*." He babbled a litany of pleas as Noah sucked him at a nearly punishing pace. His thumbs dug into Max's hips, tongue swiping against the sensitive, leaking head as he bobbed up and down. It took all his effort to keep his eyes open, to watch as the spit dripped down Noah's chin and onto his cock, the swollen, red skin disappearing between slick lips.

Max didn't stand a chance. When Noah curled his back into the air, adjusting the angle and adding a hand to the base of his cock, fingers firmly wrapped around him, and slid his hand and lips together to create a tight ring of pleasure, Max collapsed against the bed, body *screaming*.

He barely had time to tug on Noah's hair, let alone get the ragged "gonna—Noah—gotta—" before he was coming, hard, the warm, wet swipe of Noah's tongue never letting up as he came and came and came. Stars burst across his vision, throat closing as he called Noah's name again and again.

When he was done, body twitching and softening cock so sensitive he whimpered as Noah moved off of him, Noah quickly climbed up the bed, and pulled Max to his chest. He slid a knee between his legs, curling around him, and softly swept his hand through Max's hair.

"Such a good boy," he complimented softly in his

ear. Max snuggled closer, breathing evening out. The last thing he felt before he gave in to the calling urge to sleep was Noah's lips against his hair, mouthing that he loved him.

BIBLIO

Lin Devon

The simple apparatus of keys can become an unwin-nable puzzle when they're soaked by a sudden rain-storm. Just water from the sky, but with an armload of books, Bel Graves had lost all dexterity. Her key ring jangled with useless options as she tried to jam the right key in the book depository lock. If she'd had her druthers, she might have just said, "Speak friend and enter," but she managed to get the stubborn thing open without magic. She was a friend. Not to many humans, but to books. She was a patron and, in her imagina-tion, a patron saint to the volumes and tomes, weath-ered antiquarian and crisply bound alike. Books, and the institutions that housed them, were her sanctuary.

She hustled her bounty inside and sighed happily. What some might call a dusty old closet, Bel saw as the coziest treasure trove in town. Scents of binding glue, paper pulp, worn leather, and faded cloth greeted her like the arms of a familiar lover. When she'd gotten the annex manager job at Tome After Tome, the little bookshop still holding ground in the thriving downtown flower district, it had been on the merit of her passion. The ancient bespectacled bookseller, Mr. Gordon, had recognized the bibliophile in her by the glint of wonder in her eye. It took one to know one. Her bookshop-heavy resume and a minor degree in library science had opened the door, but her reverence had sealed the deal. What Mr. Gordon could not know was the true intensity of her obsession.

Bel set the stack of books on the table beside the door and examined them. A first edition Samuel Clemens from 1876 gleamed up at her from the top of the stack. She blotted three raindrops from the plastic book cover with the hem of her skirt.

"There you are, Samuel."

In the theater of her imagination she saw the man himself, bushy mustache arcing up in a smile and wild eyebrows raised to drop a wink in flirtatious thanks. Cheeky, but he always had an irreverent streak.

Waiting just beneath that was a pristine signed copy of *Delta of Venus*. Anaïs Nin shrugged up from the dark to coo into the cup of Bel's ear, "I am so thirsty for the marvelous that only the marvelous has power over me." And it was just as if the woman had swept through the room, black chenille wrap moving like smoke over the flesh of Bel's calf. Bel would spend all afternoon here researching rarified work and trying like hell to keep her wits about her. It was hard, though, with masters like these.

There were many others in her haul, but she set that indulgence aside. She slipped out of her coat and scarf to pull books for online cataloging. Part of her job was showcasing the gems in the depository to the wider internet-savvy public. The small space provided scant room to maneuver between towering shelves. She couldn't get lost in here, but she could lose herself. The collected history of human spirit hurling against the confines of a human life was here, raging "against the dying of the light." Dylan Thomas smirked at her, his famous line slurring through his thick Welsh accent. She held the small volume of his collected poems like a talisman to her chest as he sauntered closer to whisper, "If you think that's good, you should lay your greedy hands on Keats."

But from beside her ear Henry Ashbee, in gruff English said, "No, what you seek is in *The Romance of Lust*, right here under the name William Potter." A hand, as real as flesh, held her by the wrist and guided her fingers with gentle accuracy to the book. Bel turned her face and brushed against a bristly smile. He pressed a kiss to her ear and faded away.

That she was recognized in her fantasies as peer to these historical bibliophiles, people who knew the power of the book, was intoxicating. It was a wire in the blood. She thought, *I am yours in legacy and you are mine in heritage.* Her breath was short as she rested her palms across the spines so neatly placed one against the other. What Dickens subverted sat beside what Michael Field, pseudonym for a lesbian couple, writ large. Bel's earlobe under Katherine's lips and Edith gently kissing the side of her neck, they beckoned her to *open and know*.

When Bel laid her fingers on Thoreau, the cool breeze off his beloved pond lifted her skirt to tickle against her panties. He hummed behind her shoulder, "All good things are wild, and free." Her hand slipped and she clutched at Emerson, who echoed his friend at her other side, urging, "Trust thyself: every heart vibrates to that iron string." Hands slid upward along her thighs, pulling her wool skirt up around her waist. She ran from the aisle crowded with its excitement of ideas. Rounding the corner she fell against Hemingway, Miller, and Fitzgerald himself sipping champagne from one hand and guiding her into a dance with the other.

Bel's blouse had fallen open. Vaunted men and women who had moved her now crowded in for their due. She leaned against the shelves and they clamored in planting kisses along her clavicle, down the thundering flesh between her breasts. She laid down amongst them and some bearded genius found her crux, nuzzling wet lips with his prickly ones. Fingers rough from their type-writers and pencil nubs and keyboards penetrated her tight wet heat. Sappho in Greek robes smiled over Bel's exposed nipple, singing, ". . . all at once a faint fever courses down beneath the skin, eyes no longer capable of sight, a thrumming in the ears . . ."

She let herself go. Words became hands and mouths plying her body as they had her mind. Their ideas, ripe and throbbing, coaxed her to open and know, open and know. They delved the depths of her understanding, then further. She couldn't catch a breath, couldn't hear but for their resonant murmurings vibrating somewhere deep. Voices rose as she clutched at tweed shoulders and homespun blouses, their machinations coiling something tighter and tighter. She could cry, the tension was so delicious. Hammering against her hunger, relentless forces of wit and verité plied on. She threw her head back, howling as Ginsberg and Kerouac looked on. They all hushed at once and watched as she burst open in a rain to rival the storm outside. On the floor of the book depository she was riding rippling concentric waves that beat against her shore one after the next until they calmed and settled like a pond pristine again after the disturbance of a stone.

This is how Mr. Gordon found her an hour later when she hadn't returned, curled up and snoring peacefully with a fat book on the Beat poets under her head. He smiled, covered her with her coat for warmth, set the cup of tea he'd brought beside her, and left. He was charmed. She reminded him of his younger self and his own afternoons in that space. It did indeed take a bibliophile to understand a bibliophile.

WHAT GREW BEFORE THE SUN

Z. S. Roe

"Will you tell them that I'm blind?" he asks over breakfast.

We're naked, sitting up in bed, with the drapes pulled back and the sun hot on our bare knees. There is a tray between us, empty now, save for the crumbs and two teacups.

"I don't have to. How *should* I describe you?"

"As I am. As you found me."

I'm quiet for a moment.

And then he adds, "As you've dreamt of me."

We wake, but there is always darkness.

And so he comes to me by touch, feeling his way through the sheets with slow, tentative sweeps of his hands. There is a restrained, quiet unease to his searching, as if he needs to reassure himself, as if he needs to be sure of me.

In this way we find each other: in the dark, desperately.

I'd like to think that I know his hands, the curve and bend of each finger. I pretend that I do, that I have felt his touch all my life, and can tell his from any other's.

It is the lover's dream, to be so completely known and to know completely.

We pretend at it, hoping that time will fill in the blanks.

I went to school with Jared's brother, and knew Jared only by name, from stories, from the other kids' whispers. The blind boy. He was, unfortunately, a footnote in the day-to-day drama of my adolescence, there, but only on the periphery, like a phantom haunting an empty building.

Yet we found each other in our thirties, both of us moving into the same apartment building, living only a hallway apart. At first, we barely knew the other was there. For months I heard the slide-tap, slide-tap of his white cane against the hallway floor tile whenever he left and returned to his apartment. It was a sound that was distantly familiar, though I hesitated to seek it out.

Still, he found me. From the shadowed deep of forgotten memory, his name rose in my dreams like a great prehistoric fish. And like Jonah, I waited to be swallowed whole.

* * *

We dated, though we worked opposing times, him at night and me during the day. He worked at a radio station, and I delivered mail.

This left us only the first hour or so of each morning, during breakfast, to see each other, usually with the sun still down.

At first, his kisses were hungrier than mine and sometimes clumsy in their hurry. Often, he kissed my nose and chin before he found my mouth. More than once he bit my lip in his eagerness, though I never told him if he didn't notice, not even when he broke the skin. Instead, I would make him kiss me again and then lick my warmth from his open mouth.

It's hard to believe that he so rarely noticed.

Surely, he tasted me.

Surely, I wanted him to taste me.

Looking back, I guess I assumed that it would be me to first lead us to bed, but instead he led me to his on the third morning. He had never seen himself naked, and knew himself only by touch, and so he had me touch him.

After, I brought his hand between my legs so that he would know me, and when I came I closed my eyes and held his hand against the heat of my orgasm and wondered how all this darkness could shine so fiercely.

Before, my breakfast was never more than a cup of coffee, usually bought in a rush on my way to work. But with Jared, I learned to slow my pace, to ease myself into the morning.

We began each day at a quarter to five. Sometimes I cooked for him; other times he cooked for me. Occasionally we wouldn't cook at all, but instead satisfy ourselves with fruit or Greek yogurt drizzled with honey.

Inevitably, though, we always found our way to bed.

Now and then, when the time had gotten away from us and I had to leave for work, we'd lay in bed together just a little longer, our dirty dishes momentarily forgotten in my sink or his. I would hold his hand and he would breathe deep of my scent like I was an exotic spice.

I shared that with him once, that simile, and he'd laughed and said that maybe it was true. The next morning, after he'd undressed me and laid me on the bed, he'd sprinkled cinnamon over the swell of my breasts and nipples. I shivered as he licked them clean, curling my toes as his tongue made lazy circles around my spiced areoles.

Even now I still dream about him, dreams both bizarre and luring.

One night I dreamt of a large porcelain bowl of mixed blueberries and strawberries and blackberries, all of them fat and ripe. I scooped the fruit out with my hands, filling my mouth, relishing how each tart berry burst with juice as my teeth bit into it.

Near the bottom of the bowl, I felt something out of place. I brushed aside the few berries left, and discovered Jared's disembodied penis, curled in on itself like a sleeping child. It was warm and responsive, seeming to stretch as I ran my juice-stained finger along its side. I was teasing it, curious to find its potential, to discover the sweetness of this strange fruit at the bottom of my bowl.

It needed coaxing, of course, so I coaxed it; my one stroking finger became two, and then I added my thumb, and when it began to respond more diligently, I took it fully in my palm. Soon it stood proud and firm, rising from the bowl like a sprouted tree, the berries circling it at the bottom like its dropped fruit.

Later that morning, in Jared's apartment as we lay naked in his bed, I slid his penis into my mouth, surprising him, amused at his sudden gasp, charged as he became hard and hot against my tongue. He tried to pull away before coming, but I wouldn't let him. I was still taken by the dream, still lost to its sweetness. I wanted nothing but the taste of him.

I skipped work that day.

He called in sick that night.

Now it is morning again, and he lies against his pillow, sated and grinning.

"You want to tell your friends about us?"

"Only a few."

"Will you tell them that I'm blind?"

After we've talked, I pull myself into his lap, and then kiss him between his eyes and then on the ball of his nose. His breath is heavy and warm against my chin. Gently, he places his hand between my breasts, feeling the steady rhythm within. He leaves it there for a moment, and then he kisses me.

The sun through the bedroom window is warm on my face, but his kiss is the only thing I feel.

ROLL THE DICE

Cassandra Cavenaugh

'd left a little note by the door for Claire; a simple, handwritten phrase: "Would you like to play a game?" I knew she'd laugh at the reference, but I hoped she would understand the invitation stood regardless of the 1983 classic's merit. Typically, it was she who made the games, devised their rules, and enforced them, but today I decided to play a game of cat and mouse. I needed to feel her eyes on me, to have her full attention as my mind and body shatter into a million pieces. When the door clicked, I knew the game was already afoot.

The dice were purple with flecks of pink and blue throughout; seven pieces were in the set but only one was laid out on display. I rolled the twenty-sided die between my fingers; the cold, tactile feeling soothing my nerves as I waited. Footsteps tapped down the hall

as I placed it gently in the center of the coffee table. I'd
set out two cups of tea, as we always shared after she
returned from work, but beside her cup I laid our black
leather paddle. It had been awhile since we'd used that
particular toy; it isn't the pain I wanted, but to be of
service.

I could hear Claire's quiet laugh as she approached
the door. I smiled brightly and motioned her to the
armchair across from me. A look of confusion and
anxiousness flickered across her face. The game-master
hadn't made the rules and that uncertainty was an all
too familiar feeling for me. I'd written my little game
out on a plain white piece of paper which I handed to
her quietly.

"It's just a simple game I thought we could play, but
the rules are up to you. I know you've been busy with
work, life, and everything in between and I thought
a little play was in order," I said softly, a small smirk
escaping through the seriousness. I could see Claire
relax in that moment; the certainty returning to her
world and her control recognized as she prepared to
enter the world I'd created.

When you ask me to, I will roll the die. If I roll a one,
I lose. If I roll a twenty, I win. Anything in between, I
still lose. If I win, I would like permission to orgasm. If
I lose, you can spank me that many times.

Claire read the rules carefully and looked up at me
with her head tilted to one side. I knew that look, just as
I knew before her lips started to move that I'd more than

surprised her. I didn't like pain, but I very much enjoyed being her submissive. I knew she'd be over the moon at the chance to spank me, but I daresay she was happier to have me volunteer. Of course, selfishly, I aimed to win this game.

"First roll, pet."

I rolled the die, and watched it dance across the glass table, clinking against the glass as it rolled. The odds weren't exactly in my favor; that was kind of the idea, really. It wasn't about winning or losing, but rather about submitting completely in the moment, as curated as it might be. I rolled a five.

Claire motioned me to her lap, and I stood to meet her. She bent me over her knees and slid a warm hand up the skirt of my dress. Her fingertips trembled as she caressed my ass like a prized possession. The paddle came down without warning; the crack of the leather against my bottom stung, but soon I'd taken my lashes and the soft caress returned.

"Are you okay, pet?" Claire asked with concern in her brow. I nodded happily.

"Yes, miss. I'm quite well."

We sipped our tea and nibbled on the chocolate biscuits I'd laid out for us. There is nothing so soothing and peaceful as a warm cup of tea. Well, there is one thing. Claire set her teacup down in the saucer. "Roll again, dear."

I let the die once again skate across the table, and it skipped right into Claire's tea.

"I'd call that a natural one if ever I saw one," Claire giggled and returned to her tea. Soon she'd finished the cup and pointed to the die at the bottom matter-of-factly. A natural twenty. The irony was thick, but Claire called me over once more and instinctively I laid across her knees.

She obliged me, but the paddling never came. Her hand slipped up my dress once more, but her fingers slid between my legs and closer to where I'd wanted them all evening. The other hand lifted my dress and caressed my bottom as the right inched closer to my growing wetness. Her fingertips started to enter me as her left struck my bottom, her bare hand colliding with the paleness of my ass. My body quivered, the dichotomy of pain and pleasure serving as means to a perfect end.

Claire quickly found my center and playfully struck my clit as she stroked my bright red bottom. I could feel it coming like a wave cresting in the ocean, ready to break and crash into the beach. Holding it back as best I could, I bit my lip and squirmed in her lap. I sensed the smile in her voice as she said it. She knew.

"You have permission."

I shook as the climax crested and washed across my body while Claire's fingers continued their ministrations. Knowing that I had arranged this capture, that I had brought Claire back to me with her firm and gentle hands, made my release that much sweeter. I could hear it in her labored breathing and feel it in the way her hand stayed steady, pausing to draw out my pleasure, exerting her control even then as I fell into the after-glow. Claire was in her element, in full control, and had no intention of letting it go.

She did not release me in that moment, continuing to push me further and over the crest of the next wave into another orgasm. My body pressed against her embrace as the electric endorphins rushed through my already saturated self. Turnabout is fair play, I suppose. I had forced her into this scene to please her, and she had returned the favor in kind. My body could take no more and went limp in her arms, glistening from its labors.

Still laying in her lap, my breath uneven and panting, I savored her fingers running through my hair as she waited for me to return to her. Claire knew just what I needed and ran her fingertips down the small of my back before gently caressing my still stinging bottom. There was something tentative about this aftercare that told me the scene was not over, though.

"One more roll," Claire whispered as she held the die in her palm in front of my blushing face. I took the piece between my lips and let it fall to the floor.

A natural one.

TRAVELED
SO FAR

Max Turner

This was not the first time Kai had let Anders lead him into trying something new and unusual.

Kai had come to adore the near obsession Anders had developed with Kai's often hypersensitivity to touch, his potential to be physically and emotionally overwhelmed. It was something Kai had rarely trusted someone enough to explore in this way. With Anders, Kai reveled in the mutual exploration, allowing himself to become overwhelmed but still safe and cared for in Anders's hands.

Kai had never before found someone as compatible in the bedroom as out of it. They enjoyed each other's company. He liked the way Anders talked so eloquently whether they were having dinner or fucking. In turn, Anders liked how open and eager Kai was with him.

Unusually, on this occasion Anders had told him

little except that they'd be "heightening their experience." He'd otherwise simply asked if Kai trusted him, which of course he did. Now the anticipation was arousing, not least because they were currently vacationing at Centauri Prime's most luxurious sex resort. The possibilities were endless.

Both of them had been to this planet before, though this was their first time visiting together. Kai had been excited to accept the invitation, prepared to allow himself to be led into something he'd only want to attempt with Anders.

It was their final evening in a week of ever-increasing sexual exploration and fine dining. They'd particularly enjoyed partaking in the tea ceremonies that were tradition amongst the Centauri residents, with many teas growing differently in this planet's soil.

Kai entered the room in their suite that Anders had set up, wearing nothing but a wry grin and the thin robe Anders had requested. He savored the feel of the cool turquoise and white silk against his bare skin.

Anders approached him with a smile, wearing his orange and floral print robe, open at the front. Anders loosened the robe's ties as he led Kai to the floor cushions in the center of the room. He let Kai's robe fall open before encouraging him to take a seat.

Anders hummed his approval when he saw that Kai was wearing a cock. Anders was always supportive, whether Kai wanted to wear his cock or not. More often than not Anders enjoyed helping his lover insert the small bulb end into his slick heat, teasing him by pressing the silicone shaft just right to create friction against Kai's small natural cock.

Kai began to lightly stroke himself, enjoying Anders's mesmerized gaze as much as the way each pump moved it inside him and against him.

Finally, Anders broke the silence with a gentle tone.

"Many Earth teas are grown here on Centauri Prime, but the native tea is said to have extraordinary and unpredictable effects on humans. It's an expensive, rare treat with a long tradition of being used in sexual encounters. To heighten the experience."

"Mmm." Kai bit his lower lip, already eager and aroused.

Anders looked like he'd planned to say more, but instead his eyes roved over Kai's body and he was betrayed by his wanton expression.

Kai could sympathize.

Silence fell as Anders joined him on the floor and prepared tea on the blanket before them.

Eventually, he handed Kai a teacup before taking up his own.

"The flavor will be bitter, but do endure."

Anders was right, the flavor was bitter, almost undrinkable, he drank nonetheless.

Kai was unsure how much time passed. Slowly the room became soft and blurred at the edges. He was unsure whether he was hallucinating as Anders opened a box containing seven large, live snails.

Kai had trouble concentrating as four were placed on his lower legs and began to work their way up his body. The sensation was bizarre, air cooling the trails they left, and his skin tingling in anticipation ahead of them. As one reached the top of his thigh and then moved up to his abdomen, Kai drew in short breaths.

He knew, vaguely, that Anders was talking, picking out words here and there.

". . . local tradition of erotic ritual . . . increased popularity of Earth cephalopods . . . heightened with *centauri sinensis* . . . sensation . . . *mollusca* . . . *Achatina fulica* or giant land snail . . ."

Their bodies were now entwined on the cushions. One of his lover's thighs rested between his own as they reclined away from each other, their cocks almost touching, Anders's hot flesh tantalizingly close to his own soft silicone.

Kai's thoughts were drowned out by his moans as the sensations became intense. The fastest of the creatures was sliding up his face toward his increasingly sweat-damp forehead. How much time had passed that it had traveled so far?

One was now inspecting the light hair around his navel. Another had stalled at his knee. One of Anders's feet was in his hand and he stared down at it for a long while, wondering how it got there.

Kai blinked, panting as he tried to focus on his lover.

A snail was making its way up Anders's leg towards the man's torso. It took him a moment to find the others.

One was trying to find purchase on Anders's balls, the other had slid to the tip of Anders's cock. He held his hard length steadfast in his hand, a look of bliss on his face as it slithered on his crown. Kai wondered how such a thing might feel, then stilled his breath as his last remaining companion found his own cock.

The sensation couldn't be the same, of course—he couldn't feel it against his flesh—but the weight of the creature moved the bulb of the toy inside him, pressing it against his G-spot.

A startled breath escaped him at the sensation, both like and very much unlike the drag of Anders's tongue when he sucked on this cock.

Wet, sticky, cool and warm at once as they climbed his body, lapping at what salt they found.

Kai closed his eyes, overwhelmed.

On his face, his waist. On his knee. On his cock, his insides throbbing and clutching at the heft of it, making his cock twitch.

He shook as his senses flooded.

Anders's shaky, thick words broke through the haze. "Give yourself over to them."

Kai moaned as he arched up into the sensations prickling over his skin. He wanted to pump his cock and feel the grind of it inside him, but instead he held it steady for the creature sliding along. When it slid back onto his body, Kai spread his legs and it grazed over Kai's true, hard and wet cock.

With a cry, Kai shuddered.

When he came, his inner muscles contracting and making his cock flex with each pulse, Kai could only feel the slow movements of the snails over his body. His mind a haze and his flesh singing, only the parts that the snails touched seemed to exist in that moment. Any bitter notes had faded and Kai sank back into the cushions, body spread, the only cognizant thought in his mind—*no one but Anders could introduce me to pleasure like this.*

STRUM

Jsin Graham

"You rang?"

"Jerian. Don't do that, it . . ." She paused. "It makes me feel some kinda way," Gwendolyn replied as she let him in.

Gwendolyn Hill was a lawyer, philanthropist, and head of the angel investment group that purchased a majority share of Miko's Blues Alley three months ago. From the night she happened into the club to see its star attraction up close, she'd been fighting every urge in her being to get her hands on him.

No, she couldn't risk falling into a cliché situation with a sarcastic, sexy as fuck savant of a musician. Especially one with chaotic eyes and lips that said the most poignantly nasty things imaginable without uttering a word.

Jerian "Apollo" Adams was the electric bass player for Revol, the house band at Miko's on the famed U Street corridor in NW Washington, DC. At twenty-six, he was one of the most famous, highly sought-after guitarists in the world.

Apollo shared the Greek god's frame. Chestnut brown skin stretched over broad shoulders and down a tatted, muscular six-foot frame, tapering to a sinfully pronounced Adonis belt that was frequently displayed whenever he performed.

Over the past month, Gwendolyn had conjured up reasons to see him. Ten minutes here. A half hour there. Just enough interaction to quench her thirst—until he kissed her last week. What had started off light and flirtatious quickly grew into an expression of animalistic hunger that scared her with how it made her feel.

"My apologies, Ms. Hill. What can I do you for? You called the club between sets," he said nonchalantly. His gaze moved across her curves, searing a startling scene of delicious manhandling across her frontal lobe.

Without a word, Gwendolyn walked up to Jerian, grabbed his hand, and led him to her bedroom. His eyes widened, then strained to drink in the natural sway of her hips.

"Make yourself comfortable. I'll be right back," she said.

She returned to her moonlit bedroom with two glasses, handing him one and placing the other beside an ashtray with remnants of a pre-rolled funnel inside.

"What do you have us listening to?"

Gwendolyn lowered herself onto the bed and stared at his physique. He had stripped down to a pair of crimson boxers that, paired with his skin and the duvet cover on her king-size platform bed, created a cinematic sight.

"Prince's *One Nite Alone* . . . the live album," he replied, tossing his phone on the nightstand.

The look in her eyes was different from anything he had seen from her before. There was a longing, a need, a curiosity. Jerian leaned forward slowly and grabbed the edges of her tank, easing it up over her head. His tongue curled wickedly against the right side of his top lip at the sight of her breasts.

"It's ridiculous how much you put these young women to shame," he said. "Come here."

She leaned her bare back against his chest, allowing free passage to her body. His tongue and lips lightly traced her earlobe and neck as he caressed her skin while Prince performed in the background. Though not a singer, Jerian hummed along to certain parts. The vibrations sent sparks across her closed eyelids as he trapped and teased her nipples between his fingers, applying just enough pressure to pull more nonverbal approval from her.

Gwendolyn swayed, her breathing becoming ragged as his hands found a home between her thighs, expertly massaging over her shorts. The wetness that resulted drew melodic sounds from the woman sitting between his legs.

"You should take these off," he whispered.

How long have you been waiting? Well, I hope I can make it up to you.

Prince uttered the words before his guitar whined, and his band began playing a slow, sexy, moody tune that he strode over effortlessly.

Jerian responded to the slight tensing of Gwendolyn's body by wrapping both his arms around her, squeezing gently. "Trust me." He kissed her ear. "Trust me." He kissed her neck. "Trust me." He kissed her shoulder. With each mention of those two words, his voice grew softer, more sensual, relaxing her.

Raising her hips off the bed, she eased her shorts over her ass and down her legs.

"This is my favorite song."

The slight rasp in his voice was more pronounced when he whispered. His tone, mixed with the mood and the warm, pulsing thickness pressed against her now-bare ass, had her so wet that she strongly reconsidered her no-penetration stance.

Nerve endings she never knew existed were ignited as his middle finger eased across her clit, down in between the slick wetness that welcomed him, then dragged upward without warning. The movement was so smooth and sudden that her eyes closed. She was licking her lips before she knew what was happening.

"Fuuuuck, Jer . . . that . . . don't stop, baby, please," she begged. "What . . . is it . . . about this song?" she whined.

Jerian expertly moved back and forth from one long finger to two, dragging the length of her. Occasionally, he curled his middle finger, penetrating her warmth to the rhythm of Prince's "Joy in Repetition." When Prince cried out on the record before making his guitar sing, Gwendolyn came so hard that she dug her nails into his thighs, pushing up off the bed to try and meet his hand. She wanted the pressure from the strength of his palm and desperately sought the length of his fingers.

Wrapping his other arm around her, he held firm while the wave ripped through her before she relaxed back onto the bed.

"I hope I wasn't too loud," she said in a mildly embarrassed tone, her thighs widening for him subconsciously.

He couldn't help but stare at her back, turned on to no end by the entire scene.

"It's the multiple guitar riffs," he said. "The live version of this song is ten minutes of black magic."

While he spoke, Gwendolyn opened her eyes and looked between her thighs. Jerian's tattooed arms held an array of images that she tried to make out, but her brain wouldn't allow. What she could see were the fingers of his right hand playing along with the music, just above her warmth.

Gwendolyn decided to tempt fate, using her hand to bring his back down between her thighs.

"Show me why you love this song."

Jerian played along with an iconic three-minute

guitar solo that moved from long, heavy chords to hypnotic guitar strums between Gwendolyn's lips and against her clit with a brooding fervor. Mixing in methodical, deliberate movements in and out of her, he shifted between massaging her nipples and pulling on her thick mane, exposing her neck. A neck that he kissed, licked, and sucked, sending her into a fit of breathy curses and slow whines against him.

The second time she came, she ran away from his reach. He hadn't stopped moving, and she could feel herself losing all control.

On the floor on her hands and knees, she looked at him, bewildered, the moonlight now allowing her to see the size of what the man with that hunger in his eye was gripping over the fabric of his boxer briefs.

Mmmph, this motherfucker is going to ruin me if I'm not careful, she thought.

A THUNDEROUS PASSION

Erica Smith

Anna lay on her back as a lightning bolt flashed and brightened the room.

"One, two, three, four, five," she whispered as a crash of thunder stopped her from counting further. It rumbled as it shook the house and resounded through her core. She fondled and squeezed her breasts in her hands. Her fingers brushed her nipples, and she pinched them until they were stiff peaks.

She wiggled her body, and gasped as a gush of wetness soaked her panties. A snore made her tense, and she squinted at Dean's outline. He shifted and snorted but remained asleep, unaware of her actions.

She sighed as she grabbed the waistband of her underwear. She slipped them from her hips and tossed them to the floor. Then she rubbed her thighs, before touching her labia.

At the next crack of lightning, she closed her eyes as she circled her aching clit. She panted and gritted her teeth to stifle a moan from passing her lips, trembling as her passion rose at the clap of thunder.

She tensed, stopping her hand as she felt the mattress shift. Her heartbeat raced in her chest as the snap of a switch reached her ears. She blinked, and saw Dean staring at her with wide eyes.

"Oh, Dean," she gasped, "I'm s-sorry, I-I didn't mean to wake you."

He grinned, then laughed as he shook his head.

"Fuck, baby, don't apologize," he said. "Keep going; you're hot."

She studied him, smirking at the distinctive bulge in his lap.

"Are you enjoying yourself?" she asked. "Do you want to watch or join me?"

He threw the covers from his body as he shoved himself into a sitting position.

She smiled at the wicked grin on his face as he removed his boxer shorts.

He tossed them to the floor, then he rolled on top of her.

"Yes, I wish you had woke me," he said. "It's unfair for you to play by yourself."

He kissed her, then slipped his tongue between her lips.

She closed her eyes, clasped his face with her hands, and she hummed. She nipped his lip and sighed as she broke the kiss.

"Hurry," she urged, "before the storm passes or stops."

He chuckled as he ground his hips against her with a groan.

"I love a challenge," he replied. "Now let me blow your mind."

She felt his cock press against her thigh, pre-cum wetting her skin. She whined as she raked her nails across his shoulder blades.

He hissed, then chuckled as he stared into her eyes.

"Easy, sweetheart," he said. "I'll give you what you need." He cupped her breasts in his hands and squeezed them until she moaned.

She wrapped her legs around his waist and locked her ankles. "Please, don't tease me," she begged. "I'm too excited right now."

He released her breast, dragging his fingertips over her stomach, until he reached her pussy.

"Wow, you're wet," he said. "How long have you been playing with yourself?"

She gasped as she held onto his neck and bucked her hips.

"Since I woke up and heard the thunder," she answered. "Hurry, I want you inside me."

He stroked her folds, then lifted his fingers to his lips and sucked them.

"Hmm, delicious," he purred, "I've always loved the way you taste, baby."

Anna huffed and shook her head. "Please, Dean, do

something," she begged. "You're driving me crazy."

He undulated his hips as he pressed their bodies together.

"Fuck, you're so eager," he growled. "I can't wait to take you apart."

She nodded as she met his gaze, playing with the hair at his nape.

"Yes," she replied. "Now quit stalling and put your cock in me."

Dean leaned toward the nightstand and opened the drawer. He reached inside, then showed her a bottle of lubricant.

"I stopped at the store today and bought you a special treat," he said. He flicked the lid open and squirted a dollop on his fingers.

She shifted as her excitement rose within her while she waited for him to act.

He lowered his hand and touched her clit, rubbing it in circles.

She hummed, shivering as he slipped a finger into her pussy.

"Oh, it's warm. What did you do to it?"

He chuckled as he added a second finger, sliding them in and out of her pussy.

"Relax, baby. It's a warming gel, you'll love it."

Anna panted as he pushed in a third finger and thrust them inside her.

"Okay, I'm ready," she told him. "Now shove your dick in me."

He withdrew his fingers, slicked himself with the lube, and lined himself up with her entrance.

"Here it comes, babe," he said. "This will be the best fuck of your life."

She whined as his cock rubbed against her folds. As he thrust into her, thunder filled her ears.

He started with a slow rhythm, but soon quickened his pace.

Anna grunted as his thrusts became faster and harder. She squeezed her eyes shut as her pussy clinched around him.

"Oh, yes, I want to come!" she cried. "Please, make me come!"

He growled and huffed as he snapped his hips, pounding his cock into her.

"Do you want it, baby?" he asked. "Are you going to come for me?"

She let out a strangled sound, her fingers aching from gripping his shoulders.

"Oh, God, yes. Make me come." She whimpered as he hit her G-spot and her orgasm rocked her body. Her pussy clenched on his cock as she shuddered through it.

She gasped as he pulled out and her legs twitched. As her eyelids drooped and she went limp, she heard the distant rumble of thunder.

"The storm passed us," she said. "Wow, I haven't climaxed that hard in a long time."

Dean groaned as he rolled to the side and stared

at her. "Damn, honey, that was great. Wake me when another thunderstorm hits."

She giggled as she shoved his shoulder. "Okay, I will, but what if you're at work and I'm here alone?"

He chuckled as he winked at her.

"Send me a text and I'll come home—or a naughty video clip." He wiggled his eyebrows and flicked his tongue.

She laughed as she shook her head and poked him in the stomach.

"You're crazy, but I love you," she said. "Now it's late. We should go to sleep."

He smiled as he kissed her, then flipped the switch on the lamp on the nightstand.

"Sweet dreams, sweetheart. The weatherman predicted rain for the entire week."

She hugged him and closed her eyes, eager to share her passion again soon.

SERVICE

Lee Cairney

Making sure she was watching, I shuffled back a little in my kneeling position and jogged the delicate table with my elbow. Green tea showered onto the floor.

"Oh. Sorry." I thought she'd tell me to clean it up or even better, bend me over her knee straightaway.

"Stand up." I'd seen a flash of anger pass over her face but now she seemed beautifully calm.

I did so.

I'd liked the way her gaze had locked on me in the hotel lobby. And hadn't I made an effort? I was wearing black jeans, black vest, black boots—the kink uniform. I was tan from a summer of not doing much more than lazing about the lakes outside Berlin and I'd had my hair cut in a fresh fade. But this wasn't how she was looking at me now.

"Did you deliberately knock that over?"

I considered a lie but guessed that the penalties would be worse. "I did."

"I did, *mistress*."

"You did, mistress." I held down a smirk.

"Have you forgotten what I said about screwing up on purpose?"

Must have done, I wanted to say, but instead bit my lip.

She looked genuinely angry. "Get up, collect your jacket, and leave this hotel room. I don't have any more use for you."

Her words were harsher than the slap of any cane or tawse could be.

"No, wait, I'm sorry. I thought—"

"I asked you to leave."

There was no mistaking her tone. I left.

As I walked toward the U-Bahn, I took out my phone and texted. *I'm so sorry. I misjudged the situation. Please give me another chance.*

It was evening before she replied, six slow grinding hours. *If you're truly sorry and willing to be obedient, come to my hotel room at eight p.m. tomorrow.*

She let me in without saying anything. Her mood seemed different, as if she'd clicked into a glossy, more polished mode. The few glimpses she'd trusted me with yesterday of her more homely self—easing her feet out of her high heels in front of me—were gone. The curtains in the high-ceilinged room were drawn.

"This is Neil. Say, 'hello,' Neil."

"Hello," said the big man robotically, belly cinched into his shirt by his belt. He was handsome, with a short graying beard. His crinkled eyes flickered nervously over to me.

"Unlike you, Neil has a strong understanding of what it is to obey, don't you, Neil?"

"Yes, mistress." His eyes stayed trained on one spot on the wall.

"And unlike you, Neil would never subject anyone to the pitiful charade you had the nerve to parade in front of me yesterday under the name of service. Would you?" She rested the end of her whip on the point of his chin.

"No, mistress."

She made me sit at her feet on the floor while Neil brought and served her a cup of green tea flawlessly.

"So you see"—she strode across the rug before turning sharply back on her heel—"this is how it's done. But because your attempts were so contemptible I had to ask Neil to come and serve me instead. Now you owe Neil. Do you see?"

"What do you want me to do?" I said slowly.

She cracked the whip. "Don't speak. I've had enough of you. Take Neil's cock out of his pants. Put a condom on and kneel in front of him."

"What?"

"I thought you told me you were attracted to masculinity?" She gave me a wicked smile.

"Yeah, but I'm queer," I said, despite being flooded

by an unsettling wish to obey. Following her orders turned me on, no matter what those orders were.

"So's Neil, aren't you, Neil?"

I got on my knees slowly, telling myself I could stop whenever I wanted. I was kneeling to buy myself time to think. I wasn't going to do this—or was I? I could feel my cunt getting wet with the desire to please her.

"Nice and slowly. I want to be able to enjoy this." Venezia was sitting on a low chair, legs crossed, flicking the handle of her whip against the rug.

Level with Neil's crotch, I could see the bulge in his jeans. I'd had boyfriends before, when I was younger, but hadn't been near a real cock in years. I'd sucked plenty of dyke dick, though.

I had to wrench his underpants round to get his big cock out. He flinched and went a bit softer. I was glad to roll the condom down so the plastic hid his musky smell.

"What are you waiting for?" Venezia gave me a sadistic smile. "This is for my pleasure, not yours. My obedient boy being rewarded by my disobedient boi. Go on then, Neil."

Neil's dick jumped as he thrust forward and I obediently opened my mouth. The head of his dick grazed past my lips as the chemical taste of the condom filled my nose.

"Neil, don't come, don't even think about coming unless I give you permission."

"Yes, mistress." His voice shook as I slid my lips further down the shaft of his cock.

His cock was warm, the skin yielding softly in a way that was unfamiliar to me. I moved my mouth up and down, licking in places. There was something uniquely humiliating about giving a blowjob, silenced, my mouth filled while my cunt throbbed emptily.

I resented what she was making me do as the minutes ticked past and I did my sorry best. Who did she think she was? I was about to pull my head away when a strange desire kindled. Suddenly, I wanted this; I was hungry for what I was doing for her. It wasn't about Neil, but about me and Venezia, continuing our ongoing kinky game, one she always won—but I did too. I reached a hand down my jeans and began to touch myself. Neil kept jerking his hard cock in and out of my mouth. I heard him groan, and it wasn't long before I was close too.

"Stop. Stop." One minute Venezia was lying back in her chair, one hand moving languidly down the front of her leather trousers; now she crossed the room, took a fistful of my hair, and yanked me away from Neil's cock.

"Ahhhh," he shouted.

She slapped my face and pulled my hand away from my cunt just as I was about to come.

"Neither of you have earned this but I'll let you watch." She began to touch herself again under her leather pants, as she stood, legs spread, eyes closed. It wasn't long before she threw back her head, jet black hair flaming out, and we heard her shout.

It was a few moments before she opened her eyes

again but when she did she thrust her hand toward where I knelt. "The sight of you two made me come hard. You may lick my fingers clean and if you're both very good, I might let you try again tomorrow."

"Yes, mistress." I could see Neil's gentle half smile as I bent my head to where she held out her hand, a similar smile on my face.

EXPERIENCED APPRAISAL

Brynne Blackmoore

Hope looked around the crowded barn, stuffed door to loft with furniture, linens, and pottery. Dozens of people shifted and scooted, finding deals on this muggy afternoon. Caught in the crowd, she craned her neck to find her friend, Sarah. Hope spotted the familiar bleached updo by the quilts and headed over.

"Look at these!" Sarah cried. "A broken dishes pattern and a crazy quilt!" She tried to hold them up, but her arms were weighted down.

Hope didn't have an eye for the patterns—they all looked like geometric rainbows—but she recognized their quality. "Beautiful," she said.

"Haven't you found anything?" Sarah asked. "Along with these, I'm eyeing up that dining set." She gestured with her head to a heavy pine dining table and six chairs.

"I can't decide," Hope said. "I know I need to furnish my new cottage, but I just downsized."

After a messy divorce, and with her sons grown, Hope had sold her four-bedroom Colonial and most of its contents. Too many memories. She'd found a cute two-bedroom cottage close to the lakefront, and had moved in with only the bare essentials. So far, she'd only gotten a new bed and a folding table for the kitchen.

"You can't camp out in an empty house forever," Sarah said. "It's time for you to pick out what you like. You're only fifty, my friend. Get back to living."

Hope thought that was easy for Sarah to say—she took vacations, splurged on spa days, and changed her hair color every month. Hope looked down at her own khaki slacks and thought of her dull brown hair, always in a ponytail. Her outspoken friend had a point.

"Alright," Hope said. "I guess I could live less like a squatter. I'll look around."

She wandered away from Sarah and her quilts, into the back of the barn. There, she saw two salvaged church pews, about six feet long, worn by years of use but ornately carved. She stepped closer, running her fingers over their dips and ridges.

"Gorgeous, aren't they?" said a rumbling male voice behind her.

"Yes," Hope said, not turning around. "I know they're pews, but they'd be perfect seating for my kitchen. If I could just find a table."

"Allow me to help," said the man.

Hope looked behind her then, into the face of a man who could've been Paul Newman's brother. Not quite so striking, maybe, but with warm brown eyes that exuded kindness.

It took her a moment to find her voice. "I wouldn't want to trouble you," she mumbled.

"No trouble at all. And it wouldn't be a selfless act. I'm a vendor; these pews are from my stock. Though I am a sucker for a pretty face." He smiled.

Hope felt a flush of pleasure, then panic. Did he want a date or a sale?

He read her mind. "Well," he said, "who says we can't mix business with pleasure? And it's George. George Upton."

It may have sounded sleazy from a different man, but Hope saw the way his eyes crinkled at the corners, inviting her to laugh with him or at him.

"Okay," she said, and took the arm George offered. "And it's Hope."

After an hour that felt like ten minutes, Hope and George had stuck "Sold" tags with her buyer number on a small maple table for the kitchen, a vintage loveseat that needed upholstering, and a tallboy dresser, along with the church pews.

In that time, she'd spilled the main plot points of her life and divorce, and George told her about his first career as an investment banker, and his second as an antiques dealer.

"There's not much money in it," he'd admitted. "But boy is it fun. And after the obligations of our earlier years, why shouldn't we treat ourselves?"

He'd smiled then, deepening the creases Hope recognized as evidence of that frequent happy expression. Her own lips turned up to match.

"Why not, indeed?" she'd replied, surprising herself by giving his arm a flirtatious squeeze.

Hope and George had just gotten coffee at the refreshments booth when thunder clapped overhead, followed by drumming on the barn roof.

Sarah appeared, flushed and panting. "Hey you," she said, then noticed George. "And hey *you!*"

Hope gave her a gentle kick, and Sarah shook herself.

"Right! Well, I got that dining set, and I couldn't leave the matching sideboard. I have a tarp, but it won't keep the rain off long. Are you"—she looked at George—"not quite ready?"

"George, this is Sarah. Sarah, George," Hope said quickly. "I did find some furniture, but I can arrange for delivery, if you're ready . . ."

"Please, allow me to be of service," George said. "My van is almost empty, and I could see the lady and her purchases home."

Hope noticed how gallantry didn't seem old-fashioned coming from George. Just sexy.

"Good idea!" said Sarah, winking and hurrying away.

* * *

A half hour later, purchases loaded, Hope rested on a church pew in George's van. Rain turned to downpour, and George jumped in to join her, dripping. He shut the back door to keep the weather out, and sat across from her on the other pew. Their knees touched.

"You're soaked!" she laughed, reaching up to trace rainwater on his cheek.

He grabbed her hand and held it there, against his face. Hope's laughter faded.

Here goes, she thought. She leaned forward and kissed him, allowing her lips to part, her tongue to explore, stopping only when she'd spent all the breath in her body.

George pulled back to look at her, every laugh line and eye crinkle on his face engaged.

Hope laughed. "I guess I've been saving that up for a few years!" she said.

"What else have you saved up?" asked George, not breaking eye contact.

Hope eyed the loveseat next to them and grinned. "Let's find out."

And then the gentleman in George gave way to something else. Something more demanding. He had her blouse and bra off in three seconds, her khakis off in three more.

He marveled at her nearly naked body.

Hope blushed. "Well?" she joked. "What could I go for?"

"Dear lady," he said. "I wish all appraisals were this exciting. Classic lines, pristine condition. As for desirability . . ."

He massaged his lengthening manhood with one hand and reached forward with the other, slipping capable fingers past her panties, deep inside her.

"Oh!" gasped Hope, surprise and pleasure mingling. Then need took their place and she pulled George closer.

Hope knew anyone stopping in the downpour long enough to look at the van would see it rocking from the force of their thrusting bodies. She knew the thunder might not cover the sounds her throat made—sounds new to her. Passersby might hear George yell her name, shouting it like he was calling her home. As her pleasure reached a climax that shuddered through her body, she screamed "Yes!" and didn't care who heard her. It was an answer to all life still had to offer, a celebration of what her body could still take and receive. After all, why shouldn't she treat herself?

KNOCKOUT

D. Fostalove

Ajani saw the punch barreling toward him with such swiftness he wouldn't be able to block the move. Before it connected with his chin, he knew the blow could change the dynamics of the fight. He hadn't lost yet in a bare-knuckle backyard brawl and had no intention of making this match his first.

He threw a wild right that hit air while his opponent's uppercut connected. Seeing the glimmer of hope in Pablo's swollen eyes as his lips curled into a twisted smile was all Ajani needed to end the fight. He wouldn't lose, not at the hands of the disgraced former *luchador*. Ajani shook off the unexpected stunner before he swung with his left, knocking the smirk off his opponent's face.

Seemingly unfazed, Pablo waved his hands in the air to hype the crowd. That cockiness propelled Ajani forward. He pummeled Pablo with a barrage of punches.

The fist to the face sent Pablo flying backward into the crowd of rowdy spectators. They shoved him back toward Ajani but the fight was over as Pablo tumbled face-first into the dirt, motionless.

The crowd erupted as Ajani leaned down and lifted Pablo up by his hair.

"This the best y'all got?" he yelled.

The host entered the clearing as Pablo unsteadily climbed up onto his hands and knees, blood pooling in the spot where his head had been. The host stood next to Ajani, held his hand up, and announced, "The African Assassin, still undefeated . . ."

The crowded yard of onlookers roared at Ajani's victory.

"Is there anything you want to say to the crowd or your fans online?"

"Stop sending these weak motherfuckers to battle me." Ajani glared at the man filming the event on his phone to upload online. "Now where's my money?"

When Ajani entered the house, battered from the battle, the only thing he noticed was him. He wasn't part of the crowd of family and friends cheering when he stepped inside. He didn't have a beer or plate of food like the others. He was set off to the side on a barstool, preoccupied with his phone.

"Who's that?"

"That's my cousin, Julian, the one I told you about," Jeremy said.

Julian glanced up from his phone and smiled as they approached. Jeremy introduced them before turning away when someone called his name.

"What's up?"

"Hi," Julian said. "Congratulations on your win."

"Appreciate that." He winced from pain in the hand that was wrapped in a blood-soaked towel.

"Let me look at that for you." Julian grabbed a bag from the floor and stood.

Ajani nudged Jeremy and told him he was going to let Julian patch him up in the spare bedroom. They would be back to celebrate with everyone else shortly. The pair navigated around well-wishers to the back of the house. Once inside, Ajani closed the door behind them and tossed the bag of his winnings onto the floor.

"Have a seat."

"This good?"

Julian nodded as he wheeled a chair across the sparsely decorated room. He sat where Ajani was planted on the edge of the bed.

Removing the towel covering Ajani's hand, Julian inspected it closely. "Flex your fingers for me."

Ajani held up his hand and stretched his fingers with a grunt.

"On a scale of one to ten, what's your pain level?"

"Like a six."

Julian assured Ajani his hand wasn't broken, just swollen.

"Good."

"If you'll go wash your hands, I can sterilize the cuts and wrap your hand."

When Ajani returned from the bathroom, Julian had removed gauze, tape, and a few other items from his bag. Sitting back on the bed, Ajani held out his hand. Julian began dabbing at the cuts with alcohol while Ajani flinched.

"Why haven't I seen you at any of my fights?"

"They're too brutal for me."

Ajani glanced at the bag with the cash prize inside. "It pays the bills."

"No judgment here."

Julian tossed the bloody cotton swabs into a nearby wastebasket before he began unraveling gauze to wrap Ajani's hand. Ajani sat silently, watching as Julian handled him expertly, with care. He smiled to himself, tuning in momentarily to the loud music and chatter up front.

Breaking the silence between them, Julian admitted he'd seen one of Ajani's clips online.

"I know."

Julian looked up after taping Ajani's hand.

"Jeremy told me, said you thought I was cute."

Averting his eyes, Julian muttered how embarrassed he was.

"Why? It's cool."

Julian shrugged. "It was a random observation."

"Want me to share something with you?"

"Sure."

Ajani reached for Julian's hand and placed it on the

erection barely contained behind his sweatpants. Julian pulled his hand away, taken aback.

"Now we're even."

"I don't know what to say."

"Nothing," Ajani said. "Can I touch yours?"

"Are you serious?"

"Yeah."

Julian was quiet for a moment before he asked about the people up front. Ajani assured him no one would bother them. Besides, he had locked the door when he returned. Julian glanced at the door.

"You sure?"

"Yeah."

"No penetration."

"Cool. Now take them clothes off."

Julian stood, slowly removing his shoes, shorts, and T-shirt. Ajani lowered his sweatpants and boxers and palmed his erection as Julian stood before him in his underwear.

"Damn, you so sexy. Come here."

Julian approached. Ajani leaned forward and kissed the series of star tattoos that adorned his stomach before pulling down his underwear, revealing a curved erection.

"This is just a warning." He kissed the tip.

"What?"

"I swallow."

Ajani told him having a man's essence in his system did something to him. He couldn't explain it.

"Okay . . ."

"That cool with you?"

Julian nodded. Ajani gripped him at the hips, opened his mouth, and engulfed Julian's member. He bobbed back and forth as Julian placed a hand on his head. Ajani reached up with his bandaged hand, rubbing his fingers over Julian's hard nipple. Julian flinched from the initial touch but relaxed while attempting to steady himself from Ajani's vigorous sucking.

"You like how I suck this dick?" Ajani asked after he'd pulled away to tongue Julian's tight sac.

Julian uttered something inaudible. Ajani smirked before inhaling Julian back into his mouth, using his one hand to guide him back and forth, deeper down his throat.

"I'm about to . . ."

Ajani pressed Julian deeper into him, feeling the release. He gripped Julian's hips tighter, forcing his hairy crotch into his face violently as Julian moaned. Julian shook in Ajani's tight grip before he pulled himself out of Ajani's warm, hungry mouth.

"You all right?" Ajani asked as he wiped the corners of his mouth.

"Yeah . . . sorry about that . . ." Julian panted. "That was incredible."

"I have that effect on dudes." Ajani rubbed a thumb over Julian's still oozing erection and brought it to his lips. "Glad you liked."

"I needed that."

Ajani leaned back on the bed and began jerking himself. "Lay down here with me while I beat my shit."

Julian plopped down next to him, exhausted but satisfied. "Mind if I return the favor?"

Ajani glanced over with a sly smile. "It's all yours."

PUSSY BREATH

Giselle Renarde

Odessa tried hard to sniff her pits without alerting the receptionist. New client meetings were nerve-wracking enough without the added stress of pitting out a satin blouse before nine in the morning.

She tried to convince herself there was nothing more empowering than walking into an important business meeting with the scent of pussy on her breath.

Somehow, she remained unconvinced.

Would her new client approve of hooking up with an ex before work?

Odessa couldn't say what had come over her. She wasn't normally like this. To her credit, she'd planned to be forty minutes early. That's how she knew she had time to pop up and see Jalisa.

This hookup was entirely unplanned. Entirely.

Well, not *entirely.*

When she'd mapped her route, she noticed the client's office was dangerously close to Jalisa's condo building: down the street, around the corner, then along the way just a couple blocks.

Dangerously close.

Still, Odessa didn't plan to leave extra early so she'd have time to show up on Jalisa's doorstep. She just happened to wake at an ungodly hour and leave the house with plenty of time to spare. These things happened.

She'd arrived in the vicinity far too early. What choice did she have but to visit Jalisa?

Jalisa opened the door wearing dark gray yoga pants and a turquoise sports bra. That shade of blue really popped against her golden-brown skin. She flicked her black ponytail behind her shoulder and said, "Took you long enough."

Odessa didn't know how to respond. They'd broken up three years ago. She figured her ex would have moved on in a heartbeat. Jalisa was such a catch: fit and fun and drop-dead gorgeous.

Jalisa turned away from the door. She walked across the small living space, where a fitness routine played on the television screen. When she hit the yoga mat, she stripped off her sports bra.

Odessa quickly closed the door so the neighbors wouldn't see.

Jalisa pushed down her yoga pants, bending low

enough that Odessa caught sight not only of her sculpted ass, but her large breasts as well.

A peek was more than enough to get Odessa pulsing with anticipation.

Naked, Jalisa made her way to the sturdy granite countertop that served as an eating nook. She hopped up, spread her legs, and beckoned Odessa to eat.

Odessa sped toward her ex, climbing gracelessly onto the nearest barstool. She hadn't removed a strip of clothing.

Jalisa raised those legs in the air, leaned her elbows back, and steadied her feet against the counter.

Odessa knew she was merely there to serve.

She planted her face in her ex's pussy and inhaled deeply. She could smell sleep and the start of an exercise routine. The aroma made her wild inside, and the soundtrack from whatever fitness program was on TV didn't hurt. The music had a rapid pace and thumping bass, which suited the moment.

Odessa inched her lips closer to Jalisa's shaved pussy and fought the urge to wrap her mouth around those gleaming lips, bite down hard, gnaw and tug.

Jalisa's pussy looked perfectly presentable.

A knot developed in Odessa's stomach when she wondered who that was for.

Silly question. Jalisa kept her pussy shaved because that's how she liked it. She felt comfortable that way. It wasn't for anyone but her. Jalisa acted only for Jalisa. She was her own greatest advocate and representative.

Enough thinking. No time. *You're on the clock, Odessa. You've got a meeting to get to. Just eat this pussy and get the hell out!*

Jalisa sped things along by cupping the back of Odessa's head and pressing her face into that sweet pussy.

Odessa couldn't complain. There was nowhere else she'd rather be. She circled her lips slowly around Jalisa's clit, then picked up speed, expanding the loop. Jalisa liked that, oh yes. She groaned like she hadn't been touched in many months.

Possibly years.

But that was impossible. A beautiful woman like Jalisa? She'd be fending them off with a stick. She could have anyone.

Odessa opened her mouth as wide as she could and sucked every inch of pussy inside. Not just Jalisa's clit and inner lips, but the outer ones, too. She sucked in pulses. This was the most efficient way to make Jalisa come. Her ex wasn't one for licking. When you went down on Jalisa, you had to make a statement.

This was Odessa's statement: *I can vacuum your pussy between my lips. I create suction like no one else.*

Did you miss me?

Jalisa dropped both feet on Odessa's shoulders and leaned back, so she was lying flat on the granite, with her head falling into the empty sink. You had to utilize every bit of space in a small condo. Odessa remembered having sex in every corner of every room.

They'd done it everywhere, all over, when Jalisa first moved in.

She sucked ardently at her ex's pussy, making Jalisa squeal and moan. That's all it took. Just keep sucking. Doesn't take long to make Jalisa come.

Odessa didn't stop just because her ex hit a climax. She kept at that sweet pussy, sucking down its fluids, enjoying the hold she had over Jalisa in that moment. It wasn't often she felt in control, but when she wrapped her mouth around this clean little pussy, she felt her own power.

She sucked Jalisa's pussy until Jalisa kicked her away, panting and moaning, her labia engorged, her inner thighs slick with juice.

They turned, both at once, to check the oven clock.

"Shit," Jalisa said, sliding off the countertop, nearly falling to the floor because, clearly, Odessa had left her weak with orgasm. "I gotta get ready. I'm running so late."

That's when Odessa really started to sweat. The idea of being late didn't sit well with her. "I need to go, too. I've got a meeting."

Jalisa had already fled to the bedroom. Odessa made no further attempt at conversation. She slipped from her ex's condo and punched the elevator call button four thousand times.

The receptionist interrupted her reverie by saying, "I'll show you into the meeting room now."

When they arrived, the room was empty.

The receptionist had already walked halfway back to the waiting area when Odessa said, "Oh, sorry—hi? There's nobody here. I'm supposed to be meeting the senior accounts manager. I don't have a name on file."

Turning, the receptionist tilted her head. "I meant to tell you Jalisa's running late."

Odessa's stomach dropped. "Jalisa?"

The receptionist nodded before walking away.

When Odessa dropped into one of the white leather meeting room chairs, she felt as though she were floating. Did Jalisa realize they'd be meeting this morning? Or were they both unaware they'd be seeing each other, professionally?

Odessa cupped her hand over her mouth and smelled her breath.

Smelled like pussy.

She sat a little taller and waited for Jalisa to arrive.

MILE MARKER 88.7, JULY 15 2015

Shane Ackley

Kyle flipped on the turn signal and looked out the Subaru's rear window as he eased into the right lane on Interstate 95 way north of Baltimore. As he did, he slid his right hand onto Kari's left knee and slid it up her thigh and inward until he reached the stitched-edge bottom of her dark blue cotton shorts.

"It's mile marker 88.7. The bridge is just ahead," Kyle said.

"Is it?" Kari said with a wry smile, and closed her paperback legal romance.

"Is the detective banging the DA?" Kyle asked.

"Yeah, pretty much." Kari smiled as she wedged the book in the door compartment.

She looked down at her shorts and straightened them a bit.

Kari got the shorts in the '90s and was proud of every pair she still owned. They looked like junior high gym gear, with an elastic waistband and the semi-circle cutout detail of the bottom of each side, but to a former elite gymnast like Kari, they were a security blanket—the shorts she grew up wearing over leotards at practice. Kari rocked them as a thirty-five-year-old, donning them on weekends like an old, comfy sweatshirt.

Kyle loved those shorts too, even though he teased Kari relentlessly about how '90s they looked, because they reminded him of eighteen-year-old Kari, an adorable, fit gymnast he met on the sand in Ocean City, New Jersey.

The shorts gave her wicked panty lines, but she didn't care. She'd refused thongs for years, never bending to fashion pressure from college roommates or Kyle. "I don't care if people know I'm wearing underwear," she would say of her bikini undies. Long before Kylie Jenner rocked full-butt, white Calvin Klein underwear on Instagram, Kari O'Malley was the white cotton panty queen, in Kyle's world, anyway.

They were on their way back to Jersey from a weekend visit to see her parents outside Baltimore, sans kids. Mile marker 88.7 meant getting ready for "the bridge thing." And the shorts made "the bridge thing" work.

Kari was, on first look and on most mornings, an on-her-back missionary sex girl. No hours and hours of lovemaking. Just get to it, come, and get back to life.

Rarely other positions, and maybe a finger to help things along. Kyle described their lovemaking as a "series of extended quickies."

Rushed sex, though, gave way to quickie orgasms too. Kari's side kink was short, sneaky sessions, like rubbing her clit on the couch while Kyle cooked dinner. He believed she did this because every gymnastic routine of her younger days took two minutes, and that was how Kari saw everything physical—a short burst of intense performance.

As the Subaru approached the bridge over the Susquehanna River, Kyle asked again, "You gonna—"

"Yes," Kari said firmly, and pulled her shorts to the right with her right hand, so Kyle could see her panties —today, a triangle of white cotton, taut and smooth.

"Mmm," Kyle murmured.

The bridge, nearly in Delaware, is one hundred feet in the air and just a mile lined with way-too-low Jersey barriers. Kari and Kyle always talked about how dangerous it seemed. Figuring other motorists' eyes would be fixed with their eyes ahead, one year Kari suddenly pulled her panties to the side and started rubbing her clit. "Holy crap," she remembered Kyle saying.

Kari would pop her right foot on the door near the window, open her lips with her left hand, and slightly penetrate herself with her left ring finger, while her right hand took care of her clit. It worked.

The image was burned into Kyle's mind: by the time

they reached the Chesapeake service area, a few minutes past the bridge, Kari bobbed her head up and down and grunted a few times from the back of her throat, and came as fast as she started. She slid up, straightened her shorts, and kissed Kyle on the cheek as he pulled into the rest stop.

She only did it northbound, on the way home on Sunday afternoons. Heading down 95 from Jersey on a Friday night just didn't have the vibe she wanted, even though it was dark.

This time, Kari tugged on the top of her panties a few times as the car approached the span. She'd done that before—really a treat for Kyle—and after a final check for truckers, she yanked her Calvins to the side and started her two-finger method. "Hands ten and two," Kari joked, and threw her leg onto the door.

This day was instantly different from her past endeavors. She was wildly wet, even embarrassed for a second. Halfway across the span, as her exhales grew louder, she threw her head back and rubbed harder.

"I might need some help," Kari said. Kyle planned to pull over at the rest stop and kiss her. That usually put her over the edge, and sometimes he got a quickie hand job out of it.

Kari grasped at Kyle's shorts for any hardness. "I can't, well, this is a girl but it's becoming a boy," she said, louder with each word.

Kari called her orgasms boys and girls. Girls were the wavy, not a definitive end type, which she mostly

had during intercourse, and the bridge. Boys were
when she had contractions, a real ending, usually from
masturbating with a toy or when Kyle talked her into
longer lovemaking.

"Pull over, now," she said. "I need your penis." She
always used real terms.

Kyle's eyes bugged as he jammed on the blinker, then
the hazards, and lurched into the shoulder.

"What if a trooper comes up behind us?" said Kyle,
a sudden pragmatist.

"I'll be watching, this won't take long," Kari replied
as she pulled her right leg out of her shorts and panties
and climbed onto his lap. Kyle started to unbutton his
shorts, but Kari took over, pushing them down and
pulling his balls above his waistband.

Kari reached down and held Kyle's penis up, positioned her labia above it, and sank down. She tried
planting her feet on either side of the seat so she could
lift her butt up and down, thinking it would make Kyle
come quicker, but her feet were wobbly so she abandoned it. She dropped her legs to the side so her knees
were at Kyle's hips and ground inward and down. "Oh,
yeah," she said.

She grabbed the headrest as she thrusted and grunted
in rhythm. Kyle had no reason to move. It was all Kari;
he literally sat back and enjoyed the ride.

With three final thrusts, she was done. Kari briefly
closed her eyes, wiped a brief tear with the back of her
right hand, and rested backwards, her back up against

the steering wheel. "Wow," Kyle mustered. "So proud of you."

He felt bad about saying "proud," but he knew Kari knew what he meant. "I feel bad, you're like, you're not close," she said.

"Totally okay. You just rode me on the side of the road. Let's go." Kari plopped back into her seat with a full case of cottonmouth.

"I need a drink," Kari said. "And a kiss."

"I know. Rest stop coming up."

WANNA BET?

D.J Hodge

"How many skin cells you think are in that candy bowl?"

Placing the candy down on the coffee table, I turn and scowl. Mike looks at me, laughing. It's a full laugh, the kind that has him doubling over and showing his teeth. He leans back on the sofa and smiles, deep dimples on display.

"You might as well finish it. You've already had, like, five of them."

"Please shut up, Michael."

He stares at me as I chug my water. If it were anyone else, the intensity would be unsettling. Unfortunately for him, I know he peed his pants during a dinosaur movie in the fourth grade. Instead of looking away, I lean back on the bright blue sofa and tilt my head. Our brown skin is reflective against the soft fabric. Smirking at me, Mike mimics my position.

"Niecy."

"Hmm?"

"You still seeing that guy who thinks your clit is on your thigh?"

Reaching between us, I grab a pillow and slap him with it. He reaches out, pulling on a curl that's managed to escape my industrial-strength scrunchie. "I bet I can find it," he says.

I narrow my eyes, and he laughs, sliding closer. Snaking an arm around my waist, he leans forward, bringing his lips to my ear. "I *know* I can find it."

Raising my hand, I push against his chest. It's an impressive chest. Hard and defined from years of football and a healthy relationship with the gym. He buries his face into my neck. I know if I don't stop this, it'll get out of hand. So I do the logical thing in this situation—I twist his nipple.

He leans back, grabbing my wrist. "Really, Denise?"

"Since when do you call me Denise?"

"When's the last time you fucked with a guy and didn't need a vibrator chaser?"

"Nice. Did you come up with that on your own, or did you overhear your sister say it?"

"My sister, obviously. Answer the question."

"Like, seventy-five percent of women need a vibrator chaser. I'm hardly an anomaly."

Hooking his large hands under my thighs, he pulls

me closer so that I'm tucked underneath him. Fearful I'll fall off the couch, I cling to him. Softly, he nips at my bottom lip. I feel warmth to my toes. When he kisses the tip of my nose, I know I'm going to let whatever this is happen.

"I'm gonna make you come on this Smurf couch," he quips.

Tucking my head in his neck, I laugh. "Sure, if you say so."

"Wanna bet?" He raises an eyebrow. I roll my eyes, and he smiles. It's deceptively innocent. "If I win, we do it again. If you win, we do it until I win."

Throwing my hand over my eyes, I groan. "Yeah, sure. Whatever." Grinding against him, I raise my hips. He doesn't remove my leggings like I expect him to. Instead, he moves one of his legs in between mine, pulling me on top of him. Moving his hands up my body, he settles one around my neck. I shiver, and he grins at my response.

"Is this okay?" he asks, pulling me closer.

Staring at him, I nod. Instinctively, I rock against his leg. His grip tightens around my neck, causing me to push down harder. He leans into me and whispers, "Remember junior year of college, when you spent the night?"

Before I can answer, he grabs my ass, forcing me down. I gasp at the pressure, clutching his forearm. His eyes molten, he continues, "We were hugged up under those covers, then you got up and disappeared for twenty minutes."

Then I feel it, a soft build between my legs. His hold on my neck makes it hard for me to breathe. I whimper, squirming on his leg. My leggings, now thoroughly soaked through, cling to my thighs.

"You were playing with yourself, weren't you?" he asks.

Yes, I was. Slightly embarrassed, I shake my head. Mike licks his lips and sighs heavily. "Do you really think you're in a position to lie to me, Niecy?"

My body vibrates. I'm on fire, burning from the inside out. Moaning, I clutch his leg with one hand and his chest with the other. He slightly tightens the grip on my neck. It nearly takes me over the edge.

"When you came back, I could smell it on you. I should have fucked you right there on the floor."

I gasp for air. He lets go of my neck and kisses me. His tongue slides into my mouth, and I push forward, trying to get as close to him as possible. Grabbing my face with both hands, he pulls back. The gesture is somehow more intimate than everything else we've done.

"Look at me." He tilts my head back so that I meet his eyes. I squirm under his gaze.

"Please," I whisper, holding onto his wrists.

Mike chuckles, reaching for the hem of my T-shirt. My lace bra leaves nothing to the imagination. Small brown peaks strain against the pretty pink fabric. He hums his approval, his hands circling my rib cage. Then, lowering his head, he covers one with his mouth. I nearly jump out of my skin.

"Fuck, Mike."

Sick of his shit and ridiculously wet, I beg him to stop fucking around and get on with it. I'm so desperate for release that any embarrassment takes a back seat. Launching forward, I lean my thigh into him. He groans, nearly lifting me off of him. Biting my neck, his hand slides into the back of my leggings. I grind into his leg as his talented fingers play with me from behind. When he grabs the back of my neck, I know he's going to win.

"You're gonna come, aren't you?" He smiles at me. I close my eyes and nod.

"Jesus," I whisper.

"Come. Right now."

He pushes his fingers inside of me, and I go over, gasping and grabbing at him. Then he pulls me close, anchoring me while I ride it out.

"Good girl." He smiles against my neck, stroking my hair. A switch flips and everything I'm feeling bubbles up to the surface. I feel exposed. I bury my face in his chest, afraid the tears will come. Sensing the shift, he cradles me in his arms, softly peppering kisses all over my face. He rubs my back, assuring me that this isn't an ending; it is a new beginning. He's the most gracious winner.

"Niecy?" he whispers.

"Hmm?"

"Let's order Chinese and then celebrate my victory in your bed."

He wags his eyebrows, and I giggle. It feels like a weight has lifted. I'm reminded that, above all, Mike is my best friend. Our foundation is solid. Everything else is extra. Plus, he definitely knows where my clit is. Grinning stupidly, I lay my head on his shoulder. "You're paying, right?"

"Of course. I don't expect that to change." He smiles and kisses me on my forehead.

ALL IN

Mx. Nillin Lore

"How many is that?" Reese asks through panting breaths. He lifts his head from the mattress to look down over his enormous, heaving tits and around the vibrating wand he has pressed firmly against his clit dick. A crowd of voyeurs stands mere feet away watching him, as well as glancing around the rest of the room at the variety of explicit sex acts and scenes unfolding in real time.

After a long day of conference workshops, presentations, and debates on kink etiquette and safety, this was what everybody was most excited for: the public dungeon playspace. It was easily the conference's biggest draw and allowed for participants to engage in hardcore, explicit kink and fetish play within the confines of the large community hall at a picturesque ranch just outside of Saskatoon.

"That's all five," Theo, his good friend and kink partner, replies with most of their lube-covered hand already inserted into Reese's nicely trimmed up boi cunt. "Are you ready?"

This is what they had been preparing for. Months of size play with various fantasy dildos ranging from a small-scale, rainbow-colored dragon cock to a formidably thick, deep-red werewolf dick with a huge flared knot, all leading up to this moment. Reese is determined to take Theo's full fist for the first time, right there in that room surrounded by new friends and strangers alike.

He doesn't immediately respond, instead deciding to take in the other play scenarios happening throughout the large room. It wasn't often that he found himself in an environment like this, though he suspected not many of the others surrounding him had either. Sex dungeon parties at fetish conventions in rural Saskatchewan aren't exactly a common occurrence given that the province had a reputation for being God-fearing, with strong Catholic roots and conservative family values.

As if that didn't narrow his options for exciting sexual experiences, Reese is a queer demiboy with a boi cunt, an engorged clit dick, and huge, hairy tits. That sadly puts him in the demographic of "too queer and weird" for small town kinksters and swingers who dominate the region. But this convention is different than your typical non-monogamous, sex-optional house parties or barn orgies. Here all are genuinely welcome, which meant he's finally getting his chance to soak in some explicit semipublic play.

Directly to Reese's right stands a big, hairy bear in assless leather chaps, his arms and legs spread apart and bound to a St. Andrew's Cross, screaming in pain as his partner, equally large and wearing a leather dog hood, beat his back. To Reese's left is a fabulous drag queen who he and Theo had befriended earlier in the day, naked except for the glitter fairy wings strapped to her back. She sits on a naked man hunched over like a chair while another two individuals take turns servicing her girl cock.

On the other side of the room lays a tall, slim woman on a blue tarp wearing a white bra and panties that become increasingly see-through as several of her friends pour and rub oil all over her body.

Diagonal from that display sits a heavily tattooed person with long curly hair hanging over her large breasts. She grimaces in pain then moans with pleasure as her friend, a nurse wearing plastic gloves and a head-lamp, carefully sews her mouth shut with surgical thread. Almost equally as jarring, though mostly because of the contrast, is the fully clothed young couple on the floor, facing each other with their legs intermingled, as they slowly make out and sensually caress one another with their fingertips.

All of that isn't even half of it. Not only is there plenty more happening in the room but the ranch hall isn't the only active dungeon going on. Just outside the building, a short walk across the property, past a field where everybody had parked their cars, sits a small wooden church powered by a generator.

It was there that Theo got to enjoy their particular brand of pleasure. While one of the conference presenters was ritualistically fucked on an altar at the front of the small church, Theo sat in a pew along with several other evenly spaced out individuals who all mutually masturbated together as they watched.

"Reese," Theo says impatiently, applying more lube to the exposed parts of their hand not currently buried in Reese's boi cunt. "Focus. Are you ready?"

Reese snaps back into the moment and nods. He's ready. With a flick of his finger he increases the vibration setting on the wand pressed firmly against his clit dick and lets out a deep moan. Theo smirks, pulling the sleeve of their flannel further up their arm and then grunts as they force the rest of their hand inside of Reese, then firmly closes their fist.

The pain and pleasure of that sudden stretch are enough to make Reese come right then and there. He cries out, clenching down hard onto Theo's knuckles as they rub against his insides.

"Yes! Fucking get it, boy!" calls the fabulous queen in fairy wings, who is now watching Reese and Theo as she stands triumphantly over one of her boy toys, her own come dripping down his face and chin.

Reese sighs and lays his head back, knowing that isn't everything. "Do it, fuck me hard." He speaks only loud enough for Theo to hear. They're more than happy to oblige. Theo positions themself a little better, then begins to roughly fist Reeese's boi cunt as hard as they possibly can. They know he likes it hard. He likes it to hurt. Within seconds, Reese feels another wave of pleasure crashing over him. He grunts, his face contorting, his whole body straining so hard from the orgasm that he pushes Theo out and squirts all over them and the floor.

Cheering and applause erupt from the viewing gallery, making a smile spread across Reese's face. He lays there with his eyes closed, catching his breath, basking in the exhibitionist bliss he's just experienced, and nearly dozes off to the cries, moans, slaps, and gasps happening all around him.

LIGHTS UP

Veronique Veritas

"You do that just with different colored gels?" Genevieve asked, looking down from the walkway above the stage.

Samuel laid on his stomach and slipped a piece of translucent cobalt into the hanging stage light, catching his breath as he stood.

"When I start my new job, I'll get to use some of the better software they have to automate the lights." His voice softened. "I'll be in the big leagues, Genni. You think I'll be okay?"

Genevieve gave him a hug.

"Of course!"

She gazed down over his shoulder and watched the stage glow a moody blue. The lights made the marble she'd painted on the wooden set look mysterious.

"You need to have more confidence," she insisted.

The embrace broke. She took in the long, already graying hair tied into a messy ponytail. He looked older than his thirty-two years; she, three years his junior, often gave him advice.

"It's not that I don't know that," he said. "If I could I'd do a lot of things different . . ."

Genevieve knew what he meant, remembering the time he admitted he was pretty sure he was gay, but terrified to ask anyone out.

"I just don't want you to have regrets," she said. "Anyway, you ready for your move?"

"I am. It may be hard, but I know it's time," he answered.

The next few weeks blurred together as Genevieve slept in the mornings and alternated nights painting sets at the small theater and working her waitressing job. The day of the move, she drove the small moving truck around the block a few times before finding an open space. Samuel's apartment door was open, boxes waiting. Samuel's father stood there, too, his face flushed bright red.

"How dare you leave me?! For what, your stupid lights?" his father fumed.

"Actually," Genevieve interrupted, "it's impressive that he's been hired on Broadway. You should be proud!"

His father glared at her before storming off down the stairwell.

Genevieve and Samuel rode in silence after loading the truck, unloaded his things again, and returned the truck. By the time they got back to his new place, he was ready to talk.

"Thanks for everything today. There's something else I've been thinking about that might actually help me move forward. But I don't want it to change things between us . . ." he started, before revealing his most intimate fantasy. He picked at the tape on one of the boxes, before he looked her in the eyes. "If you'd be okay with it, I really want you to penetrate me. You know, with a strap-on."

Genevieve flashed back to the times she'd worn a strap-on in the sex club she went to on her nights off. Both women and men enjoyed doing scenes with her, but she'd often had to reassure some men that doing something like that did not automatically "make them gay." She'd told Samuel about all that before, and even offered to bring him along to meet someone. But he'd always blushed and refused.

"I know you have that club you go to," he continued, "but I really think that would be too much for me right now. You know how awkward I am."

"I understand," Genevieve answered. "Although it is a welcoming place if you change your mind."

He nodded.

"I get that, it's just that I'm already starting a new job and I'm in a new place. It's been a lot for me, and you've been here for me through all of it. I feel safe with you," he explained. "Even when I dated Lindsey in college, there's no way I would have felt comfortable asking her this."

"So this would be your first time?" Genevieve clarified.

"Yeah," he whispered. "Look, just forget I said anything."

Genevieve touched his cheek.

"No, it's okay," she said. "I'd love to do this for you."

They agreed on a safeword and more specifics, then scheduled for the next night they both had off from work. When the night finally came, she could see from her bedroom window that the light in his window was on, glowing invitingly. Something warmed her as she laid in bed, moistened her first two fingers with lube, and rubbed them in circles on her clit, pressing harder each time she inhaled. The numbers on the clock flashed, and she realized she was running late. She didn't stop.

By the time she'd orgasmed three or four times, she carefully stood and finished getting dressed. She gathered her supplies and headed downstairs, then across to Samuel's apartment with his spare key.

When she opened his apartment door, she found him kneeling with his forehead pressed to the floor. Seeing him naked made her realize the full extent of his bulk, and why he'd been nervous about going to gay bars populated by so many model-pretty guys. But she knew he would find someone who appreciated him.

She closed the door behind her and saw him shiver,

but he didn't say the safeword they'd discussed. The long jacket came off and she watched the way her black latex shimmered as she moved.

"How long have you been waiting?" she asked, pulling a small painted canvas out of her bag and resting it against the door.

Samuel kept his head down, but she heard him clearly.

"Not long."

She walked behind him, brushing her fingers lightly along his hips.

"That's a lie. You've been waiting too long for someone to fuck you the way you want," she said, before lightly spanking him.

He gasped as her bright red handprint rose on his skin.

"Did you like that?" she asked, as she watched him nod. "Want more?"

"Yes," he begged. "Genni, please . . ."

She took the strap-on out of her bag and adjusted it to fit. It rubbed against her already primed clit, and she nearly came again before reaching into the bag once more.

"Get ready for my cock in your ass," she whispered, as she covered the appendage generously with lube. She spread him wide and searched for where to enter, feeling a resistance that gradually eased the further in she went.

He cried out as he moved against her, taking her cock deep. She steadied herself with his hips and once they were in a rhythm, she lowered her hand to hold his cock.

"Yeah, just like that," he said with a sigh. She firmly pulsed her hand up and down his shaft as she felt it harden.

When he admitted he was on the verge of coming, she pulled out and commanded him to sit up and look at the painting she'd brought. His come splattered across the painting of two male nudes embracing, coating it with a sticky sheen. He trembled, drawing in another deep breath as Genevieve gently brushed the hair out of his face.

She removed the strap-on and touched his shoulders as they got cleaned up.

"I hope you like your housewarming gift," she said, and he squeezed her hand.

"More than I'd ever imagined," he admitted, a peaceful smile illuminating his face.

FIXTURE

Evie Bennet

When I excused myself to wash my hands, you stood up. "Let me take you. I have to grab something, anyway." You held my hand and led me past the kitchen and guest bath to your old bathroom upstairs. "This should have everything you desire." You winked. "And no need to hurry; I'll keep your food warm and keep the others busy." You caressed the curve of the bannister on your way down the stairs to entertain your guests.

Large, marbled tiles made the bathroom feel more spacious. Tiny beads sat suspended in the clear gel soap. And then I saw *it*, your elegant faucet, and I remembered.

I'd been to your house dozens, if not hundreds, of times when we were in school, before your parents retired somewhere in Florida, leaving you this "modest but fabulous" property.

Sleepovers filled with laughter no longer had to be muffled so as not to awaken them. Back then, your breath had been hot on my face while you swore that *technically,* you didn't masturbate.

"You use a vibrator?" I clarified, rolling onto my side.

"I fuck my faucet."

The alliteration struck me as beautiful, unique. But the semantics brought me back down to earth, trying to fit pieces of the puzzle together. "You . . . stick it in?"

"No, I grind it." Your hands disappeared beneath your covers, resting on your hips. "It has these *ridges.* And it's hard. If I'm using the hot water, it gets warm enough to, uh, to feel good." You shrugged, not meeting my eye. "It's different than using a showerhead."

I snorted and grinned. "How many pieces of furniture are you fucking?"

"Just the ones that get me off. They have to give off the right energy."

"Makes sense. Any of them are probably better at it than Gex," I teased, referring to the ex whose fingers cramped after five minutes of fumbling around. "What about this bedpost?" I tapped it with a sock-clad toe.

You shrugged and bit down on a guilty smile.

Cackling, we rolled onto our stomachs, and you talked me through the dos and don'ts of getting off on household objects. I hung onto your expertise, riveted, staying up all night as our tales twisted into teasing, our limbs tangling in slumber.

And seven years later, there we were. You, in the kitchen, entertaining our other friends, while I washed my hands, lathering and rinsing under warm water. Licking my lips, I touched the faucet.

Hot, but not enough to burn.

It was juvenile to even think of our past conversations.

But . . . you'd spoken so highly of it. And my sink wasn't like this. With your wink as my blessing, I twisted the nozzle to a lighter stream, then wagged my hips as I stripped.

I stuffed the leggings on one side of the sink and my shirt on the other and clambered on, using the guest towel handlebar for leverage. My breasts knocked against the mirror. Squatting, half-naked, I shook my head at the idea that you used to go to all this effort.

For all I knew, you still did.

With renewed determination, I sank down, pressing my slit against the warm metal. The gentle vibrations combined with the white noise of the faucet relaxed my tense muscles.

I tilted my head back and rocked my hips.

When did you first notice how smooth and perfect this fixture would feel gliding against your sex? How had you been brave and reckless enough to try? Why were you sharing your partner with me, now?

My clit caught the edge of the architecture you

praised and fucked. The dull pangs of arousal had me biting back a moan.

No wonder you were happy to live in this house forever. Or at least until your joints gave out.

My clothes dug into my knees as I humped the curve of the faucet, then the head, my clit throbbing from the stimulation. *Fuck*, I wanted to rip the towel bar off the wall. Crush the mirror into a hug as that delicious, tight energy stretched under my skin. Cry in victory as I came.

My nails dug into the glass, and my muscles clenched, a wave of pleasure coursing through my nerves. I angled my hips, accidentally knocking the handle with my knee. The hiss of flowing water rattled the faucet. I sank onto it, melting atop the molten curves as starlight burst behind my eyelids. My hungry pussy gushed and throbbed and gobbled at the sink.

It was slippery. Trembling like me.

As long as I worked at it, ecstasy flowed and ebbed. My breath fogged the mirror, and my tits kissed the glass. I ground my pleasure out until the cabinet shuddered worse from wear. Oh, I would fuck your house down to the ground and rebuild it again.

But they were waiting for me downstairs. For us, perhaps. And that's why I came, wasn't it?

Warmth lingered with the syrupy satisfaction of a lazy morning as I clambered down with the gracefulness of a drunk, laughing at the mess and my stiff thighs. Streaks of cloudy and clear fluids mixed, so I squirted soap in my hands and jerked the faucet clean. And you did this every other night, you little sneak. Or at least you did back then. I found your stash of towels and got to work, throwing the used ones in the hamper after I'd wiped my palm prints off your mirror.

My reflection shined with the new, glowing secret we shared.

A fixture. Our friendship. Whatever the future held for you and me and this strange, wonderful energy.

I AM ALSO YOURS

Kei X. Griot

"That's a good boy," Master Adrian said as he finished the knot securing Dev's ankles together. His knees were on the floor and his hips pressed firmly against the foot of the red velvet bed. His arms stretched the width of the king-size bed, wrists tied to either wooden post. His ankles were tied so he could gain no leverage and any movement was nearly impossible, had he wanted to move. His flesh came to attention as he thought of nothing but the feel of the black rope and what his master would administer.

"Now, take one last look," Master Adrian instructed just before tying a red silk scarf over Dev's eyes. On the bed lay a bamboo spatula, rope gag, crystal plug, and black leather collar. Now sight deprived, Dev pictured all he had just seen. He throbbed and hardened against the soft velvet covers. Master Adrian picked up the collar and fastened it tightly around his neck. He sealed it with a heart-shaped lock, a larger version of the one Dev wore at all times on a chain choker. He grabbed a handful of his thick, short hair, slowly yanked his head back, and bent down to whisper in his ear.

"If you scream too loud, the gag is next." Dev contained a smile, bracing himself to scream louder than ever before, remembering what day it was. He began to salivate, then bit his lip as Master Adrian ran his fingernails roughly down the length of his arms, back, and legs. Not hard enough to break the skin, but enough to inflict the sweet sting of pain. With his strong hands he squeezed both of Dev's cheeks, then parted them. "You're wet," Master Adrian declared as Dev quivered. He felt a cool sensation as Master Adrian teased him open and thrust the crystal in. Dev bit harder on his bottom lip and moaned. He tried to rock his hips and grind against the bed, but the futile effort was quickly thwarted by Master Adrian. "Did I tell you to move?"

"No, master."

"Hold still then. You will obey absolutely. Won't you?" He placed one hand on Dev's back and took the spatula in the other. He carefully put his weight onto Dev's lower back as he knelt beside him.

"I will, master," Dev replied, nearly drooling.

Master Adrian raised the spatula high above his head. "That's my good boy," he said, and came down fast with a controlled, almost gentle, stinging thud. Then without pause, six hits, each with increasing intensity, struck Dev's reddening butt cheeks. His muscles tensed and he refocused on the feel of the crystal comfortably snug in place as he exhaled and waited for more.

"I have something special for you," Master Adrian said with a smile. Dev could not see, but could hear and feel the smile in his master's voice, the voice that simultaneously alarmed and aroused him. Master Adrian went to the candleholder, selected one lit, red candle, and held it over Dev's body, staring at the ripe flesh below him. He slowly put the flame close enough to Dev's skin for him to feel the heat and moved it along his back, letting the wax slowly drip.

"You will get your brand today," he said and awaited a reply. Pleased with the silence, he continued, "Did you remember?"

"Yes, master." Dev had not forgotten anything since their relationship began. That rainy night he'd had a flat tire on his bike after a class two years ago. The older man who approached asking if everything was alright, if he needed help. The long car ride home they shared listening to Sade. Taking his number in case Dev needed anything, he had said. That alluring subtlety which somehow commanded his actions. Dev remembered how often, like now, he felt cared for, exhilarated, free to be afraid. He focused on the heat from the flame and wax dripping on him.

"And how do you feel?"

"Happy about it, but nervous."

"Do you want to see?"

"Yes, master."

He put the candle back in the holder and untied Dev's arms from the bedposts. "You may remove your blindfold." Dev bent his arms toward his face and removed the scarf. While he did this, Master Adrian untied the rope from his ankles. He stood and said, "Kneel."

Dev turned around and knelt facing his master, who was holding a thick metal wire. He curled one end of the metal around, forming a spiral. He held the spiral over the flame until it turned red, then let it cool.

"Do you still want it on your shoulder?"

"Yes, master." Dev took his free hand and began massaging himself, noticing how wet he was in anticipation.

"First, I want you to get yourself off. Then the brand, okay?" Dev leaned back against the foot of the bed. Master Adrian stepped forward and over him, pressing his pelvis against his head. Rubbing himself in a circular motion, Dev closed his eyes and pictured sucking his master off. He reached up with his free hand, touched his crotch, and could feel through his leather pants that he was packing. "I'll give you that later, but come for me now."

Dev rubbed himself faster and harder until he felt he might squirt. "It's all yours, master," he said in a medley of moans and heavy breathing. While Dev continued to play with himself, trembling and panting on the floor, Adrian looked down at him and remembered their first time.

When he'd received Dev's call, he made sure to tell him upfront exactly what kind of relationships he had. After that call, he knew Dev's offer for coffee insinuated more. One coffee date turned to weekly, then daily, hangouts. The boyish naivete was as much a seductive role Dev played as the stern authoritative nature Adrian exuded. Before their first time together, they went to get rapid tested and then to the park after. It was there that Adrian explained what it would mean for them to be together.

"Before you are mine, you are your own." He said it then, and again throughout their time together. Just as he said it while pressing the hot spiral to Dev's skin. Dev took in a big inhale. His skin sizzled for the few seconds the metal touched. "Are you okay?"

"Yes, it only stung for a moment." Dev had thought it would hurt a lot more, but was relieved it didn't.

"Good, I have a surprise for you. You're giving me the same brand." Master Adrian placed the spiral back into the flame, letting it get red. "As you know, I am also yours." He handed the wire to Dev, who didn't hesitate to take it. He unbuttoned his leather shirt, revealing his tattooed chest, ran his hands along his scars, and pointed to his heart. "I want it here." He knelt with Dev, who carefully pressed the hot wire to his master. Soon after, Master Adrian dressed both of their brands while sweetly kissing all over Dev's skin and rubbing him with shea butter. Then he bent him over the bed and kept his word, rewarding him with the strap he craved.

AT IT AGAIN

Dani Mignon

"They're at it again," Max told Pauline. "Showing up the old folks."

"I don't think they're doing it to make a point," Pauline replied. "I think they're just horny. Anyway, we're not old folks."

"Compared to them, we are." Max gestured out the window. "You know why those two make love with the curtains open? They're stickin' it to us!"

Pauline tsked. "Nobody's sticking it to anyone."

"*He*'s stickin' it to *her*. Look! There's the stick!"

These neighboring houses were incredibly close together. Couldn't be five feet between the two. Never was a problem until those sorority sisters moved in next door. What kind of people don't close the drapes when they're making love?

Staring at the young couple next door, Pauline said, "Anything she can do, I can do better."

Max didn't catch his wife's drift.

"If you think they're sticking it to us," Pauline explained, "we'll stick it right back."

He wasn't too sure what she was plotting until later that evening, after the young man had departed and the woman sat alone at the desk by the window, tapping at her computer.

Pauline came out of the bathroom wearing a sheer black negligee. Max had seen it before, and he knew what it meant. He was already in bed, having closed the blinds before undressing.

His wife made a show of sauntering toward the window, pulling down on the blind, and releasing.

"What are you doing?" Max hissed. "Our light's still on. The girl's right there. She'll see—"

"Precisely," Pauline said, raising an eyebrow. "You want in, yes or no?"

Max looked, with alarm, out the window. His gaze met that of the young woman who loved showing off her naked body in the throes of wild lust. Why not give her a taste of her own medicine? Show her the old folks could still get it on?

Casting off the covers, Max strode naked across the bedroom. He kissed his beautiful wife. Was the exhibitionist next door getting a good eyeful? Could she handle the sight of two lovers in their sixties, who knew precisely what felt good?

When Max kissed Pauline's neck, she nipped at his cheek, catching his silver beard in her teeth and tugging gently. She grabbed his bare ass as he slid his hand down the sheer fabric of her negligee.

"You look gorgeous tonight," he said.

She offered a throaty chuckle. "You look gorgeous every night, and you don't even have to try!"

He didn't contradict her, though her assessment was wildly incorrect. *Trying*, for him, meant hitting the gym every day, without fail. Trying meant trimming his facial hair so it wouldn't get in the way when they kissed. He didn't wear makeup or lingerie for her, the way she did for him, but that didn't mean he wasn't trying.

When his knees buckled, he tempted her to bed. Was the girl next door watching? Would she eye their every move?

Pauline said, "You have no idea how attracted I am to you."

He knew why she made a point of saying such things: same reason he went out of his way to assure her that he found her incredibly alluring. She didn't often get wet for him and he didn't always get hard for her. Age was to blame. They discussed the matter often enough. It helped to remind one another the attraction was still there, even if the response was hard to come by.

Tonight, they got lucky. He was already at half-mast by the time Pauline started stroking him. When she climbed down his body to put him in her mouth, Max very nearly snuck a peek out the window. No, he decided. He didn't want to know whether they were being watched.

He focused on his loving wife, certain his attention would pay off in spades.

Often, they made love with the lights off. It wasn't deliberate—they ended up in seduction mode once they were already in bed. Watching his wife devour his dick was a rare treat, and he couldn't get enough. All the same, it wouldn't be fair to make her do all the work—or let her have all the fun, depending how you looked at it—so he slid his finger along her shoulder and whispered, "How about a sixty-nine?"

Pauline climbed eagerly onto his face. The world grew a tad darker, thanks to the negligee. Max found his wife's clitoris easily, and offered soft licks to start. Pauline wasn't having it. She ground her lower lips against his tongue, going for what she wanted, no signs of waiting for him to catch up.

Her arousal increased his. With her mouth wrapped fully around his shaft, her lusty words were muffled, but he could always interpret her level of arousal by the frequency of her shrieks. At first, they got higher in pitch. Then, they went low. That was stage one of her orgasm process.

Max never felt as though he were doing any work when his wife rode his face. She knew what she wanted. She knew how to get there. She used his tongue as a toy, and he didn't mind one bit.

Her intensity boosted his.

She sucked with fervor at his solemn erection, wrapping both hands around his shaft as she pressed her breasts against his belly. Shame they weren't naked. He loved to feel her skin against his. But the negligee felt nice, too. He knew how lucky he was. He got the sense his friends' wives wouldn't ride their faces in front of the girl next door.

"Your beard feels so good!" Pauline growled as she stroked herself firmly against his tongue. "So good, Max! So good!"

Sometimes it seemed as though Pauline's orgasms went on forever. She rode them like waves, one to the next. Max was really rather jealous of that. He wouldn't mind trying out an ongoing orgasm.

But he couldn't begrudge his wife her extended pleasure when she brought him the kind of climax he sought. He felt it on the horizon, in his spine, traveling closer. Pauline's ongoing cries sped the sensation along, until it gripped him by the balls, clutching and twisting most enthrallingly—or was Pauline doing that? Hard to tell what was happening.

The thrill of orgasm took hold, forcing him to thrust his hips unwittingly, and fill his wife's throat with the froth of his pleasure. Sexual delight went on and on, explosion after blissful explosion, to the point where he felt that perhaps he was riding his wife's lustful wave. Perhaps they were riding together.

Pauline didn't move from his face, even after they'd taken their time panting and moaning, assuring one another that no other orgasm had ever felt so intense. She rested upon him, her juices and his saliva mingling in his beard.

Max resisted the urge to turn his head, to gaze beyond his wife's bare thigh.

The girl next door—was she sitting at her window? Had she been watching all this time? Did she like what she saw?

Perhaps it was better not to know.

A BIRTHDAY GIFT

Kristan X

It happens just after her thirty-fifth birthday. Nothing marks the change. No shift in mood, no breakouts, no heavy period. Her weight doesn't change. No hot flashes or headaches. The transformation is so unmarked, in fact, that it almost scares her when she first realizes what has happened. Her body has altered. Shifted. Quietly and coolly and without her knowledge.

Now, suddenly, she can come from just the slightest touch.

She's used to masturbation taking time. Effort. The wand makes it happen, but it takes a long time. She must relax her body piece by piece. Put everything out of her head and ride the slowly building waves of it until something finally unlocks. Afterward, she usually feels almost numb from the vibration, exhausted from holding her breath.

But now she comes just from reaching down and parting the lips of her cunt with her fingers. It's like a firework, one of those ones that screeches, goes silent, then explodes. She parts the lips of her cunt and there is a moment of rising tension, a moment of silence, and then . . .

She explodes. Gasping and clutching herself on the bed, stunned by the abruptness of it.

She tries again a little later, thinking it must have been a fluke. That orgasms cannot come so easily, not to her. And it takes a little longer this time, but seconds only. She gets her fingers inside herself, and she's wet beyond belief, and she comes like that, with her cunt clutching down in spasms on her fingers.

In the first week she tries to refrain as much as possible. She is afraid that if she overuses this newfound ability it will disappear as quickly as it came. And, to tell the truth, she's a little frightened of it—of how easily she can provoke from her body such a cataclysmic shudder.

In the second week she gives in. She masturbates eight or nine times a day. Before bed. In the morning. After breakfast. In the shower. In the bathroom at work. She's constantly wet; she even has to take a spare pair of panties with her to the office so she can change in the middle of the day.

She gets getting off down to an art. She can come by touching herself through her skirt, pressing a seam of fabric into her cunt and grinding, tensing her thighs.

It takes less than a minute every time. She can do it silently, with barely a grunt. She can do it standing, sitting at her desk, sprawled in bed.

Constantly, now, she feels like she's glowing from it. Rarely is she more than an hour from having come. Never more than an hour from coming again. In between, the pleasure suffuses into her skin and tingles there like electricity, waiting to be discharged.

In the acts of ordinary things, now, she finds pleasure. Pissing is pleasurable. Showering is pleasurable. When she sits on the bus and the seat vibrates beneath her, she has to try quite hard not to come right then and there. It's good, of course, but it's also frightening. She feels naked, stripped bare, denuded of all protections. Anything can take her over the edge now. Anything can make her lose control.

Perhaps that's why it takes her so long to try it with another human being. It's a different prospect, here on the other side of whatever transformation has taken place. A warm body and the thrill of being wanted are still exciting, sure. But the idea of going out, dressing up, flirting and talking and bringing home a man or woman of her choosing seems like a hassle. She could stay home instead, and make her own body perform a miracle a dozen times over.

For a while she does this. She flirts with Tinder, but cannot muster the effort to do more. It feels pointless, lackluster. She exchanges dirty messages with a tall, aquiline man whose profile consists of pictures of him vaping. Young looking, oddly handsome. His messages are greedy, self-centered, demanding. She replies to each: obscene lists of what she wants, what she'll let him do, what she needs. Masturbates while she waits for each message. Comes three times, the last almost suffocating. Blocks him and deletes his number after the third, and never thinks about him again.

It's not until she runs into an ex that she tries it with someone else. They haven't seen each other for years; she thought he'd left town. But here he is. Back. They go for drinks—more drinks than she intended, and before she knows it they're at her flat, naked and on the bed and giggling.

She intends to warn him. Wants to warn him. But there's not a chance to do so before it happens for the first time. His thigh between her legs. She grinds down, clutches his ribs, breathes in the olive oil scent of his skin, and comes explosively. One long swooping drag in the pit of her stomach and then she's floating. Her insides fill with stars. She loses the edges of herself. He's holding her tight and she's holding him and in that moment of weightlessness she feels like the two of them could melt together, become one, become jelly, become white light.

She's aware that he's seeing her come. Feeling her come. And that's a warm, bright pleasure all its own. As the long throbs of pleasure fade out a little she falls back into her body and sees the look on his face. He seems surprised. Not just surprised. Astonished. When she's done, finally, he kisses her on the lips and she comes again. A smaller orgasm—almost lazy; a spurt of stars in her belly and a moment of sensation: lift, lurch, shiver.

After that they fuck for hours.

By the time they stop to rest and drink water and talk a little, her legs are weak. She's lost count. Her head feels light and her skin enervated. She's cloaked in light. All the orgasms have sunk into her skin and she's warm and tender and richly happy. He flops on the bed beside her.

"So," he says, "what happened?"

She doesn't know how to answer that, so she doesn't answer. She rolls on top of him and kisses him again, and they dissolve into one another. She feels the tug in the pit of her stomach. The rise. The fluttering excitement. And she thinks of an answer she could have given.

It's a gift, she could have said. Although that doesn't quite capture it. That's not quite accurate. Is a thing still a gift if you give it to yourself? She doesn't know the answer. She doesn't know if it will stay or go away again after a year or two. She doesn't understand and she doesn't need to. It's a gift. If it's the only gift her body ever gives her, she'll be more than happy with that.

THE
PHALLACY

Allison Hope

C adie felt choked by anticipation.

She nervously adjusted her collar and smoothed her jeans, running her thick fingers from the tops of her thighs slowly down toward her knees, a quick shake of her shoes to help settle the excess pant leg at the bottom.

Fancy meeting you here. She practiced in her head how she might greet Emma when she arrived. *Cool and collected,* Cadie told herself to try to appear, the right edge of her plump lips upturned slightly to relay bemused and playful. *Act accessible, but not too accessible,* she scolded herself as the ice was rapidly melted on her scotch on the rocks.

It had been fifteen years since they last saw each other. Cadie could still feel the sharp pain of missed opportunity. They were in their early twenties, full of bravado and swagger, all flirtation and no action. For months, they worked across the loft from one another, the object of her affection leading the editorial department of the magazine, while Cadie ran the publishing department. They had outsized roles that spilled over the edges of their experience and maturity. It made their dance all the more exciting.

They were smart, full of potential, with the world and the city at their fingertips. They wrote each other little notes that they passed during meetings, and found excuses to cross the spacious downtown office to enter one another's orbit.

Cadie was intoxicated by Emma's unassuming beauty, the stunning features she bore likened to a Greek Adonis, etched face, flowing dark hair, eyes that could penetrate you like a thousand shooting stars. Plus she was brilliant. Ivy League grad. Had traveled the world. Translated old Sanskrit texts for fun.

For half a dozen years they danced this tiptoe tease, flirting, backing off, coming in again for more. They dated different people—Emma, always boys, too lanky and immature for her. Cadie, a rainbow variety of queer people who never felt quite right enough.

Once, when they were out drinking, celebrating Emma's appointment to a doctoral program, they came the closest they ever had to kissing. The last thing Cadie remembers is Emma leaning in close enough that she was completely absorbed in the scent of her hair, the sensation of her sweet breath on her face. Then, nothing. She blacked out. Didn't remember the rest of the night. Was too embarrassed to ask.

Then it was time for her to leave. They stood in the vestibule connecting the office to the darkness of the city streets on a winter night. They stared at each other for a long time, too long for friends, not long enough for Cadie. She wanted a lifetime with Emma. She leaned in, the heat between them palpable. She turned slightly, and they brushed against one another's cheeks.

Then, Emma was gone.

Post-graduate degrees, marriages, and kids. They'd both had lived several lives—apart—since then.

But now, she was about to walk through that door of the bar, a decade and a half later. The only thing harder than waiting for Emma to arrive was the tug of her clit against the strap-on she had boldly worn, which she could feel through her underwear.

"Cadie? Is that really you?" Her voice cracked. *She must have come in through the back door.*

"It's me," Cadie said, laughing nervously. *Way to blow it with playing cool.*

"You look gooood," Emma said in the same sexy, raspy voice as ever, and she slid into the bar stool next to her.

Cadie took stock of herself in that moment, a butch lesbian with a square jaw and admittedly more round around the middle. She felt a surge of electricity, her enlarged clit filling with a fever pitch against the strap-on hiding under her jeans. It was as if the dildo tucked between her legs was capturing all the sexual excitement and was ready to unleash it in her.

"Yeah? You like this version of me?" she asked with a sheepish grin. *That's the right line to take,* she thought and adjusted her posture to sit a little taller.

Emma leaned in and brushed her delicate fingers across her cheek, sending shudders down her spine.

She looked the same, like exactly the same.

"You haven't changed one bit," she said.

"Well that's a damn shame!" Emma said. Always self-deprecatory. It made her even more desirable.

"Let's drink to damn shames!" Cadie said and motioned for the bartender.

They fell into easy banter, filling each other in on all of the mundane and excitable plots on their divergent paths and reminiscing about their free-flung days at the magazine, the nights out, two sheets to the wind.

She wanted to tell Emma how much she'd thought about her all these years, that a jagged boulder had sat in the pit of her gut ever since that night when they said goodbye. How she knew Emma might have considered her differently if she were a man, rather than an awkward lesbian.

She couldn't let another fifteen years go without trying harder.

"I have a room upstairs," she said, brushing her hands across Emma's. "And a bottle of good scotch."

"Well, I guess I can come up for one," Emma said,

lowering her eyes to meet Cadie's squarely, the intensity slicing through her body, drawing a line of heat from her forehead down to her pulsing crotch.

They hadn't even finished their first drink upstairs when Emma climbed onto Cadie's lap, straddling her still jean-clad legs. She reached around and took her shirt off.

"We've wasted enough time," Emma said.

Cadie glided her fingers across Emma's soft back, expertly unclasping her bra and sliding her hands back to cup her luscious breasts, nipples now erect and eagerly pointing toward her.

Emma pressed her vagina and ass down into her and pulled Cadie into a tight embrace.

She unbuttoned her own shirt, one button at a time, pausing to look into Emma's eyes. She moaned and put her pointer finger under Emma's chin, pulling her face gently up towards hers. Their lips met, softly at first and then with a fervor matching fifteen years of pent-up desire.

Their tongues swirled in a choreographed routine, as if they had practiced. *We're good at this,* she thought.

Cadie stood slowly, with Emma still wrapped around her hips, and laid her down on the bed. Their pace quickened as they tugged each other's clothes off. Emma rubbed her wet vagina on the dildo, the sensation sending chills up Cadie's back.

Emma sat up, pushing Cadie down hard and working her mouth down her body, licking and then sucking her silicone dick. Cadie cried out in pleasure and then drove herself into Emma, hard and deep, with increasing speed. She screeched in pleasure, pulling her hair and her nipples, squirting clear across the bed as she came.

When they were done, they lay in one another's arms and sipped from a single glass of scotch. Then they dressed silently and stood facing one another.

Cadie leaned in; her lips pursed. This time, Emma didn't turn her cheek and neither did she. Their lips met, seamlessly, spectacularly, softly.

Then, she was gone.

MY FIRST SHARED ORGASM

Suzannah Weiss

When you knock on my door, I'm nervous for multiple reasons. The first is that you've traveled six thousand miles to visit me after a one-week vacation romance, and it's hitting me that I barely know you. The second, I've never told you, because it's a secret: I've never had an orgasm with a partner.

I've had plenty of orgasms on my own, but nobody else has gotten me there. I feel too embarrassed to bring it up, so I just feed myself clichés about enjoying the journey. And I do still enjoy sex, but I sometimes wonder . . . well, I don't want to get my hopes up.

You enter my apartment with an awkward hug, then we go walking. As we stroll through Times Square, I keep wondering if I can kiss you. Finally, at the Central Park boathouse, you make that decision for me. My breath catches as your hand runs up and down my leg. "I can't stop kissing you," you say, laughing. I'm not nervous anymore.

When we arrive home, you lay facedown on the carpet, gazing up at me with your big brown puppy dog eyes. I kneel down to kiss you, and a wide grin fills your face, as if you're the lucky one. "I'm going to take a shower," you say.

"Can I join you?"

"If you want."

As if you could get any more attractive, the water makes you look like you belong on the cover of a romance novel. It drips from your pitch-black hair down your perfectly tanned arms and the peach fuzz on your muscular chest. I lather up your soft hair with shampoo, then glide my soapy hands all over your smooth skin.

Afterward, in keeping with the romance novel look, you pick me up and carry me to the bed, where you plant gentle kisses on my mouth and then reach down with your hands. I lie on my stomach to give you my favorite angle, and you slowly, deeply penetrate me with your fingers. You reach up high, fucking me so hard I can't help but shout into my pillow. I won't come this way, but we'll have a whole week to figure that out. For now, I can just bask in the feeling of your warm wet fingers caressing places I've never reached myself. When I'm spent, I tell you I've had enough, and we go to sleep.

The next morning, we work across from each other in a cafe. You get up to order me a second iced coffee, putting in two brown sugars like you saw me do with my first. Once we're done, we eagerly head back to bed. You cup my head in your hands like I'm a precious jewel as we kiss, and your hands wander down again, lingering on my clit this time. This is a better start. You've been so sweet; I can't help but get my hopes up.

"Mmmm," I say to encourage you. My face contorts in deep concentration.

Just as I begin to worry it looks strange, you say, "You look so hot." I smile.

The pleasure radiates from my clit throughout my body. It builds, then falls, then builds, then falls. I wonder if I should just give up and fake it. I'm afraid of giving you carpal tunnel. But the look in your eyes tells me you love this. You want it to keep going. So I let it.

My mind begins to wander. It's a habit. I enter bizarre fantasies that pop up when I'm alone, settling on one where I'm on a spiritual retreat, masturbating with a group of nude women on a mountaintop. One of them starts moaning, then the other joins in, all harmonizing in their expressions of pleasure. I can feel their ecstasy; it connects me to my own. My voice joins the harmony. "Mmm!" I say louder as I grab your arm.

I think I might be close now, but I'm afraid it'll fake me out. That fear becomes a self-fulfilling prophecy. I fall back down just as I start to reach the edge. But you don't seem to notice. You just keep rubbing your finger, a look of wonder in your eyes. I squeeze your arm harder each time I get close. I find myself back on that mountain, the other women cheering me on, knowing I can do this. I squeeze harder. I can tell you're as determined as me. If I cut off your circulation, I think you'll understand.

The pressure builds up in my clit again, rising and falling. I'm starting to feel embarrassed about all these false alarms. But then, it rises again—and it doesn't fall this time. Now I know it will stay. And it does. I finally release your arm as orgasmic waves undulate through me, laughing with bliss and relief, then I squeeze my legs together so you'll let go. I tilt my head up and smile and kiss you. You don't know I've just reached a milestone.

In fact, for you, it's not enough. You keep going, two fingers inside this time, your palm pressing against my clit. *It won't work,* I think; I'm not multi-orgasmic. But anything seems possible now. I give it a chance. Sooner than I expect, I arrive back at that edge, squeezing your arm again as I ride this pleasure roller-coaster. Then another one hits. My hips repeatedly thrust upward, rising up to greet your powerful hand, before relaxing back down. Once I catch my breath, recovering from another trip to the stars, we kiss again, and I fall into a blissful sleep.

When I wake up, you ask, "Can I play with your pussy again?" How can I refuse? You alternate between rubbing the outside and putting two fingers in. I'm not thinking anymore about whether I'll come; it's doubtful given that I just did twice. But sure enough, my climax builds up again. This one takes me by surprise. "Oh,

God, I'm coming," I announce it this time. You get an excited sparkle in your eye as you take me back over the edge, not stopping until I can't take anymore, and I melt into your arms like pudding.

As we shower afterward, I can see our reflection in the mirror: you behind me with your big arms wrapped around me and your strong hands fitting right over my breasts, me beaming and glowing like I never have before. When it rains, it pours, I think—which is wonderful when it's raining orgasms.

Once you've discovered what makes me tick, you want to do it every morning when we wake up and every night before we go to bed. I don't stop you. One day, over drinks, I admit I'm self-conscious about making you do all that work. "I don't care if my arm falls off," you say.

Before long, it becomes easy! I can't believe I thought this wasn't possible. I'm elated to know that I'm not broken. But it's not just me I have to thank. Finally, I have arms I can relax in—arms that won't stop until they fall off.

ENJOYING THE DARK

Rose Jordan

The glamorous invitation from her new friend Deb in her inbox intrigued Andi. She'd mentioned something about a gathering, but now Andi could see that this erotic free-for-all was just the kind of party that she and Paul had always wanted to attend. "If only he didn't have a company party that night . . ." she mused to herself, her mind already picturing bodies pressed together in the most intimate of ways. "We'd have a blast. Maybe I should go anyway."

"Let's check it out." The handsome man next to her near the front door of the nondescript building took her hand.

A ramp along the side led to a back door. The sign said, "Grope Room." Andi had heard of these before.

Her new friend seemed eager to go inside with her, and she knew exactly why. Here, he would get at least some sort of play with her.

Andi peered into the darkness. Once the door was shut, the room turned pitch black. Andi could hear that they weren't alone, but she couldn't see anyone.

"Feel around a bit to get your bearings." The voice floated across the room from nowhere and everywhere at the same time. She did as instructed and located a table on each side of the entrance, and an open area in front of a king-size bed. Andi had no idea how many others were in the room with her.

Immediately, hands brushed against her. The first one startled her but confirmed her understanding of how this room worked. Hands stroked her from all directions. They touched her ass, her breasts, the back of her neck. She couldn't tell if her eyes were closed or if it was just that dark.

Andi reached out, bumping against male chests. Figuring she should get in the spirit of this adventure, she let her hands wander across the chests, and the bare skin of two very different arms. One was thin, the other smooth and well muscled.

Hands slipped under her shirt, removing it and her bra. Someone reached under her skirt, discovered that she had arrived commando, and murmured approvingly.

Andi lowered her hands and felt a hard cock protruding from unzipped pants on either side of her.

Damn, this is hot!, she thought. Whichever guy had his hands under her skirt was finding out how aroused she was, his fingers were dipping into her wetness, spreading it through the entire area between her legs. Then, someone stood behind her, lifted her skirt, and pressed a naked cock against her naked ass. The taboo thrill of exposing herself spurred her on. *I love this! I want to get fucked so hard,* raced through her mind, along with thoughts of how much Paul was going to enjoy hearing about her escapades.

Whoever's cock was ramming against her ass reached around her, unzipped her skirt, and let it slip to the floor.

Once the skirt came off and the group realized she was naked, they eased her to the bed. She let herself be guided back until only her feet were hanging over the edge. She was on her back, her legs spread wide, and there were hands on her breasts. There were fingers between her legs. There were cocks bumping against her shoulders. Everywhere she reached she found naked chests or, even better, hard, naked cocks. She stroked and squeezed and moved from one to another, never sure whether she was returning to someone she had already touched, or if the cock in her hand was someone new. The realization that so many wanted her was intoxicating. She embraced her inner slut and knew her boundaries had just moved farther than she'd ever imagined.

Finally, someone whispered, "I want to fuck you.

You want to get fucked, right? You want to feel this hard cock inside you, don't you?"

Quietly yet matter-of-factly, Andi said, "Absolutely, but you have to be wrapped. Condoms are in my skirt pocket."

"No problem," said the voice as he moved away. She felt him leave the bed. Moments later, he knelt between her legs. She heard the condom wrapper being ripped open.

She briefly grabbed his cock, feeling the smoothness of the condom stretched tightly over his hardness. "Okay, you're good." And with that, he slid his long, hard cock into her wet pussy. As he did so, he asked her name. "Andi," she said quietly.

As he entered her more forcefully, she cried out, not in any pain, but because without the ability to see, all of her senses seemed to be on overdrive. As he thrust into her, Andi stroked the cocks that found their way to her waiting hands. Someone moved close enough to her head that she was able to take him in her mouth.

Even as she reveled in these new sensations, she was thinking, *I can't wait to tell Paul about this. He would love it!* As mysterious cock number one continued to fuck her cunt, she stroked and sucked the others. Suddenly, she felt a lubed-up finger sliding into her ass. She'd been curious about anal play, but had never tried it before. The fullness was overwhelming in the best way. A cock in her mouth, a cock in her cunt, and a finger in her ass! Every opening was filled, and Andi couldn't get enough. She came loudly, but she didn't care who heard her. In fact, she hoped that the crowd outside was hearing every noise she made as she reveled in the cockfest.

The thick cock kept thrusting into Andi's pussy, every stroke sending flurries of delight through her body, until he gasped and came while still inside her. She felt him pulsing against her, savoring the sensation of the warm liquid through the condom. Then, a gush of liquid released from her pussy. She panicked for a moment, but it was happening in the middle of one of the most intense orgasms she'd ever experienced. She'd squirted—another first!

The fun didn't stop or even take a break. As soon as one guy moved off her another took his place. One of them started licking and sucking Andi's pussy, while others were sucking her tits. Between his mouth and fingers, the guy between her legs brought her off four or five times, and during each one she squirted more fluid, which only encouraged him more. The puddle under her ass grew, but she didn't care.

Finally, she'd had enough, and extricated herself from the orgy. She had no idea how long this had been going on, but she was tiring, and faced a long drive home.

Andi located her clothes easily, but took her time getting dressed as she transitioned from her most wanton to her everyday self. When she stepped outside into the light, several men stood on the ramp. Had she just screwed one or more of them? Would she ever know? "Thanks, Andi," said one. Knowing these men could have just seen her at her most raw and intimate sent another flush running through her, her greedy pussy throbbing once again. She couldn't wait to tell—and show—Paul all about it, and return with him soon.

ACTION AT A DISTANCE

Helia Brookes

"This separation won't change our relationship."

D said nothing.

"It won't. I will not let it," K insisted.

"I do have my own life. I'm not just your plaything."

"You belong to me, though. You are mine." K grabbed D's hand insistently. "You agreed to those terms."

"I like being yours when we're together. It's hot . . ." said D, feeling the old familiar tingle, "but we are separate people."

"I'm going to keep you. I won't let you go. We'll be connected. Deeply." K squeezed D's arm, shoulder, waist.

"You mean sexting?"

K locked eyes with D. "Something new."

"Sexting's not very old."

"Really new. Haptic technology—vibrations."

"Vibrations . . . a vibrator? Sorry, that's no substitute." D looked dubious.

"Not a vibrator." K pulled out a soft matte black ovoid. "It's like a special Ben Wa ball. But remote controlled."

D hefted it. The texture was smooth, firm yet a little squishy. "Looks like a butt plug."

"The shape's adjustable for the best fit. In any orifice."

"And you expect me to . . . insert this?" D's mouth quirked.

"I'm telling you to insert it. I *expect* you to enjoy it." K stared intensely, eyes level, tone commanding. D laughed, with an underlying shiver of anticipation. K continued inexorably. "You *will* enjoy it. You will come like a geyser."

"A geyser!" D said. "You're ridiculous."

"We can't be together for months while I'm on this assignment. I want to keep you hooked, and I'm going to. Here, I'll show you."

K put on a black glove and toggled switches on the wrist. "Just pair it with the Bluetooth on your phone." D did so and felt the device come to life. As K moved each finger, the object extended and bulged in that direction, shifting its center of gravity as the smooth surface rippled. It writhed like an octopus when K engaged multiple fingers. K made a fist and the device contracted and pulsed.

D held it gingerly as it moved around. "It's like a cartoon hand. I'm going to call it Mickey's Glove."

"Hey, what's Mickey doing in this relationship?"

"Okay, K's Glove. But not mine."

"Come on. Please put it in." K edged over and began gently rubbing D's back. "You like this, don't you?" Rubbing progressed to caresses, lower and lower. "And *this?*"

"Not saying," D panted, engulfed in heat.

"Tell me. Use your words."

"Observe me and deduce what my words would be," muttered D, trying not to moan in pleasure.

"You would say . . . I like it, don't stop! And you're going to like this too." K wrestled down D's pants, coaxing, licking, fingering. K brought the glove into play and D began to lose track of what stimulation came from flesh and which was something else. Between two climaxes, K inserted the object.

"Aaahhh . . . yes . . . but you're here, you're doing it to me." D moaned and writhed. "I smell your pheromones or whatever. God, you smell good . . . come closer . . ."

"Come? You come. Come!"

"Not until you do." Like two magnets, they smashed together, reluctantly at first, each fighting the other's attraction, then giving in to the rush.

* * *

They lay together in a sweaty tangle, panting and laughing.

"See?" said K. "Just follow my directions and I'll show you a good time. Geysers, like I said. On my command. I control the glove, I make you come."

"You can't *make* me."

"We'll see about that."

"No, really, if I'm not in the mood, it's just going to be an irritating tickling."

K's eyes bored into D's. "My desire triggers your mood! You want to be wanted, admit it. Right now, you'd say you were done, but if I wanted more . . ."

D tried to avoid that fiery gaze, but felt the tingling surge again.

K kept staring. "If I'm ready, you'll be ready. I'll turn it on whenever I want."

"Then it might be buzzing and thrashing in a drawer."

"Spoilsport."

"I think you mean 'Wow, I admire your great boundaries.'"

"Your boundaries are flimsy. Transparent ice sheets that melt under my heat. My gaze, my will, my thoughts. I engulf you . . ." K pulled D back down into the blankets.

"I might turn it on at any point. But to build anticipation, I'll set a daily time. Three p.m."

"What if I have a meeting?"

"Mute your audio and lower the lights. Everyone's looking at their own video anyhow."

"Could be that once I'm out from under your spell, your domineering won't be so attractive."

"Just remember—geysers."

D's phone buzzed with a text.

K: is it in
D: wouldn't you like to know
K: tease
K: you'll be missing out if not...
D: oh really?
K: are you in a meeting with it in you
D: maybe

D put the phone down and tried to ignore both it and the tingling that strengthened as three p.m. approached.

K: i'm going to get you fired and it will be worth it
K: you will thank me

D snatched up the phone again.
D: you can't predict the future

K: i can
K: i have that power
K: 5 more minutes

K: 4
D: *stop that*

D had the illusion the phone's buzzing was getting stronger, as though it also was anticipating three p.m. and its sibling gadget's sympathetic vibrations.

K: 3
K: 2
Now D could barely type.
D: *shut up*
K: 1
K: *blast off!*

Deep inside, the ovoid began to writhe, filling D with what felt like the essence of K's caresses, warm and insistent and unstoppable. It was as though K's force of will reached through the miles separating them and engulfed D in an explosion of involuntary pleasure. The phone fell on the carpet as the waves of sensation took over.

K: *that was good for me, was it good for you?*
D: *yes, damn you*
K: *3pm tomorrow if i can wait that long*

K: *can't wait*
D: *oh thank god*
D: *damn you*

D: *don't say I told you so*
K: *who me?*

"C'mon, admit it," said K on the phone.
"What?"
"I *can* make you come. Say it."
D smiled. "I can make you come."

THE RED SLIP DRESS

Suzanne Jefferies

The red slip dress sat too close. The material pulled in the wrong places, the emphasis on her swollen hips, the pouch of her belly. Her bra underneath had slackened from too many spins in her automatic, and the faded straps shadowed the red silken ropes that held the dress's satiny fabric.

Outside, the evening traffic white-noised the room's silence, the breathing—his breathing—so soft and so heavy.

Antony had loved this dress. He'd said she looked red-hot sexy, and he'd slipped the dress from her shoulders, making it shimmy into a pool of liquid lust at her feet. She'd *felt* red-hot sexy in this dress, the way it danced over her body's dips and crevices, a ripple of satin temptation. A cloak of sexuality that promised its wearer infinite desirability.

This man had to help it over her head; his too large hands easing the dress past the wideness of her thighs. Her arms rested limply at her sides, her shoulders shifting in awkwardness. The dress didn't fit as it once had. And with it, her wiles diminished, vanished even.

He dumped the dress to the floor, a crimson stain on the bare-bleached floorboards. Stripped.

His face dipped to kiss her again. He kissed softly, with a tender kind of passion that made her insides itch and twitch. Could he not throw her on the bed and ravage her in a violent lust rush? Or bite and nip at her neck, his hands rough and heavy? Have his way with her?

Yet his fingers were defter than she'd given them credit for as he unhooked her sad bra.

She quickly pushed her unfettered pendulous breasts against this man's chest, pulled him back to the safety of her open mouth, and kissed him hard, the way she'd kissed so many before him. His hands wandered over those rounded hips, to her waist, to her panties's elastic. She sucked in her stomach.

With infinite care, as if she were something delicate, this man beckoned her to the bed. Her bed.

Her hands fluttered across her chest—with the scarlet dress on the floor, her inhibitions clothed her. If he had been Antony, she would have been curling her legs round his, grinding against his cock, teasing him, taunting him.

This isn't how it goes . . .

Her sheets, worn soft with wear, thrummed with oversweet perfume. He resumed the kissing, his tongue insistent in her mouth. She couldn't look at him. It was too much. Eyes closed, she pictured a different lover. A harsher lover. A more familiar lover. Someone who would sink her to her knees and demand she suck.

The soft swelling between her legs temporarily surpassed the gnawing in her head. She kept her eyes closed and surrendered to a foreign receptivity.

Her breasts slipped to the side, traveling fast into her armpits. She made an effort to arch her back and lifted her hands behind her head to feign youthful voluptuousness. And yet what for? Breasts were no more than an amuse-bouche—a prelude to the feast to come.

They wanted? Oh, yes. They ached. Gluttons for attention, yet always discarded and starved. Even now, when they no longer delighted the eye.

He sighed. "Beautiful, beautiful, Jay." He continued his quiet, slow caress across her cheek, her jaw, and down her neck. So close. The warmth of his breath on her skin almost claustrophobic. The words could have been anything—nice day, there's the cat, where's the dinner—all men said the same. But the warmth behind this man's endearments were built on months of close friendship, whispered secrets, shared confidences. There was a truth there that deeply discomforted something in her. Something hidden. Something dark.

Tender.

Something that didn't need the courage of a red satin

slip dress, or a body poured into some preconceived ideal.

His mouth busied itself on her nipples, the swelling between her legs intensifying as if he'd pushed his mouth against her folds. And sucked.

Her hands lightly rested on his head, the wiriness of his hair beneath her fingers as he focused on her overfull breasts that sagged sideways. The sensitivity coiled in those tight peaks braced for an increased pleasure that would not arrive, not this way, never this way. Who had time for her breasts, any breasts?

She gasped. Her breath hitched.

. . . *could she even?*

At some point, an intrusion flickered, a reminder of her duty to perform, to reciprocate. To be a good lover. The best. His best ever.

Then it faded under this man's dedicated, gentle persistence to pleasure her breasts. Her goddamn breasts.

Pinched, released, pinched, released, her nipples tightened with an unexpected exquisiteness of sensation that pulled her clit, her core. Fuck. Her hips ground into her sheets. Her clit begged for his tongue, his fingers, his cock.

What's in this for him?

And yet, he did not move onward.

A plane sauntered overhead. A curtain rustled with the promise of a late evening thundershower.

Minutes collapsed.

Inch by inch, she unraveled.

She let go of the Rolodex of porn clips that got her off. She dropped the need to insert her fingers to the right spot for just the right climax.

She surrendered to his fingers that never stopped at their casual assault on her nipples, so hungry for attention they swelled harder still. His tongue lapped and sucked as her fear poured into pools of longing.

Her orgasm, so unexpected, started from that somewhere deep inside her. That quiet, shameful spot. So slight, so almost insignificant, a pleasure, yes, but not a fire burst of explosion. Something deeper. Something stronger.

It rose from within her, higher, higher, and steady. She was sure it would dissolve, fade away before it broke.

But no. It warmed through her, reached in and pushed her further, higher, until it crashed down over her in waves and waves of amazement.

From her breasts. Her goddamn breasts.

And closeness.

Tenderness.

An intimacy that was almost unbearable.

This man who'd sought to know her through that soft slackening flesh of her breasts, with his tongue, his fingers, the nip of his teeth.

She turned her head away, the tears painful and unexpected, but so worth it.

MOJAVE SKY

Louise Blaydon

S lap bang in the middle of the Mojave and Jeff's sweat-soaked, thrumming, the wicked vibrations of the engine thundering in his ribs. The desert is hot, empty. The scrubby landscape stretches out around him in this yawning swathe of dead-dirt wilderness, and Jeff could be alone, here. Jeff could be discovering America, marking out the McAllen line.

The thought makes him laugh and he shifts, lets his thighs splay open a little further around the saddle of the Harley. It's kind of awe-inspiring, this loneliness. Jeff's hair is curling over his collar, his shirt and leathers moving palpably, uncomfortably over his skin, making all his sensory neurons wake up and take notice. *I am Man*, is what they're getting. *I am conqueror.*

God, it's dumb, but Jeff can feel his dick starting to

fill, lifting from the root, steady and sure. Some primal urge, wanting to claim, to mark up this empty landscape as his own. Jeff's half-embarrassed, but not embarrassed enough to keep his hand from creeping up to his inner thigh, palming the sweat-damp denim. The long muscle twitches under his palm. The sun beats down on the back of his skull, the exposed nape of his neck. Beneath him, the motorcycle is singing songs of love.

The bulge of his cock is clear and straining in his jeans now, spurred on by the heat and vibration and the raw sense of being exposed, being out here in this gorgeous emptiness that is his, claimed and yet vulnerable to intruders. A car might spin into sight any minute and catch him, palming the press of his dick.

Jeff lifts his chin at the thought, a hot flash of want lancing his stomach. He tilts up his hips into the flat of his palm, the cradling grasp of fingers. He's harder now, blood pulsing, and the slow slide of a thumb down the spine of his dick sets him gasping, flushing hot and cold for more. Fuck, yeah, he needs more of this, and it doesn't fucking matter that the silence might be shattered any second, the foreign hordes flooding in.

He pops the button on his jeans. It's a tiny gesture, insignificant, but he feels it like a jolt to his heart, setting his pulse ratcheting up. It's another step toward nakedness, being broken open, and some nasty, twisted part of him wants that, wants this act to be seen. Jeff knows he's got a nice cock, fat and heavy and long. It's pushing up through the splayed V of his fly by the time he's got the zipper down, straining for his hand; Jeff doesn't mean to deny it—fuck, no, not now. He's got all the time in the world, or maybe he hasn't. Who cares? He's horny, the rumble of the motorcycle like a second heartbeat in his pelvis. Jeff's going to have this.

There's a tiny damp place on Jeff's boxers where the head of him rests, slick pearling from the slit; he rubs at it with his thumb, hissing dry through his teeth. Fuck. Too late, now, to question it; already, he's snapping the waistband down under his balls, spreading his fly wide. His dick strains hard and upright against his belly, wetness glimmering at the tip. Jeff curls his fingers around the shaft of it and jacks it slow at first, working the foreskin back and forth over the head where it's red and gleaming.

The low pulsation of the Harley is enough to amp things up, keep him on slow burn. The first touch of his thumb to the head makes his hips buck up off the seat, his voice break. "Shit," he grits, pressing his toes harder into the asphalt and spreading his legs wider over his mount. Jesus, *yeah*, heat flashing through him like the last of summer, and his cock thrusts easier now into his palm, slickness from the crown smearing down over the spine, glistening along the curve of it.

"Oh, fuck," Jeff mutters, body jerking, head tipping back as his hand slides smoothly right from base to crown, his long fingers a certain tight tunnel to fuck himself into. It's good, better because he can't help thinking that if anyone were to show up, they'd see all this, the shiny red head of his dick emerging through the circle of his fingers, slipping back home into his fist. Orgasm tugs at his belly, too soon and too deep, and God, Jeff could get there just from this, spurt all over the road, spend himself in the dust. He bites his lip, works his fist faster. No time to linger, after all.

Anywhere else, he'd have brought his other hand into play—snatched it up off the handlebars of the motorcycle and worked it back behind his balls, teased his perineum. Maybe he'd have gone back further still, worked the tight clench of his hole, but he's in the middle of fucking nowhere and the bike is doing that for him, cradling him in its perpetual motion, sparking off his skin. He can feel his dick swelling, hardening impossibly, and he knows there's no goddamn need for that right now, not with the way he's sliding faster through his fist, thumb catching at the slit, thumbing the nerves below the head. Jeff grits his teeth, biting back a cry, and his dick jerks, something rough and half-vocalized creeping in under the edges of his harsh, broken breaths.

"Jesus," he gets out, toes curling in his boots. A hawk circles above. As the sun beats down on his back, his orgasm is arrowing down, growing huge in his belly, the push of conquest awaiting him. "Jesus," he repeats, and then his back is arched and he's coming, shooting white on the brown dirt in long, sticky pulses.

He comes down slowly after, heart pounding in his ears while his cock goes soft and still against his thigh.

By his left heel, the desert's soaking him up, taking him in. *Mine.*

He's almost got his breath back before the car goes past, a station wagon with two passengers in the back.

Jeff laughs breathlessly, pushes his sticky hair back off his face, and tucks himself back into his jeans.

COAL ROOM

Olive Barnes

"You want to go down to the coal room? Now?" Faith asked in disbelief. They were both nearly undressed, bodies intertwined and buzzing with the thrill of new intimacy. When Faith had tugged at Liz's boyshorts and whispered *What do you want, baby*, this was not the answer she'd expected.

Liz gave a coy shrug, "I'm curious." She looked up at Faith with eager eyes, dark and sparkling.

"Later." A hot excitement had just begun growing inside her, and a trip to the coal room was a surefire way to extinguish it. She preferred to pretend the coal room didn't exist. It made living in the old, shadowy house much easier. She leaned in, brushing her lips against Liz's slender neck, trying to recapture the mood, but before she knew it Liz was wiggling out from under her.

"Come on." She slunk towards the door, wearing a mischievous grin.

An hour into their first date, and already she felt that inexplicable pull toward Liz, that giddy attraction that made her say, "Fine, toss me my dress."

"You won't need it." Liz bit her lip. "Let's finish this."

"Wait." Faith's eyes widened with understanding. "You want to hook up in the coal room?" Now that was a much harder sell, even with those dark, pleading eyes.

"It'll be hot. Exciting."

"I don't know. Sounds like the start of a bad horror movie."

"I thought you didn't believe in the hauntings," Liz challenged as she reached for Faith's hand. Her lips drew tickling lines up and down Faith's arm. "Although in my opinion it's much better when you do believe. That fear gets the adrenaline pumping and makes for insane orgasms." Now her lips were on Faith's neck, her hands reaching between her legs.

Faith let out a nervous laugh. "You sound like you've done this before."

"I'm telling you, there's nothing like it. It's a little kink of mine."

Of course. Faith finally meets a lesbian her age who's attractive, funny, interesting . . . and she's got a fetish for fucking in haunted houses. She sighed. "You're lucky you're so damn sexy."

* * *

The staircase leading downstairs was steep and narrow. As they descended, the temperature dropped. Liz was nearly glowing with excitement, the pools of her dark eyes growing deeper in the candlelight. Once they reached the bottom, Liz took Faith's arms into her urgent hands and pushed her up against the stone wall. She seemed more alive than ever. The warmth of their bodies pressed together, lips meeting in the darkness.

A whistling sound, almost like a laugh, made them both jump.

Liz brought her lips to Faith's ear. "What if that's her?" she whispered. "You know, the woman who was killed down here had a female lover. There are letters to prove it, dozens of them."

"Really?"

"I'm surprised you don't know more about the case, being that you own the house."

Faith thought of the tattered folder she'd borrowed from the historical society sitting unread on her bedroom dresser. She'd go through it eventually, but she'd been putting it off, somehow believing if she didn't know the story of these doomed souls she could remain free of them. "Three people murdered in the coal room eighty years ago, a married couple and a priest. That's all I know." And all she wanted to know. She tried focusing on Liz's hands as they slid over her body.

"The priest was there that night at the husband's request, to perform an exorcism on the 'homosexual demon' inside his wife. Records show the wife was already dead before the fire had been set, though that little detail was not made public until years later. By that time nobody was interested in the case except ghost enthusiasts and scared tenants. Many believe it was the other woman who set the fire after seeing what had been done to her lover. Poetic, if you ask me. Those men thought she'd go to hell but they were the ones who burned." Her voice turned playful. "Are you here, little priest?"

"Don't do that!" Faith tried to mask her fear with a laugh, but the tremor in her voice betrayed her. She felt trapped, her back flush against the wall, the pounding of her heart booming in her ears.

Then, the candle went out. "Don't be afraid," Liz whispered. She dragged her teeth down Faith's neck and chest, pausing to flick her tongue over Faith's hardening nipples. And still her hands worked fervently between Faith's legs, tugging at her panties until they were at her ankles.

Familiar heat began to swell at Faith's navel, spreading in all directions. At the same time, rousing nerves intensified the building passion. That passion fused with the surrounding eeriness, creating a dangerous, delicious cocktail. Each of her senses felt magnified. The tiniest sounds echoed in her mind, stealing her breath and making her cling tighter to Liz. Liz's soft, stroking fingertips felt electric, her kisses otherworldly. Every touch sent a frenzy of chills over her body, the sensations of lust enhanced by the unsettling feeling that they were not alone.

Faith slid her fingers over Liz's pussy, letting the wetness guide her inside. After a moan of approval, she began pumping her fingers to the rhythm of Liz's quickened breathing. She kept her own eyes tightly shut. Liz brought her hand to the base of Faith's neck, grasping her hair in a loose fist, urging her on. Their open mouths met while hands caressed and explored. Squeezing. Stroking. And when it happened, it happened fast, Liz gasping and clinging to Faith as her body jolted in delight. The pleasure noises made Faith wetter than she already was, amazed at how hard Liz had just come.

Soon, Liz had fallen to her knees, and moments later, Faith felt hot breath between her legs. Her clit throbbed with anticipation, her pussy aching for the wetness and release of Liz's tongue. Liz teased her for a few torturous moments before finally making contact, fingertips digging into the flesh of her hips. She took Faith's slick pussy into her mouth and gave her what she needed. Even before Faith expected it, the orgasm began. There, in the darkness of the coal room, she reached a high she had never known before. She floated there at the peak of it, breath stolen and body stiff as the climax consumed her.

Faith woke the next morning dazed and alone. She stumbled out of bed and grabbed at her dresser for stability, fingers grazing the tea-colored folder from the historical society. With a groan, she opened it and began flipping through the contents. Her eyes skimmed the police reports and newspaper articles before settling, awestruck, on a grainy photograph of the female victim. Those deep, dark eyes. A boyish grin. It took her only moments to place the familiarity. Liz.

And stranger still, tucked beneath the photo was a letter written in faded handwriting that looked eerily similar to her own.

My Dear Elizabeth,

They paid for what they did, my love. Someday we will meet again, in this lifetime or another.
    Have Faith,

F.T.

ADDICTION

Abigail Lambkin

As I hold the pink, vibrating toy in my hand, I sigh and resign myself to yet another impulse buy. I'll probably regret the purchase—I always do with sex toys—but my shopping addiction has kicked in again and I suddenly need the pleasure hit I'll get from buying this thing.

"I don't really need another sex toy," I say to the cashier as I hand her the device.

"*Trust* me," she says with a conspiratorial smile, "you need this one."

Just like I needed all *the other ones you've sold me,* I think, and pull out my credit card. Yet I can't help it; there's that always present thought that comes with shopping—that *this* time it will be different. *This* will be the product that changes things. This new dress will make me sexy. This new makeup will make me confident. This new sex toy will make me come for the very first time. The minute that thought hits me it's like I can't resist. I'm lured in by the siren song of the cash register.

I frown as the price comes up on the machine. That is a seriously expensive vibrator, even if it does claim to use "super high-tech sonic waves."

"There isn't a chance this is going on sale anytime soon, is there?"

"Definitely not. That's actually the last one we have in stock. They went like hotcakes."

I raise an eyebrow. Does anybody actually *like* hotcakes? But looking at the vibrator in its pretty paper bag, tied up with a pink ribbon, I feel warm all over. I swipe my card and a thrill runs down my spine. *This time* . . . I pick up the bag and walk back to the car, the waves of pleasure lasting until I get home, and then the buyer's remorse kicks in once again.

My fiancé laughs when he sees I've bought something new. "Don't you have enough sex toys?"

"Apparently not," I say, pulling my T-shirt over my head.

He smiles at me a little sadly. "Sorry I can't make you come."

I frown. "Nonsense. That's my body being a bitch. It has nothing to do with you. Lord knows it's not like you aren't trying." I lean up against him and kiss him until I'm sure he's too horny to be feeling insecure. It's true; he'll go down on me for ages and play with my clit until his hand is sore. It feels *good* and *intimate*, but I've still just never hit that peak. Honestly, I'm beginning to think it's a lost cause.

He reaches around and unhooks my bra and I let my mind relax, forgetting about the shopping trip, the new toy, my wish that I could just return the damn thing if it doesn't work on me. I give in to the play of his fingers down my spine, over the globes of my ass, and back up to my breasts.

He's amazing, he really is. Every touch makes me wriggle. I can feel it building inside me as he moves downward and his tongue makes circles inside me— that endless want, that need for something more, the climbing up the ledge sensation. I'm wincing already, waiting for it to do what it always does—plateau and then fade away, never giving me what my body craves. Then I hear unfamiliar buzzing.

Oh, right, the new toy.

He's looking at the vibrator curiously as he twists his fingers inside me, and I don't blame him. It's odd looking, with a little mouth that's supposed to provide a sucking sensation. He puts the mouth against his nose and jumps back, eyes wide.

"This feels *weird*," he announces.

"Let me feel?" I beg, because begging is about all I'm capable of when I'm waiting for the orgasm that never comes. He laughs and puts the toy's mouth to my nipples.

Oh.

It feels just like there's someone flicking their tongue against my breasts, but with a speed and intensity human tongues could probably never achieve.

I close my eyes and wait for him to move the toy down to where it belongs, but sweet, wonderful bastard that he is, he keeps playing with my nipples. Finally, I kick him in the shin. "Don't tease!"

He laughs again, warm and kind and all the things I love about him, before bringing the toy down between my legs. It feels good, a rumbly, sucking sensation that gives me shivers. "Come out, little bean," he murmurs to my clit, and I'm laughing despite the pleasure.

And then he finds it.

And, again, *oh*. That tongue flicking sensation is right there, but there's also this incredible sucking, like there's a tiny tornado against my most sensitive part, pulling me into it. In fact, it feels like my entire *body* is being pulled into it. I realize I'm shaking. The noise that starts coming out of me is guttural and foreign. I've never heard myself make this noise before. I'm climbing that ledge higher and higher than I ever have before and there's something warm and wet and wonderful spilling out of me as every tightened muscle inside me seems to release at once. It's like my whole entire *body* is letting go.

My fiancé pulls the toy back as my groans turn to pained whimpers and then we just look at each other for a while.

"Did I just . . . pee?" I ask finally, not really sure what else to say.

He's quiet for a while too, before shaking his head. "Actually, I think you're a squirter." Then he looks down between my legs. "I'll change the sheets?"

When I start laughing, he does too. I pull him down beside me, despite the wet sheets, and feel the pleasure, the pure bliss, running through me.

There's a sign advertising a sale in the window at one of my favorite clothing stores. My fiancé sighs when I point it out and asks gently, "Do you *really* need to go in?"

I feel the craving running through my body, just waiting for that hit of dopamine that comes from shopping.

"If you don't go in," he offers, "we'll have time to do something after dinner. Like watch a movie?"

I frown, torn. My head is singing the praises of a new dress.

"Or we could fool around," he says hopefully, and presses his mouth to my ear. "I could make you squirt again."

One more time, I think, *oh*.

Those dresses? Those new shoes? The shiny siren song of the cash register? All have paled against the realization that I can go home and get something way, way more pleasurable. That hunger for a dopamine fix is suddenly emanating from between my legs and not from my wallet. I turn to him with a wild grin. "I hear that our bed is having a sale on orgasms."

He smiles wildly, grabs my hand, and pulls me toward the car. "I think I may have a coupon."

MAINTENANCE NEEDED

Dr. J.

While the fall scenery, a canvas of red, yellow, and orange, surrounded her, the knocking car transmission overshadowed it. She strained her neck, searching for a designated pull-off. A sign for the park maintenance shop appeared, so she turned onto the service road.

She cut the car off, wondering if it would ever crank again. Her head dropped to the back of the seat. She closed her eyes and blew out a shaky breath, one she didn't know she was holding. Once she opened her eyes, there he stood, an erotic road sign.

She blinked twice to clarify the sight. Backlit from the sun with the leaves' hues highlighting him, he might have been a sexy mirage. His unzipped one-piece coveralls dangled off his hips while his ripped T-shirt stretched tight across his broad chest. Her mouth went dry as he approached her car.

"Well, you know how to make an entrance." The fresh scent of spruce blended with this hot man's southern drawl became her instant aphrodisiac. Proof he was not a hallucination.

"What?"

"That transmission announced itself three switchbacks ago."

She grimaced. "I think I need a tow."

"Come up to the shop, I'll give you a number."

"Appreciate it."

She stepped out into the serene outdoor sanctuary, following his sexy walk in silence, and then made her call.

"No help for two hours."

"Hmm." He stretched his body. "I'm taking my break at a nearby waterfall; it's about a ten-minute walk. You can wait here or join me."

As she pondered his statement, he stepped out of his coveralls. *Boom. What a specimen of a man.* The T-shirt, shorts, and hiking boots fanned her flame. Her mouth dropped open.

He smirked. "Which works for you?"

"Ah, the waterfall. I'm here to enjoy the local scenery."

"All the scenery?" He winked.

Her face flushed. "Yeah, I appreciate *all* that nature has to offer."

"Me, too." His lingering gaze across her body lit everything inside her up. *OMG.*

With her hiking partner leading the way, the excursion provided a walking meditation. He was quiet and respectful. *Damn if that isn't a turn-on.*

Soon the trail opened to a vista of big rocks at the bottom of a glorious waterfall. She plopped on a rock.

After taking in the view, she lay back on the rock and closed her eyes, enjoying the sensation of the sun on her body and the burbles of the water below. When her hiking mate rustled, she opened her eyes. He had shrugged off his T-shirt and his skin gleamed in the sunlight. Every muscle of his back popped, a tattoo of a tree coming to life.

"Nice tattoo."

"Thanks. It signifies I'm one with nature."

This location coupled with his presence caused her horniness to surge. "How one with nature?"

"Well, that depends on your nature definition."

She gulped hard. "The sexual kind."

His big grin foretold his answer. "A true favorite."

"Then I'm taking my clothes off. I want to experience all of it."

"I'll join you."

As she worked to undress, he removed his boots and she admired how his shorts hung on his hips. *Hung?* She snickered. She was about to discover that.

After she swept her shirt over her head, her nipples pebbled. His eyes widened at the sight. She shimmied out of her pants until she stood before him in only her lace bra and panties, goosebumps forming on her skin.

She wasn't sure if it was from the air or his intense stare. When she dropped her bra on the ground, they both stood wearing only their bottoms.

"I'll go first," he said.

As his shorts fell, she spied his sinewy ass, lean like all the other animals one might find in these woods. He fit here. And when he turned, he was as hung as that elk she'd seen yesterday.

She wondered what he was thinking as she hooked her thumbs in her panties and dragged them down her legs. The hair of her bush gleamed in the sun. When the air hit her vulva, she shuddered.

"What now?" she asked.

He chuckled. "I usually masturbate."

Her heart raced. Her pussy throbbed. Her nipples ached. The scent in the air overpowered her—fresh, earthy, and full of sex. Her body was on board with whatever he proposed.

"Well, okay then. When in Rome?"

They were three feet apart as she observed him slide his hand over his cock and moan to his own touch, exact and sure. He was a man in nature pleasuring himself; the sight was exceptional.

With her arousal stoked by his efforts, she joined in. She rubbed her breasts and slid her hand into her wetness and wiggled. The contrast of her internal heat with the cooler air pressing on her skin ratcheted up her desire. She gasped.

They turned to face each other. Like mirrors, their

individual moves and reactions urged the other on. Her fingers rolled over her clit. His fingers and hand worked his cock. They moaned as their bodies bowed, performing an erotic *pas de deux*.

The birds squawked above them, then circled, serenading their earthly ritual. She soared with them. Her masturbating mate added low groans to their refrain. And like on the quiet meditation hike, he led her on this sexual path with his own nuanced stroking that caused her orgasm to build and sail.

In this ancient place, as his body flexed for orgasmic flight, the movement sent her to a spiritual realm. The energy of the rushing water expanded inside her, pulling her orgasm to heights she'd never experienced. Her clit responded to her touches like it never had. It was as if her partner was a mystic orchestrating their sexual vibration to the energy, the ozone, and the ambiance of the mountain.

They were one with nature, rooted like a tree. Together, but alone.

When their orgasms broke free, their song rolled around the rocks and deadened into the waterfalls.

A standing orgasm was just what she needed, and sharing it with another person in this place was phenomenal. They had witnessed each other owning pleasure. Each smiled at the other as their breathing normalized.

Her entire body tingled as they dressed in silence. The experience brought home a new aspect of her nature, an openness; one she wanted to further explore.

While they hiked back to the maintenance shop, a tow truck bellowed in the distance.

"Thank you for helping me today," she said.

"Thanks for adding splendor to my break."

Pride replaced blushing. She stuck out her hand, the one that had made her come. They shook, cementing their private celebration. What they'd just done was the most intimate thing; their essences mingling between their hands was an added bonus.

"I'm Jules."

"I'm Caleb."

"Maybe we can do this again sometime."

He cocked his head. "You're not a tourist?"

They turned as the tow truck rumbled onto the service road.

"No. I'm starting a new job at the university."

Caleb nodded to the driver and squeezed her hand.

"Well, if you need more natural maintenance, you know where to find me."

PHUGOID

Alexa J. Day

"I 'm going to fuck your brains out," he said. "That's probably going to take a lot of fucking."

I met him maybe two hours ago when I theorized that physicists settle for studying things they can't control. Now he's rooting greedily under my collar with his mouth. I suck in the scent of leather tangled with something sweet in his hair. My hands tremble, wondering if this is allowed.

"You're still thinking too much. I can tell." He pushes away from the door and throws his jacket at a chair. "Come on."

His bed is churned up and untidy, the thin blanket entwined with some sheets that might be any color in the faint light from his window. Two pillows meet in a right angle.

He pulls the shirt off his muscular torso with thick arms. I must have made a sound. He plops onto the bed and grins.

"You might want to take that off." His hands swallow the heel of one heavy biker boot. "I'm a ripper and that looks expensive."

I barely manage three buttons before I yank my blouse over my head. When I can see again, he's right in front of me. His belt buckle clinks when he hauls me up against him.

He shoves my hand into his pants, loose around his waist. The synthetic fabric of his underwear is stretched tight over his dick. He slides my palm up and down the length of him.

He sighs. "Fuck. Take your clothes off so I can get this in you."

My hips shimmy a little one-two, one-two dance until I'm out of my skirt. He slings me onto the bed. A baby-chick cheep jolts out of my mouth. My bra cup creaks under his hand until he shoves it over my breasts or my tits—he probably says tits, vulgar like his hands pawing at me, the lips and tongue stuffing my whole tit into his mouth. I'm spreading for him, rocking against him, when he puts my hand back on his dick (holy God, it's big) and he says, "You want that? Huh? You want it all?"

And I'm like, "Fuck yeah, I want it all," and that doesn't even sound like something I would say but at the same time I want to tell him a lot of other dirty stuff. I want to be that woman with him. He's pushing my legs apart and the air feels cool where I'm already so wet.

He smacks me there like a douchelord summoning a bartender and now I just want this, more of this. How does this feel so good? His mouth is on my other breast, his tongue flicking it, and then all of him sucking and flicking and that wet sound of his hand and I'm starting to come, but not before I can have him in me. I want to squeeze him there like my fist and I'm whining because it's too soon.

"Not yet," he says. He rubs my mound, stirring me up until I need his whole hand in me. He rolls onto his side and licks his fingers like they're covered in powdered sugar. Then he's rubbing my lips, and I smell my uniquely earthy funk, and I suck my cream off his fingers while he watches, serious as a surgeon. His cock twitches, the snail trail of his own juices cooling on my skin.

He kicks his jeans aside with broad feet before kneeling by the bed and heaving me up to his face, blowing between my thighs where I'm too hot to eat.

He laps me up the way he did with his fingers, his tongue sweeping up over one of my lips and then the other. I twist in his unkempt sheets while he kisses and sucks my other lips and I'm so wet now his tongue slips out to take my juices and a sound like singing is coming out of me as his tongue dives deep into me, delving like he's trying to get the last bit of a forbidden treat. His whole face is pushed between my legs, his mouth sealed to my pussy. I pull him into me by the hair, I can't get enough and neither can he, and God, he is literally slurping me, not eating me out but drinking me up and it's so good. He moans and the vibration has me so close and no one's ever done it like this. I'll make more and more, as much as he wants, while he pants and slurps like something wild feasting on me. His hands have me pinned down with my cunt locked to his face and I want to come so hard now. I want to come on his face, pushing down like I'm made for birthing pleasure.

He sits back on his heels, rubbing his forearm over his face. I hike myself up on my elbows. I don't want to glare but I'm probably glaring.

"Turn over."

Pleasure glows under the weight of my body. I lift up my ass, conditioned to respond to the slithery stretch of latex. His hands caress my curves before thick fingers dig into my hips. His condom-clad hard-on nudges me. I push back toward him. Finally.

I want to be filled so badly I look over my shoulder. He raises an eyebrow like he can't figure out what I want although he knows good and damn well because he's sliding his fingers into me. I don't care how many, it's still not enough. I have to breathe deep, not too deep, not before his cock is in me. He inhales like he's meditating; I breathe into the hand holding me down into the pillow that smells sweetly of cologne, shampoo, and him, and breathe out into his fingers rocking into me. Should have done this before instead of chasing that high but I'm still ready; he's sliding out of me and I'm rolling over, all blissed out.

His cock opening me up he's so deep inside me and I need to lock him in here like magnets meeting. I hitch my legs up like a jockey only underneath him, being ridden, that girth and mass pushing deeper into me. We grin at the same time and he plunges way down inside and then withdraws with the same slowness and the two of us start accelerating upward and I want to pull him down into me and it's perfect, the shape of him like a statue. He tosses his hair and pushes breath out of his lungs and then mine and the perfect shoulders/back/hips making a perfect wave that hollow pop-smack between his flesh and mine and everything falls together.

Singularity?

His cry answers to the question held in my breath and everything surges out of him into me and celebratory gibberish erupts out of me in response, organic and orgasmic and unstoppable.

"Unbelievable."

"Huh?" My contribution to the scholarly discourse.

"I mean, I knew it would take a lot of fucking." His breathless giggles ripple. "But Jesus."

CAVE WALLS

Judy Calabrese

Y ou arrived in my bedroom seconds before my baby
pushed himself out of me. The child loosed himself
from a place inside me, a chamber I housed but had
never been. Suddenly, I didn't know where I was, in the
red water of the birthtub, somewhere between here and
an invisible planet only I could see, its energy held me
in a tractor beam. When I was able to let go, back into
this world, I looked up. There you were, eyes wide and
luminescent, receiving me. A slippery baby in my arms
still attached to his cord, embedded to the placenta, his
planet still inside me.

A few days before birth, I'd asked you to lay hands
to soothe my skin stretched and bulking. You'd rubbed
my back with oil when I was so full of life that it hurt;
my skin was about to burst. When you helped me out of

the tub, you laid me wobbly in the bed and wiped blood from the floor, the insides of my thighs. You massaged my abdomen, firming my womb back to size, a little bigger than my fist.

You are my best friend. And now we find ourselves two years later here, another place I've never been. Before we sealed the plans to have sex, you told me you were still grieving your marriage to your wife and to be clear: this is just sex. We brokered this agreement just a few days ago, negotiated it like a deal, scribbling the contract over texts. You needed to discuss boundaries, *hard and soft lines,* consent and safe sex. Things I have never uttered or identified before a sexual relationship even begins? I felt my age—a teenager's age older than you and my insecurity said, *Do you need all these rules to feel safe? Aren't we friends? Don't we trust one another?* But I didn't say anything because I wanted you so much, I'd do anything to have you.

Language is foreplay, you texted. *Where do you like to be touched?*

Everywhere, I replied, as if I've never been asked before.

Then you said the thing that would dictate our intimacy, our sex. *I will decide whether or not you get to touch my pussy.* You spoke to me as a "top," the position of dominance. I went lightheaded, spinning inside, shortness of breath. Vertigo pulled my loins like tiny weights inside my pussy, drawing me to the ground.

I will not be making love to you, you wrote. *I will be fucking you. Will you do as I say when I ask you to?*

I held my breath as I typed, *Yes,* and felt any resistance leak out of me. My compliance caused something ancient and unnameable to get on its knees.

"May I bite you?" We are making out on your couch, just forty-eight hours after we brokered our deal, your hot breath at my neck.

"Please," I say with a slight squeak. Arms and legs in a tangle of hair and hips, your bites send me to a cave dwelling where I claw the walls. Unhinged, fire licks my heels and when you say, *Do you want to go to my bed?* you've rescued me. You undress yourself and then me with no apology. I want us to behold one another in our skin, but there isn't any time, we are being dragged.

You push me down hard onto the bed.

You're on top of me, grinding into my thigh. I find my hips bucking, reaching for you. My thirsty desire to heed your command is the only thing keeping me from begging you to enter me.

Finally, you say, "May I put a finger inside you?"

I swallow hard before responding, "Please."

"*Yes, please,*" you instruct me.

My clit twitches to obey. "Yes, please."

"Say my name," you whisper firmly.

As I do, you slip one finger inside my pussy.

My hips and torso twist under you and I don't hear you ask for the second or third finger—did you? I only know you are deeper and deeper inside of me, discovering places I didn't know I had, places asking to be touched, pushed, prodded, provoked. No one had bothered to look there, including myself. I slip into another state of consciousness, forgetting everything that came before.

A few days before, I'd awoken from sleep with words swirling a chant, *You are born. You are unborn. You are born. You are unborn.* I chased the voice but it led nowhere. Here with all of your fingers inside me, I am inside a cave of myself and you have lit torches. You are scrawling on shadowed walls, etchings, ancient drawings. You're burrowing inside me and I am being excavated. We are making our own language. I make guttural, animal sounds. Your capable fingers are signing the language into the walls of my cunt.

We enter the final chamber, the place inside me I was unaware existed until I take your hand—your entire hand—inside me. You and my body knew the way to this place like tour guides to an ancient burial site. I am the tourist, wandering with you, sprawled and moist, allowing you in, smelling the rain beat the earth outside your window, squinting through sweat at the spring dusk melting into the blue mountains. I gasp, as if on the brink of life and death, into a state where I am almost inhuman, I am another life form. This place inside me has no name but it has a voice, one that I now know has called to me before but I didn't answer because I didn't know what to say. No man's cock has ever reached this place. Only my babies, the ones that lived and the ones that died, have known it. Tonight, it is where centuries of deep pain slow-dances with explosive, exquisite joy in an ancient dance hall.

I am screaming. The scream squeezes all breath from my lungs, clamping down on your hand while I am also splayed open, the most open I've ever been with anyone. I am not my body, I am a light being, floating entwined with your spirit dancing in the stars outside.

When I come, I shake violently, convulse, volcanic. My body loses control. I look at your face to anchor me. Your crystalline eyes are clean, pure, and I know you've given me some piece of myself I didn't know I'd lost.

We lay in damp sheets side by side like two naked paper dolls, spent. The time to return to our separate lives drives toward us fast. You stare up at the low ceiling and say, "Sex with you is like the fulfillment of desire mixed with some kind of theology. A sacrament."

My silence is my testimony, the most potent messenger of all that is true. But I don't know what that means because I don't know who I am anymore.

You drive me home and I lay in bed alone. Our smell imprinted on my skin, soaking down deep into my bones. I think of you and I wonder if you think of me.

SEXQUESTRATION

Camille Adler

Gabi tossed her head back to take the shot of tequila and wiped her mouth on her sleeve. Liquid courage delivered. She sucked on a lime and spit it in the sink. Glancing at the calendar on the wall she noted that it was Day 47 of quarantine. Time to take action.

In the front room Jacob was sitting hunched over his laptop. Sweet, quiet Jacob, her roommate for the last two semesters. Jacob who makes polite small talk with the blandness of a Mormon on his mission, who studies constantly unless he is getting his required eight hours of sleep. Jacob who she had never seen interact with friends or love interests in all the time she had known him. Jacob with whom she now had an exclusive relationship due to the world shutting down—exclusive without benefits.

He glanced up and gave her a friendly nod before looking back down at his organic chemistry book. *No homework tonight, cutie pie.* She walked over and sat on the table edge in front of him, kicking out her legs and inching herself up on the table. "Oh, er, hi Gabi. Um, do you mind scooting down a bit?" He tried to pull the paper out from under her, but she braced down and held it in place with her firm booty.

"Yes, I do mind," she said in a calm, matter-of-fact way.

"What, er, what did you say?" He finally looked up at her eyes. She swayed a little bit and leaned in so that her breasts—showing a lot of creamy brown skin in the skimpy tank top—were just inches away from his face. He leaned back. "Gabi, have you been drinking? You okay?" She was a keto-vegan-Crossfitter whose idea of a crazy night involved a bottle of kombucha.

"Yes, I have been drinking, Jacob. All by myself. Now come to the kitchen and take a shot."

"Sorry, Gabi, I have a midterm next week—"

She jumped off the table and pulled him to his feet. She was surprisingly strong for someone barely five feet tall. "Now." He frowned but followed her orders. She poured two shots and passed him the salt and a lime wedge. With a small nod of her chin, they both shot back the cheap tequila and sucked their chasers. He turned to return to his work.

"Jacob . . . wait. I have something to tell you. We've been in this apartment for forty-seven days. And we're likely going to be here longer, for weeks." He nodded, looking concerned. "You have to fuck me or move out of the apartment." Jacob froze. Then tequila hit her (again), and she couldn't hold in her giggles.

He relaxed. "Oh, you're fucking with me. Okay, good one."

"No, I am *not* fucking with you, but I want to be— no, I *need* to be fucking you. Or you can leave and never come back." She pointed to the door and leaned back against the counter, misjudged it by a foot, and fell on the floor, laughing again. He helped her up, eyeing her hitched-up skirt and long black hair curling around her breasts.

"Gabi, I'm not going to move out."

"Great!" She grabbed a kitchen towel and started knotting it around his wrists. He stared at her, his eyebrows raised. Then she was tugging her tank top off, taking off her skirt, kicking off her flip-flops until she stood before him in her skimpy pink push-up bra and black lace thong.

Jacob looked down at the clumsy knots around his wrists and then looked up, meeting her eyes. "Gabi, you're way out of my league. You're beautiful. And smart and . . ." Before he could go on, she sprung at him, knocking him down onto the linoleum and covering his mouth with hers. His body, at first tense with shock from the fall, relaxed. She felt him kissing her back, his tongue moving inside of her mouth.

She grabbed his hand and pressed it into her chest,

his fingers coming alive as he moved her bra straps down, releasing her large breasts. With one hand he unlatched her bra.

"Wow, you are good at—"

Without warning, he shifted his weight and quickly flipped her on her back, roughly pinning her to the ground. Now it was her turn to stare up in silence at him, her pink mouth open. "Don't fuck with an ex-high school wrestler," he said. "I mean, do you want to fuck a wrestler?"

"Yes," she whispered.

"As you wish." He reached up and grabbed the ice bucket from the counter. "But first, a little payback." He grabbed an ice cube and pushed it halfway into her mouth. "Suck it." Her eyes widened in surprise. "Suck it harder." Her lips complied as little drops of melted water ran down her chin, dripping onto her tits. He suddenly pulled the ice away from her, leaving her gaping like a fish out of water. He traced the ice down her throat and around her breasts, drawing a figure eight that circled closer and closer to her nipples.

She began to shiver and moan, trying to move, but firmly held in place. He moved the ice down to her pussy, rubbing it over her clit once, then twice before abruptly shoving the entire piece of ice past her thong and up her pussy. When Gabi screamed in delighted shock, he covered her mouth with his, sucking her lips.

She laughed suddenly while kissing him and he pulled away, confused. "I can't believe this is happening," she said, pulling him back to her mouth. "I'm so fucking horny and you are so fucking perfect. Everything this year has been so hard and so wrong. And you," she said, grabbing his face with her hands, "you are so hard and so right." He smiled, and slid down her body, nuzzling her breasts before sucking on them one mouthful at a time. Just when she couldn't stand it any longer, he moved down until his tongue was lapping at her clit. She lifted her hips up and curled her leg around the back of his head, bringing him even closer. When he snaked his hand up and inched his thumb against her asshole, she growled in anticipation as he pressed inside her. Quiet Jacob seemed to have a lot of hidden talents.

"Yes," she moaned. Gabi was so close to coming she was shaking. He pulled back, moving up to kiss her mouth, making her wait for it. She sucked his lips, tasting herself all over his face. She found his eyes, pleading, "More . . . don't stop." He gave her a shy smile and returned to her clit with athletic intensity, finally dragging his teeth against it. Gabi came hard, eyes rolling back in her head as she screamed again. "I should have fucking kidnapped you forty-six days ago. Come here." She grabbed his belt and pulled him down on top of her.

DIRTY PICTURES

Rachel Kramer Bussel

Logan made the mistake of glancing at his phone during his morning team meeting. Thankfully, he held the screen beneath the table, angled so only he could see it, because there was Renee, his wife, stark naked, eyes closed, her nipples hard and pointed, the hint of red fuzz around her sex. He stifled a smile and nodded seriously as he willed his cock to wait to get hard.

When the meeting ended an hour later, he rushed to his desk and gave her a taste of her own medicine—an image of his cock he'd taken a few days ago, when he'd been rock-hard first thing in the morning, before she woke up.

They'd started the game when he'd taken the office job and shifted their work-from-home lifestyle to a more typical weekday schedule. No more lunchtime quickies or mid-morning makeout sessions. He'd worried about missing hopping into bed whenever they were both in the mood, but this penchant for surprising each other had added a new spark to their relationship.

While Logan was staring at the clock, Renee was getting a head start. Sometimes she waited for Logan, forcing herself to work with her clit hard and aching, pressing against her panties, urging her to relieve the pressure. Her favorite plug-in vibrator was only a few steps away, after all. But there was something exciting, most of the time, about holding out, letting fantasies about what she wanted to do with him flit through her mind as she went about her day.

This day, though, she wasn't in the mood to wait. Instead she saved her document, closed her computer, and positioned herself on the floor on her hands and knees. Sometimes she chose the bed, but the floor felt wilder, more animalistic, like she really had to have it right now. She lay the phone on the ground, the image of Logan's hand wrapped around his cock so near, even if the real thing was so far.

She licked her lips, picturing how he would feel and taste, as her fingers crept toward her sex. Usually she wanted everything, from masturbation to fucking, to race toward its finish, but today she took her time, mashing her clit hard, but moving slowly. She spread her legs, picturing Logan behind her, holding his dick just like he was in the photo, staring at her pink lips as he prepared to enter her.

She longed to call him just then, paint him a verbal picture of what was happening, but that wouldn't be fair. She could take a break whenever she wanted, but he couldn't. She said his name out loud, the familiar word only for her. When she said her own back, trying to imitate his deep voice, a shudder passed through her. The way he imbued so much heat into those two syllables—"Renee"—always got to her.

She kept going, her fingers sliding lower to enter herself, occasionally shifting to hold open her ass cheeks in invitation to her invisible lover. That move was part of a game she liked to play, where she did things she didn't quite dare when Logan was actually there with her. Sometimes she thought of herself as another, bolder woman, the kind who could be one hundred percent wanton with the love of her life.

She started talking out loud, speaking her most outrageous fantasies into the air, but hoping, somehow, that the real Logan could hear her. She reached for her favorite butt plug, lubed it up, and slid it into her ass, wishing there were a way to get a good photo of that sight.

"I wish it was your cock," she said, the image of him poised to enter her making her shake.

"Do you really?" she heard from the man who she was just as in love—and lust—with as she'd been twenty-three years ago.

He'd come home early! She didn't ask why he was there—the answer was beyond obvious, even in his work pants.

"Yes, I do," she told him, meaning every word. Dirty pictures turned her on, sometimes of him, sometimes of other people, but they were nothing compared to the real thing. She wanted him in her pussy, her ass, her mouth. She wanted him on top of her, whispering filthy words into her ear.

She closed her eyes, her fingers still as they rested against her engorged, aching clit, and listened to the glorious sound of his zipper being lowered and his clothes slowly being removed. She waited until she could smell him up close, knew he was right in front of her, near enough to touch, to lick, to taste. She opened her eyes to see her dirty picture come to life. He didn't need to tell her to take him between her lips; they parted instantly, her hand gliding through her slickness as he plunged inside.

She made a noise from deep in her throat, her own fingers pressing into her wetness, eager for him to fill her there, just as the plug filled her tight hole. He pulled out before she'd gotten her fill, but she wasn't going to complain.

"How could I miss out on this?" he asked as he moved behind her, not even bothering to suggest they waste precious seconds moving to the bed. He knelt so the head of his cock was poised right there at her entrance, admiring the plug even as he gave it a twist. "Renee, you drive me wild," he said softly before one firm thrust had him all the way inside her.

He squeezed her ass cheeks, watching ever move as

he pulled back, then thrust inside her warm tight pussy once again. Her heavy breaths started blasting the air, her fingers brushing against his cock as she stroked herself. Logan shifted his body so she was flat on the ground, his body pressed against hers, pinning her beneath him with the weight of his desire. She still had enough room to play with her clit, though, he found when he wriggled a hand beneath them to join her.

He offered her the fingers of his other hand to suck, his dick getting even harder the moment her lips and tongue welcomed his driving digits. Very soon, she was tightening around him, her climax seeming to rear up like a wave in the ocean, towering over them, then crashing down as her muscles clenched around him.

He wanted to come right then, to fill her with all the longing he'd felt since he'd glanced at her luscious photo, but he held off, savoring the delicious torment of being as hard as could be, knowing he would get his reward very soon. When her spasms were done, he pulled out, giving the plug one more turn, then moved back to his prior position. "Taste me," he said as he slowly guided his hand around his cock, her hooded eyes watching every move, offering her a live dirty picture as his cream shot out onto her lips, her tongue, and she in turn gave him a view that he'd never get tired of as she licked up every drop.

WITNESS

Allison Armstrong

Meredith adjusts the position of the inflatable air mattress, centering it in the taped-off section of floor. The noise of the play party buzzes around her—the thwack and slap of impact toys, the yelps and moans, the growls and gleeful cackles—but she's made herself a temple as best she can, laying her plush, black throw over the mattress, marking out the space with flickering LED tea lights and setting the tiny shop bell on the floor within easy reach.

She takes her time preparing, strips off her flowing skirt, her AmazonFest '82 T-shirt, her boots, and tucks them all away. She lets herself focus on how the warm air feels against her bare ass and thighs, and how her long, iron and silver hair brushes her bare back all the way down. She's still amazed at how well it grew back after the chemo, even though it's been nearly a decade. Meredith adjusts her socks. They're impossibly long—stockings, really—and they coil around her calves and thighs, offering a gentle, constant touch that makes her want to brush her legs together. Carefully, she kneels on the mattress, feels the trapped air shift and bubble under her ample, fought-for weight, and finds her balance.

She chooses a vibrator from her stash of toys—one with a Bluetooth remote and dual heads—lays out the lube like she's planning a date with a lover, because she is. She drips lube on the vibe and settles it snugly inside her, squeezing just to feel the fullness it provides, then selects a familiar setting that will give her lots of time. Even knowing what to expect, she still gasps when the vibe starts to buzz. The low-level hum gives her just enough of a thrill to warm her up, to let her be curious about what happens next.

Kneeling on the mattress, Meredith breathes out slowly. She touches her fingertips to the tiny bell then, closing her eyes, brings her finger down quick and light. She treats it like a holy object because it is one. Three taps, three chimes. Meredith lets the sound sing through her, a reminder to stay, to be the body she is. Meredith reaches for the East—an entirely hypothetical direction in this windowless room—to call the panting breath, the gasps and moans and howls that are Air. She lets her lungs fill softly, then breathes out hard, her asshole kissing the velvet with every breath. When the heat kindles inside her, Meredith calls the electric vibration of South, the friction and tension and body heat of Fire. She licks her lips, feels the slick between her thighs, and reaches for Water, calling to sweat and saliva, the brine of desire and the gush of fulfillment. She strokes her hands up her thighs, along her ribs, over her face, and calls on Earth, calls healing cells, muscle and sinew, the iron of her blood and the calcium of her bones.

I've come to play in the temple of pleasure, she thinks. *Will you witness me?*

Eyes closed, she brushes her hands over her body, moving slowly, deliberately, focusing on the sensation of skin brushing skin, the texture of nipple tightening under palm, of cotton meeting thigh meeting fingertip. Feeling her way, brushing her long hair to the side, she lies down, letting the plush of the throw cradle her. She strokes her hands over her thighs, tracing her fingers along the bare skin between the cuffs of her cotton stockings and the place where her vibrator pulses and thrums. It feels good, the way the pleasure ripples through her, making her shiver as the sensations start to build, but the noise of the party is distracting.

At home, cradled in the warmth of her bed, red candles flickering on her altar, all Meredith has to compete with are her own shame and anxiety. Here, she has to contend with the throb of Nine Inch Nails at high volume and the sounds of a dozen scenes. It makes it hard to focus on herself, to show up as her own lover rather than turning this into an awkward performance piece. But the velvety throw reminds Meredith to pay attention with all of her skin, to breathe all the way down to where her pelvic floor can roll and flex, down to where her insides can squeeze and grip her purring, pulsing vibe.

Meredith focuses on the vibrations, lets herself relax into the rise and fall of their independent pulses, which are heavier first inside, then outside, then inside again. She works the muscles of her pelvic floor, rolls and flexes her hips. She strokes her breasts, breathing deep and letting her belly swell, brushing her fingertips over her throat, cupping her face, then sliding her hands down her body again. She listens to the rise and fall of her breath, pays attention to the weight of her breasts as they play with gravity, and to the gentle squeeze of her cotton stockings clinging to her calves, her thighs. She brings herself back to the movement of her hands over the jut of her hips, lets the noise of the party grow distant as she turns her senses back to the rising intensity of the vibe humming and pulsing between her legs.

Meredith lets herself squirm, tracing her hands up over her belly, back to her tits. She can feel her hard nipples under her palms, the warmth of her palms on her nipples. She squeezes her tits, drags her nails across them, makes herself shiver. She brushes her thighs against each other, aware of how wet she's getting, how hard her clit is, how her hips want to grind against the rumble of the toy. Meredith licks her lips, and lets herself whimper as the pressure between her legs builds.

She palms her breasts and squeezes, letting the muscles in her hips and belly flex and clench. Meredith grinds, working the muscles in her ass and thighs, digging her heels into the mattress. She kneads her tits, arches her back, gasps, moans, growls as she squeezes the vibe inside her. When she comes, it's a long ripple of release, all the muscles in her abdomen clenching and shuddering as the pleasure takes her, riding the relentless thrum and pulse of the vibe until the programmed pattern runs out.

She slides her palms down her ribs, lies there with her eyes closed, catching her breath.

She listens to the hush of air in her lungs as they fill, empty, fill again. Her skin is hot to touch, the throw radiating heat where she's crushed it under her. She savors the wetness of her sweat, her come, soaked into the soft plush of the throw, and the warm burn of tired muscles, worked hard, the heaviness of her limbs cradled in her makeshift bed.

I have come to play in the temple of pleasure, she thinks. *Thank you for witnessing.*

Slowly, she turns her senses outward.

The noise of the party comes back.

She doesn't mind.

DO SMURFETTES DREAM OF ELECTRIC BLUE BUSH?

Amanda Earl

Clotilde received a message from an acquaintance on Facebook asking about her favorite vibrators. She was surprised, but it was understandable. She'd been posting status updates about her daily masturbation routine: showing her body on Snapchat to strangers while using her vibe hands-free. "Clit vibes give me amazing orgasms," she'd announced to her so-called friends. Clotilde is prone to oversharing, but why not, if the result is this pretty chick with blue hair asks her for vibe recs.

The thing about Facebook friending was that Clotilde did it without knowing anything about them. She felt guilty if she didn't accept a request. She had no idea who this person was. She'd never even looked at her profile.

Clotilde wasn't sure if Zo was her real name or a pseudonym. Zo had sent over a pic of a giant purple plastic G-spot clit vibe combo that reminded Clotilde of *The Texas Chainsaw Massacre.* "It's just BOOM, shic! It goes BOOM, shic! Then goes BOOM, shic!" Clotilde shuddered and shook her head at being able to remember the goriest movie from the seventies and associate it with jilling off.

She'd been a wand user most of her masturbating life, but the latest version was too wimpy. She kept burning out the motor. So she'd started on the clit vibes.

Zo messaged her a few weeks later to tell her she'd purchased the vibrator Clotilde had recommended. After wishing her a happy wank, Clotilde cruised Zo's page. Cute was the first word she thought of, but she, herself, hated to be called cute, even though she's short and busty, with silvering bangs, long legs, and an off-kilter sense of humor. She's always had a thing for manic pixie dream girls in films. Zo looks like that, but older.

When she's wanking next time, she thinks about Zo's blue hair and wonders if the carpet matches the drapes. That makes her laugh.

She's seen cam girls do performance sex; some of them dye their hoochie hair while others shave it bald and paint on a little face, making it dance for the big tippers. She doesn't share these thoughts with Zo, who's started to correspond with her regularly. They're both government workers, both single. Clotilde is divorced and Zo is a widow in her forties.

The messages become Face Time chats full of laughter. They say laughter and orgasms are similar; they cause people to let go, to lose their inhibitions. That's the way it is for Clotilde with Zo. Their shared delight led to mutual wank sessions.

Clotilde loves watching Zo turn herself on, the way she knows her own body. She takes note of every touch: the way Zo licks her finger and moves it around each of her nipples, the small, delicate tugs, the way Zo's eyes grow dark with desire when it is just right. Clotilde's body responds to every tug, every caress, every openmouthed O of ecstasy. When Zo parts her legs for the first time to reveal her swollen clit, Clotilde notes she does indeed have a blue bush that Clotilde wants to bury her face in. Zo strokes lightly along her clit and Clotilde does the same. They have different bodies but fucking this way is like fucking a mirror image of herself. It feels intimate. Private. And hot as fuck.

Eventually they can't hold back any more and decide to meet up in person at an upcoming comedy show.

On the night of their date, Clotilde sits in the basement of the almost empty club, totally nervous. She orders crappy beer and drinks it fast before Zo arrives, then orders another. Maybe Zo isn't coming. She thinks about hightailing it out of there when the show starts. She hears the announcer call a name—Zo's. Zo is standing up on the stage, at the actual microphone. Clotilde almost spills her beer. More people have arrived. Apparently, Zo is a last-minute replacement for the opening act.

Zo is hilarious. Then Zo starts on the sex stuff. She uses the word *masturbation* and some guy in the audience goes "Ewwww." His bros pat him on the back as they crack peanuts with their teeth. Zo keeps going, not letting it faze her. Somebody calls her Smurfette and asks if her cunt hair is blue as well.

Zo just laughs at the guy. "That's right, but you'll never see it. I don't fuck loud-mouthed idiots," she says, and the dude turns red and shuts up.

After her set, Zo shoots the heckler a finger and sidles up to Clotilde's table. Clotilde loves her fire and the way she copes with even annoyances with humor. She tells Zo how much she loved her act, especially the sex stuff. Droplets of sweat roll down Zo's neck and into her cleavage. Clotilde's eyes follow them down. Zo takes Clotilde's hand.

"Let's find someplace private," she whispers into Clotilde's ear, and a pang of arousal hits Clotilde in the cunt. She barely notices the dingy, butt-covered floor on the way to the bathroom.

The room itself is a single stall with a dirty urinal beside the sink and a toilet in the corner. Zo locks the door. Clotilde calls Zo "Smurfette" with a shy smile. "I think that might be my new nickname for you." Zo laughs and Clotilde joins in. Whatever self-consciousness Clotilde had been feeling immediately vanishes.

Zo presses Clotilde up against the wall. They both ignore the scrawled graffiti. That first contact of Zo's lips on Clotilde's feels soft, wet, and oh-so-fucking delicious. She can feel the brush of Zo's hard nipples against her body. She slides her hand over Zo's top. "I've been wanting to touch these since I first saw you naked on cam, Zo." Zo groans as Clotilde traces the outline of her nipples through her thin T-shirt, then puts her hand on Clotilde's waist and looks at her questioningly.

They'd spent ages watching each other on cam, legs parted, fingers on clits, talking about sex and bad lovers who didn't take the time to learn about their bodies. Clotilde is turned on but also nervous. Zo points out the mirror. Clotilde smiles. They move so they are positioned nearer to the mirror with Clotilde behind Zo. "Show me your cunt," she tells Zo. Zo gives Clotilde a deep kiss and lifts up her skirt. She isn't wearing any underwear. They both laugh again at the sight of Zo's bush, then Clotilde watches in the mirror as her hands caress Zo's breasts, rubbing each nipple the way she likes it, and tugging at them until they're stiff. She takes in Zo's open mouth, her wide eyes. Her breath is shallow, her heartbeat racing.

Then she can't resist anymore. She runs her hand down Zo's body and teases the soft cunt hair, dipping a finger into her wetness and sliding it along her clit.

Zo moans, clearly ready to come. The sound is more sensual than any of the many scenarios Clotilde had imagined. In what feels like no time, they both have loud orgasms, not caring who hears. Some dude bangs on the door and says he has to use the can. They burst into laughter.

DOT'S PEARLS

H.L. Brooks

Small Town
1946

Finally back in her room, an exhausted Pearl unhooked her stockings, peeled them off, and tossed them on the chair next to the bed. She always wore stockings, except for when rations made it impossible. Back then her friend Tildy would draw lines on her legs each day. If she wasn't friends only in the most plutonic way with Tildy, it might have been a slightly titillating process.

Pearl popped the buttons on her dress, revealing a powder-blue bra. Her dress fell, revealing matching silk tap pants, but not a girdle, because she refused to strangle her luscious thighs. Magazines would have you believe that curvy thighs and bottoms were a shame, but she relished in their gentle sways and emphatic jiggles beneath her clothing.

The newspaper kept sending her on trips across the East Coast. This particular guesthouse was the nicest place she'd stayed this month. There was a big tub in the bathroom she shared with the room across the hall, and she hadn't heard a peep from that room since she checked in so she was going to risk a soak.

Pearl threw on her silk robe, picked up her bubble bath solution, and scooted across the hallway. It was the largest bathroom she'd ever been in, with a claw-foot tub, tile floor laid with large soft rugs, and even a settee. The ledge near the sink had a row of candles on it, so she lit them.

She put the little sign on the outside of the door that declared *Occupied, Sweetie!,* and ran the water. She dumped in the solution and the water bubbled up nicely. She reached into her deep cleavage and pulled out a small silver flask that had *Two Scoops* engraved on it (a journalistic inside joke) and took a swig, then tossed it onto the bench, stripped down, and got in—glossy red toenails first.

She sighed and unpinned her hair; ringlet tips dipped into the bubbles and danced like seaweed around her tawny nipples. She leaned back and closed her eyes. Moments later there was a creak and clunk from downstairs. Then footsteps, and giggles with low talking. She caught her breath and held it when she heard the door to the bathroom crack open, and almost shouted

"Occupied! Occupied!" Instead she sunk down into the bubbles, leaving nothing but nose and eyeballs peeping over the foam.

The couple tumbled into the bathroom, attached at the lips. A handsome couple dressed for a date. They were whispering, muffled mouths pressing together. His hat tumbled onto the floor and Pearl tried not to make swishy sounds, but felt she should announce her presence.

Now the woman's hat was off, a whiff of gardenia perfume as she unbuttoned the man's shirt. "I love watching you take off your belt, Beaux," she cooed.

Beaux grinned wide under smoldering eyes and slicked-back hair. He put his hand to his belt buckle, then paused.

"Dot, these candles . . ."

They turned to Pearl, who crossed her arms against her chest and cleared her throat.

"Hi. I'm Pearl, from across the hall." Awkwardness, but then sensual energy crackled in the air. "I don't mind . . . if you don't." She gave a little nose twitch and arched an eyebrow.

Dot and Beaux consulted each other with a mix of skepticism and mischief. Beaux held his breath and raised his brows as he touched his belt buckle. Dot nodded, wide-eyed, then Pearl nodded, too. Beaux let out a gush of air, smiled, and proceeded to unbuckle his trousers as the ladies watched. Dot pushed the bathroom door shut with a hip. The rattle of Beaux's belt hardware and the creak of the leather sent a little tingle down Pearl's spine, compelling Dot to wiggle urgently out of her dress. Underneath was all sexy peach lace and silk.

Dot went to her knees on the plush mat, tugged down Beaux's shorts, and the women gasped as his hard cock sprung forth. When hungry Dot wrapped her mouth around it, Beaux let out a moan. She plunged and tilted her head while moving her hand up and down the shaft. Pearl had never seen anybody do something like that before and watched with delight and curiosity.

Pearl had never been so turned on. She shifted in the warm water, then slipped her hand beneath the bubbles and started to gently tease the excited bud between her thighs as she watched the lovers.

"Come here," Beaux said gently, guiding Dot to her feet, Dot kept her hand wrapped tight around his cock. She gave a devilish grin, her eyes twinkling and locking with his. As he gave a delighted shudder, she released him.

"You want me to take off my underthings?" Dot asked in her cutesy voice.

"Oh, yeah," he replied, deep and low.

She kicked off her heels and pulled down the strap of her brassiere over one shoulder, while giving him a little wink. She then looked at Pearl and wiggled her eyebrows. Pearl smiled, rubbing herself faster. Her other hand slid up to a nipple, pinching and teasing. Bubbles sliding and hair swimming, she could see candlelight glowing on her own wet flesh. The image made her quiver.

Dot unhooked her bra, then gave a little shoulder shimmy that made her breasts sway and swing free, rosy nipples bumped out. Beaux cupped them in his hands then their mouths pressed tightly together. He put his hands inside the back of her peach silk underpants and squeezed her round bottom. Dot pulled away from the kiss and turned around, bent over, and put her hands on the yellow settee. After she gave a little bottom wiggle, Beaux unhooked her garter and let it fall. He peeled off each stocking and pulled down her peach silks to reveal a delicious view of her flesh and folds.

Beaux kneeled down, grabbed her bottom, and licked and teased her wet slit while Dot moaned, gasped, and pushed against his face. She yelled, "Beaux! Yes!" Then she slid down to the floor and spread her legs, offering a glorious view. "Fuck me, then come all over me," she commanded.

Beaux inhaled sharply, positioned himself over her and placed the tip of his hard cock at her opening. She grasped his back hard with spread fingers as he plunged into her. Dot lifted her hips and gasped as he entered. She moved with him, pressing and pushing, gasping and moaning. She was saying, "Yes! Don't stop!" As she came to her peak and began screaming his name, he worked faster.

Pearl rubbed herself faster, too. The water in the tub sloshing and bubbles fading, Beaux glanced over, and her delicious tits and the look of lust on her face pushed him over the edge. He yelled out, leaned back, pulled out his cock, and exploded over Dot's stomach, breasts, all the way to her neck in long arching spurts. They both collapsed in sticky satisfaction as Pearl cried out, her pleasure echoing in the small room.

Pearl smiled. This would be one extra story she'd have to keep to herself.

I CAN'T
STOP COMING

Debi Frond

I *can't stop coming!*

I'm fucking Sheila Shanmugam, although to be more accurate *she's* fucking *me,* because I'm just lying down and she's on top of me working her pussy over my cock up and down and up and down and up and down and *I can't stop coming.*

This isn't supposed to be a thing. My orgasms have always followed a consistent pattern: a sudden heightening of pleasure, followed by a few spasms of release that gradually decrease in intensity until the sensations fade away. This was what it was like when I was a three-jerkoffs-a-day teenager, this was what it was like during my first time with Gretchen Lipchinski in sophomore year of college, this was what it was like with every woman I've slept with since, which should be ample evidence toward the irrefutable conclusion that this is, indeed, what it's like.

But Sheila hasn't stopped fucking me. I came fifteen seconds ago and she's still going on, still moving those surprisingly dextrous hips up and down over me. This is unprecedented. When I used to masturbate (oh, hell, who am I kidding, I still do), I'd stop once the sensations stop. When I'm doing the fucking, on top or from behind, I stop thrusting after I've come. Even when women have been on top of me, they stop when they don't have to keep going anymore. That's what you do when your partner has reached orgasm. You don't go on anymore.

Sheila is still going on, and *I can't. Stop. Coming.*

Does she *know* I'm already coming? I open my eyes. (Because I close my eyes when I come. Who doesn't? I mean, don't you?) I see the saucer eyes, the wide lower lip, and the deep brown complexion that first attracted me to her Tinder profile picture. It took a week of texting before she agreed to meet IRL, which in my book is approximately five or six days too many for a Tinder match. But something made me stick it out with her. Maybe it's the fact that she's a teacher, which makes for plenty of role-play fantasies. Maybe it's that great Nicki Minaj pun she made, when I mentioned this woman I saw in a 7-11 once that I thought was her, and Sheila said, "Guess it was just a Nicki mirage." Or maybe it's just those eyes.

Those same eyes that are looking down on me right now along with a grin that says she *does* know I'm coming, but she's still going anyway, still working my cock with her pussy and making it so that I.

Can't.

Stop.

Coming.

You know that old joke about God giving Adam and Eve a choice of two things? He says the first one is the ability to pee standing up, so Adam immediately takes it, leaving the second one for Eve, which turns out to be multiple orgasms?

Is this what that's like?

I try to tell her to stop. But I can barely breathe. I usually breathe hard when I orgasm, but that's about it as far as physical reactions go. I come quickly, silently, and with dignity. I mean, it's only women who thrash about wildly and scream their head off during sex, right? Men don't do that. I sure as hell don't do that. Hell, I'm not even a huge fan of women who do that. If I want a porn star performance, I'll watch porn.

But now I'm having literal goddamn convulsions as I come again and again, the spasms not stopping at all, my abs doing involuntary crunches, my head slamming back into my pillow over and over, gasping so hard I'm actually making sounds. My hands reach up for her. I'm not sure what they want to do. Maybe they're trying to push her off. But not the right one, because it goes to one of her perky breasts and squeezes it, and that just encourages her. The left one meanwhile runs up through her hair, then cups her face, then is joined by the right one.

And now I'm looking at the face I'm holding, I'm looking into her eyes as I come, and she isn't grinning naughtily anymore, she's looking down on me with an expression that I can only describe as fucking *beatific*, like a goddamn angel taking me to the rapture, because rapture is what I'm feeling right now, rapture that this beautiful creature is giving me with every thrust of her hips, this woman who I thought was just going to be a Tinder hookup but who I swear I could stand to wake up next to every morning of my life from now on, because that would almost, *almost*, feel as good as this orgasm.

This orgasm that is still going on, for how long I fucking can't tell anymore, making me moan now, actually moan like one of those porn stars, and maybe I should feel embarrassed or unmanly about that but I don't. It feels right—it feels right to look in her eyes as I come, it feels right to let her know with my voice how amazing she's making me feel, it feels right to let go and lose control and let this orgasm just *carry* me. But speaking of control, I need to regain a little of it now because I need to catch my breath and tell her something and say it very, very carefully, because if it comes out wrong it'll mean the exact opposite of what I want to say which, oh, God, I don't want that so I breathe and breathe and breathe through every tremble and shudder and shiver that's still going through me until I can finally say . . .

"Don't stop."

Of course, she eventually had to stop.

But that's okay, because she's lying next to me now, her silky body on mine from my shoulder down to my feet, warmer and snugger than any blanket, and I really should put my arm around her and let her know how much I appreciate this except I can't move any of my limbs.

"Holy shit," I say, which is both a horribly inadequate yet perfect encapsulation of the sex I'd just had.

She grins at me.

"Wait, you didn't come, did you?" I realize with a start. "I'm so sorry, I don't want to be selfi—"

"It's okay. I can wait till next time."

I smile back. "So there's gonna be a next time?"

"Hell yeah," she says. "You owe me. And next time?"

She gives me a look that almost, *almost* makes me hard again. "What I did to you, you're gonna do to my clit."

SKIN DEEP

Carolyn Vakesh

Ellie's husband grinned while fanning a stack of identical envelopes made from shimmering holographic paper and sealed with a scarlet sticker pretending to be sealing wax. She traced her fingers along the raised depiction of a crown atop a large tome.

"A game," Nicky said in a lascivious tone she hadn't heard in years.

"What is it?" She reached for the middle envelope, fingering its slick surface.

He whipped it away. "Greedy!"

"Always." Ellie laughed and pulled his warm lips to hers, whispering, "Tell me."

He opened the first and showed her the sheet of words. Not even words built into phrases. Raw words. She hid her disappointment. Whatever she expected from the mysterious envelopes, temporary tattoos wasn't it. They seemed childish until she caught his gaze filled with wonder, possession, and something wicked. It scraped against her consciousness like whiskers abrading her skin. She nodded, transfixed by his intensity.

He unbuttoned her blouse, aligning the first tattoo below her collarbone, and pressed a wet washcloth against it.

"Love."

As he marked her, a warm glow suffused that spot, burning away the water. The word itself took up residence, pressing itself into her like her lover's fingers, spreading inside her walls. It tingled, the sensation turning the air to roses and love.

Nicky staggered against her for a moment, his body heavy.

"Take me. Here, against the table."

Her breath came shallow, vibrating with need. But he sighed like a man satiated, his eyes dazed and dull. "Later," he mumbled.

That night in bed he plowed her with a passion she hadn't seen for years.

In the morning she touched the word, enjoying the tickle with remembered bliss. She delighted in the feeling, waiting for it to fade.

The four letters still hadn't faded a week later. Nicky laid her on the dining room table and opened her jeans to place the next word to the curve of her left hip. "Can," read that one.

The word settled into her as the air cooled her skin where the towel had been. She heard whispers of all the things she could do, all the ways to use cans, all the possibilities. She was "can" for a moment. Nicky sagged momentarily, but that night he kissed her like a man freed from prison and laughed as he took her furiously from behind.

The days between tattoos shortened until they came each night. He undressed her only far enough to apply the next word or phrase to her skin, as meticulously and with as much dispassionate focus as if he were performing surgery. The nights were wild.

She could still read "Love" in bright red letters on her chest when she gazed in the mirror months later. But now nearly her entire body was covered with words. Green words, blue words, red words, black words. All running along her body, letters almost touching. Naked, she looked like a bizarre crossword puzzle game tangled around itself. By day she wore long sleeves and tights or pants to avoid questions. Sometimes, during quiet afternoon moments, she felt the words like a half-heard, buzzing conversation tickling her skin. It was their secret, and all the sweeter for it.

Trembling fingers opened the last silvery sealed envelope. Nicky bent her over the dining room table. His fingers quested for the hook at the top of her skirt. This close his scent of biscuits, lemon, and musk inflamed her. She ached for his cock.

She bit her lip as he unhooked, unzipped, and slid her skirt down. He rolled down her tights and her panties and scrutinized the last bit of ink. Finally, he unbuttoned the long-sleeved red silk blouse she wore and kissed the first one he'd ever placed, "Love."

She gasped at the pressure of his lips. Need tightened within her as the air licked the moisture his lips had left. The air swirled with roses and sweet honeyed love.

"The first and last word," he murmured.

She started to pull her panties up, when he moved her hand away. His breath tickled her left ear as he whispered, "Not yet. I've spent a great deal of time writing. I want to read the full book."

She laughed, enjoying the new wrinkle in his game. "I'm always an open book."

"No. You were never a book before. A short story perhaps. But now you are a book of endless stories." He reached his hands around her and pulled down her tights, revealing the words along her tush and legs. He knelt and kissed her fleshy bottom, licked her and said, "Taste." He swirled his tongue along the word and as he did, the soft, warm organ tingled against her skin in sharp electric sparks. She sipped wine and sunshine and sex like an edible montage of joy.

He moved down her left leg and bit gently followed by a kiss. "Life," he said, and for a moment she connected with everything alive as if she were the personification of springtime, verdant and filled with lust for life. Her mind swirled. The inner walls of her vagina pounded in an ecstatic tattoo, a grasping hunger. She moaned lightly and grabbed his hair, pulling him toward her, but he shook her off.

He kissed a spot below her belly button. Then again. "Twice," he said, and every sensation she'd had before gave birth to its twin leaving her quivering in need.

A woman's voice, heavily accented but delightful, spoke in her ear, "We write to taste life twice, in the moment, and in retrospection." Ellie twinned with the author, Anaïs Nin, in that moment, her stories spreading from lips to labia like the sweep of sunlight across a wood floor.

He kissed both wrists and the crook of her elbow in quick succession. "Once is never enough," he said softly. She surrendered as rapturous spasms split her consciousness.

He buried his face in the corner where her legs met. She parted to him with a soft sigh and a little laugh. "Oh, please read more. I must know the ending."

In answer, he slid two fingers into the damp cleavage of her labia.

Once wetted he stroked her nub, forcing a cry from her lips and an involuntary twerk of her hips. He circled his fingers slowly across her, strumming her like a mandolin. She sang for him until he removed his fingers, wiped them wetly across her cheeks, a new way to mark her.

Emptiness radiated from her core, needing fulfillment. She seized his hair, tugging his lips to hers, slipping her tongue inside. He opened to her. "Take me," she said.

"Can't. I haven't finished the story."

"I am the story. Come into my library, love. Read me from the inside."

He laughed roughly as he tugged her hips up. "Cover to cover."

He pushed his rigid erection against her burning pussy. She guided him inside, quivering as he burrowed, moaning as he did so, coming hard.

Her passion exploded, enveloping him, sucking him in. Words shifted across her skin to his, ravishing both in endless combinations, a shared library of carnal delights, so much more than skin deep.

ABOUT
THE EDITOR

RACHEL KRAMER BUSSEL (rachelkramerbussel.
com) is a New Jersey-based author, editor, blogger, and
writing instructor. She has edited over sixty books of
erotica, including *Coming Soon: Women's Orgasm
Erotica; Dirty Dates: Erotic Fantasies for Couples;
Come Again: Sex Toy Erotica; The Big Book of
Orgasms; The Big Book of Submission, Volumes 1* and
*2; Lust in Latex; Anything for You; Baby Got Back:
Anal Erotica; Suite Encounters; Gotta Have It; Women
in Lust; Surrender; Orgasmic; Fast Girls; Going Down;
Tasting Him; Tasting Her; Crossdressing; Cheeky
Spanking Stories; Bottoms Up; Spanked: Red-Cheeked
Erotica; Please, Sir; Please, Ma'am; He's on Top; She's
on Top; Best Bondage Erotica of the Year, Volumes 1*
and *2;* and *Best Women's Erotica of the Year, Volumes*

1–7. Her anthologies have won eight IPPY (Independent Publisher) Awards, and *The Big Book of Submission, Volume 2, Dirty Dates,* and *Surrender* won the National Leather Association Samois Anthology Award.

Rachel has written for *AVN, Bust, Cosmopolitan, Curve,* The Daily Beast, Elle.com, Forbes.com, Fortune.com, *Glamour,* The Goods, Gothamist, *Harper's Bazaar,* Huffington Post, *Inked, InStyle, Marie Claire, MEL, Men's Health, Newsday, New York Post, New York Observer, The New York Times, O: The Oprah Magazine, Penthouse, The Philadelphia Inquirer,* Refinery29, *Rolling Stone,* The Root, Salon, *San Francisco Chronicle, Self,* Slate, Time.com, *Time Out New York,* and *Zink,* among others. She has appeared on "The Gayle King Show," "The Martha Stewart Show," "The Berman and Berman Show," NY1, and Showtime's "Family Business." She hosted the popular In the Flesh Erotic Reading Series, featuring readers from Susie Bright to Zane, speaks at conferences, and does readings and teaches erotic writing workshops around the world and online. She blogs at lustylady.blogspot.com and consults about erotica and sex-related nonfiction at eroticawriting101.com. Follow her @raquelita on Twitter.